BEAR NAKED

HALLE SHIFTERS BOOK 3

BY
DANA MARIE BELL

D1738894

Dana Marie Bell Books
www.danamariebell.com

Dana Marie Bell

PO Box 39

Bear, DE 19701

Bear Naked

Copyright © 2014 by Dana Marie Bell

ISBN: 978-1984304261

Edited by Tera Kleinfelter

Cover by Kanaxa

First Edition publication by Samhain Publishing, Ltd.: February 2014

Second Edition publication by Dana Marie Bell: March 2017

ABOUT THE AUTHOR

Dana Marie Bell lives with her husband Dusty, their two maniacal children, an evil ice-cream stealing cat and a dog who thinks barking should become the next Olympic event. You can learn more about Dana and her addiction to series at www.danamariebell.com.

DEDICATION

To Mom, who called my Dad "Stinky Pete" in an email recently. Do you know how long it took me to figure out who you were talking about? I thought you'd hired a pool guy to close the pool for the summer, and wondered why you would hire someone with Stinky in their name.

To Dad, who in no way stinks. Although you do kinda look like Stinky Pete, now that I think about it.

And to Dusty, who understands and embraces my family's insanity.

P.S. Trust me, if you knew my family it would explain so much.

CHAPTER ONE

Ryan Williams woke with a feeling of renewed purpose. He stretched, yawned widely and sat up, eager to start.

Today was the day, damn it.

He was going to claim his mate.

Of course he woke up *every* morning lately thinking that, but Ryan refused to allow Glory's snarly ways to get him down. She was so cute when she was trying to be all big and bad, with those long, powder-blue curls floating around her and the bangles on her arms clinking together. To Ryan, Glory was the size of a donut hole, about as frightening and just as sweet.

He adored the ground she walked on, whether she liked it or not.

He sighed and crawled out of bed, padding naked to the bathroom. It was still early out, but the sun had begun to rise, and there was no sense in remaining in bed. Better to get up, get dressed and work once more on Project Glory.

He brushed his teeth and took a quick shower, all the while trying to think of ways to get the stubborn woman to accept what he'd known since he'd stumbled into her at the hospital all those months ago. He'd looked down at the oddly dressed, blue-haired woman he'd accidentally knocked down and damn near had a heart attack. She'd blown her curls out of her eyes, glared up at him and he'd been instantly smitten.

"And hello to you too."

At the sound of her voice he'd shuddered. His Bear, still upset over his sister's brutal beating, had stilled its frantic pacing. All its attention had focused on the gorgeous fairy sprawled at his feet.

Mate.

Ryan hadn't expected to be so fortunate as to find his mate in the same town his favorite cousin had, but there she'd been, all five foot three of her. Glory had been bristling over the fact that he might have a mate, and she'd been unwilling to acknowledge the pull between them. Tabby had told her friend he was a shifter, and Glory had growled at him for the first time, winning his heart with her fierceness.

How sad was it that he'd never been so turned on in all his life? His Bear had wanted to growl back, to bite and claim and carry her off to his den where she'd be safe. The knowledge that his baby sister was in the hospital, clinging to life, while his mate stood defiantly before him had made him lose his damn mind. He'd commanded Tabby, a Wolf and the mate of his cousin Alex, to keep Glory safe and forced himself from Glory's side. He had time to claim her, to mark her as his.

But that time was beginning to run out. The mate dreams had become so intense Ryan was almost afraid to go to sleep at night. Each one had him spending in his sheets, waking lonely and cold and in need of a shower. His Bear was beginning to snap and snarl, and it had only gotten worse since Glory had been injured.

Ryan felt his eyes change, his Bear coming to the fore at the memory of being unable to get to his mate. She'd been in the hospital, shot by the man who'd cast Tabby from her home Pack, and the hospital had refused him entrance. They'd claimed he was acting crazy, that he was a disruption.

His mate had been *shot*. What had they expected, tea and crumpets?

So instead of being there for his mate he'd gone hunting, looking for the man who'd harmed Glory, trying desperately to keep from slipping over the edge and letting loose his rage on the woman who'd denied him access.

And he'd done it. He'd found Tabby's ex-Alpha holding Cyn at gunpoint and taken him down, but not before the rogue Wolf had shot and nearly killed her. Julian had almost died saving her, something that still gave Cyn fits. She was almost as protective of her mate as Ryan was of his.

Ryan returned to his mate's side, happy with the knowledge that the man who had hurt her would never hurt another living soul, let alone Ryan's tiny mate.

Ever since then, Glory's stance toward him had softened. She'd let him in a little bit, allowing him to hold her, to shoulder some of the burden she seemed to always carry with her. But she'd refused every plea for a date, every demand that they mate. She didn't understand how he suffered without her, but the last thing he wanted to do was to force her into accepting him out of pity.

Ryan wanted her heart. Now all he had to do was figure out how to win it, a task that seemed easier said than done. So far, the only place he was certain he held it was in his dreams.

Ryan needed it in reality as well. The madness the mate dreams could bring was slowly seeping in, and there was nothing he could do about it. If she refused to accept him, Ryan would leave Halle and literally pine away for lack of her.

Ryan turned off the water and stepped out of the shower. If he had to, he was willing to strip his soul bare to win her affection. He'd stop the sun in its tracks for her smile, take the moon and hang it around her neck to hear her sigh. Didn't she know she was everything to him? And if not, what could he do to make her see it?

Perhaps it's time I consulted Tabby and Cyn. The girls knew Glory better than anyone, and only his reluctance to air their troubles before her friends had stopped him before. But the stronger the mate dreams became, the more desperate he was to finally mark his mate. The girls would know what to do to win his reluctant mate. She wasn't immune to him, but she wasn't letting him any further into her life, either.

Ryan dressed, his thoughts racing. He'd talk to the girls, find out what he needed to do before his Bear decided to take matters into its own paws. Because if his Bear took over and forced her, Glory would never forgive him.

And neither would Ryan.

***

Glory couldn't believe it. It was the sweetest yet creepiest thing she'd ever seen.

Another dozen roses sat in front of her apartment, the same as the week before.

Ryan's really stepping up his game. She picked up the bouquet and took a sniff, hoping no one saw the sappy smile that crossed her lips.

The week before he'd left not only the roses but a small gold bracelet. The week before that had been a small bottle of her favorite perfume. And the week before that? A premium hand lotion that smelled of fresh pears. How he'd known it was her favorite scent she'd never know. Maybe it was that Bear nose of his.

She couldn't wait to see what was in the box this time.

Glory carried the roses and her latest present into the apartment, kicking the door shut with her foot. She needed to start dropping hints about the kinds of things she liked so he'd continue to get it right.

She tore into the box, eager to see what he'd gotten for her. Inside, she found two champagne glasses with a small bottle of Dom Perignon. And this time the note was just as beautiful as the last one. *Your sweet smile brightens my day.*

Glory stroked the note, glad her friends no longer lived in the two-bedroom apartment with her. If they could see her now, after all the shit she gave them over Alex and Julian, she'd never hear the end of it.

But… She sighed.

Damn it. The son of a bitch was getting to her.

And if she didn't get her ass in gear for work, Cyn would get her too.

Glory darted out the door and drove like a bat out of hell for the tattoo parlor she now co-owned with Cynthia "Cyn" Reyes and Tabitha Bunsun.

"Good morning, Glory." Cyn had her back to the front door, and her shoulders were tight as a bowstring. Even her voice was strained. Either she was pissed about something, or trying desperately not to laugh.

"Good morning?" Glory dropped her coat onto the coat rack, ready to open her station for the day. Something was up, but that didn't mean the girls at Cynful wouldn't be ready to roll when the doors were unlocked.

Muted giggles sounded from behind her. Glory smiled when she saw their latest employee, Heather Allen, curled up on the gray chaise, her face buried in her hands. Glory was tickled pink that the little Fox had settled in so nicely with them. She'd been shy and withdrawn when she first started with them, a holdover from a trauma she suffered as a child. Some Bear shifters had thought it would be *fun* to force a twelve-year-old to go through her first shift, something Tabby had told her didn't happen until puberty. Bunny had come upon the Bears tormenting his little cousin and gone insane, damaging several of them permanently.

There were still Bears who whispered Alex "Bunny" Bunsun's name in fear six years later. The downside was Heather had been terrified of Bunny's anger as well, and began avoiding her cousin like the plague, causing Alex to try to learn control over his Grizzly Bear temper. It had earned him the nickname Bunny, but he wore it as a badge of pride. He'd learned that control he so desired, and become a man more than worthy of one of Glory's best friends.

His only regret had been Heather's fear of him, so when the Bunsun-Williams clan descended on Halle, he'd introduced Heather to Cyn with the hopes that Cyn would see what he saw: a lost little lamb in need. Cyn had taken one look at her, and her artwork, and offered her an apprenticeship. Heather had taken her up on it, and now the shop was complete in a way it hadn't been in a long time. With the Cynful girls, Heather was open and friendly. She was even beginning to get comfortable around their customers, a feat Ryan had sworn would never happen.

Showed what he knew. Heather was a lot stronger than her relatives gave her credit for. She just needed a safe place to blossom in, and Cyn was all about taking in strays and helping them do just that. All anyone had to do was look at herself and Tabby to see that.

Glory put her hands on her hips. "What the hell is going on here?"

"Hey, Glory." Tabby slunk glumly out of the back room of the shop, her head low. Her lime-green bob easily obscured half her face, but it couldn't hide what had obviously set her co-workers off.

"Guh." Glory just couldn't stop staring. It was…

It was…*huge.*

"I know, right?" Heather broke down into breathless giggles, just two shakes away from crying.

"My God." Glory couldn't stop staring. "When the hell did that happen?"

Tabby sniffed pathetically. "I woke up with it this morning." She moved behind the counter, her expression pitiful.

Cyn poked at the *thing* sitting on the end of Tabby's nose. "You couldn't cover it up with something? It's gonna scare the customers."

"Cover it? With what, a burka?" Glory stared at Cyn. Was she crazy? "David Copperfield couldn't hide—" she waved at the humongous growth on Tabby's face, "—*that*."

Heather fell off the chaise with wheeze and a thump. Glory sure as hell hoped she was still breathing. She knew shit about CPR.

Tabby sniffled as she batted Cyn's finger away. "Pregnancy glow my lily white ass. More like pregnancy oil slick. And don't poke at it. It might get mad." Tabby's Southern drawl was thick with unhappiness. "I think I heard it growl this morning."

Cyn ignored Tabby's plea and poked at it again. "*Dios.* It's like Mt. Doom, all ready to erupt and shit."

"Ew." Heather picked herself up off the floor and flopped back on the chaise. "Just... Ew."

Glory shuddered. "Not in here, please." Just the thought of that monstrosity blowing in the shop made her want to gag. It was the biggest, *whitest* pimple she'd ever seen. "That thing should have its own zip code."

"Alex tried to be all helpful." Tabby sniffled pathetically. "He said I should put hot towels on it."

"Did you?" Glory couldn't get over how big the thing was. You couldn't *not* stare at it. It was the huge white elephant in the room.

Literally.

Tabby nodded glumly. "It got bigger."

Heather began giggling again. She was going to get a stomach cramp at this rate.

Cyn was tapping her lip in that way she had when she was really thinking hard. "What about a hot needle?"

Glory and Tabby shared a look, then both women shuddered, Tabby covering Mt. Doom with her fingers. "I thought the idea was to keep it from getting mad?"

"Yeah. I mean, why poke a sleeping bear?" Glory grinned as all three shifters rolled their eyes at her. So far, Glory was the only member of Cynful Tattoos who wasn't furry, and she planned on keeping it that way for a little bit longer. Ryan Williams might be the cutest Bear this side of Winnie the Pooh, but when it had mattered the most, he'd done what every other person who'd ever claimed to love her had done.

He'd disappeared.

Oh, he'd come back, and his sucking-up skills were excellent, but she knew the truth. Ryan was just like her family, and Glory had no intention of ever allowing anyone to hurt her that way again. The only people who stood by her no matter what were standing in front of her, discussing Tabby's pregnancy hormone woes. Even her twin…

Well. Glory tried not to think about her twin.

Cyn nodded once, sharply. "I think we should call in an exorcist."

Now Glory was the one who started giggling. Trust Cyn to try and make a bad situation better with that sharp tongue of hers.

"Bitch." Tabby pouted, looking adorably miserable.

"Takes a bitch to know a bitch, bitch."

The banter between Cyn and Tabby was so familiar Glory barely paid attention to it. Soon, one of the girls would probably wind up chasing the other through the shop like wild hyenas, and that was just the way Glory liked it. It was fun and full of life, and no one could ever make her trade in her life today for what had once been.

Not even Ryan.

"Oof." Glory rocked against the chair she'd been standing in front of as she suddenly found a hundred and twenty pounds of green-haired Wolf shifter glued to her back. "What?"

Tabby's pointy chin dug into her shoulder. Thank God Mt. Doom was on the other side of her face, because Glory didn't want to be that up close and personal with it. "Ryan and Alex are bringing lunch today. Want anything special?"

A picture of Ryan, stripped bare and covered in chocolate, sprang immediately to mind. "Nope."

Tabby sighed. "You have to give him a shot."

Glory wrinkled her nose. "I *was* shot, remember? I wouldn't do that to my worst enemy. Ow." She reached up and rubbed the back of her head. Damn Cyn and her sneak attacks. "What?"

"That boy's gonna pine away for you if you don't accept him."

"Exaggerating much?" Tabby couldn't be telling the truth.

Could she? Glory had seen the dark circles under Ryan's eyes.

Tabby sighed in her ear. "It's true. When a shifter meets their mate, it's supposed to be this magical thing, right? But if the mate rejects you, or holds themselves back for whatever reason, the magic becomes this itch under your skin that never goes away. It's a burning need you can't quench. You start dreaming about them, erotic dreams that fill you with sleepless, lonely nights because your mate isn't really there. A shifter can slowly lose their mind, pining for someone that doesn't want them."

Glory stared at Cyn, who was nodding. "Alex told me all about it, before Julian changed me."

"They're right." Heather shot her a complicated look, both sympathetic and hard. As much as they'd come to love Heather, she was still a member of the Bunsun-

Williams clan. Alex and Ryan were her first cousins, and they adored the little redhead. "Ryan needs you."

"But… That was *months* ago!" The weather was slowly warming as the small town of Halle, Pennsylvania prepared for another spring.

Cyn sighed and ran her fingers through her multi-colored hair. Julian, Cyn's mate, always seemed enchanted by the black, blonde and pink strands Cyn had sported for about six months. "Yeah. Apparently, if they don't mate us, they…" Cyn shot Tabby a hopeless look.

"Well, he won't *die*, but he'll be one unhappy Bear for the rest of his life." But the uncomfortable look on Tabby's face told her it was far more serious than that.

Shit.

"But no pressure or anything." Glory threw herself into the smoky-gray chaise lounge she'd declared her own spot months ago. She loved lying there when she wasn't busy, chatting with the women she considered closer than her own sisters. Faith and Hope were long gone, but Tabby and Cyn would be with her forever, if only because Glory knew where Tabby hid her favorite shoes.

Tabby settled carefully into one of the chairs they'd had reupholstered from the old shop. Living Art Tattoos was gone now, their lease given over to a small card- and gift-shop. Glory always felt strange walking past the place that had once housed Cyn's shop, but she had to admit that losing LA's lease had been the best thing that ever happened to them.

The new shop was theirs in a way LA hadn't been. Cyn had made both Tabby and Glory full partners, and each of them now had a say in how the business was run. They'd all decided on the new decor, the new flash art on the walls and even the name, much to Cyn's embarrassment. Cynful Tattoos was just as popular as LA had been, and Glory knew exactly who was responsible for that.

www.danamariebell.com

Cyn settled on the lighter gray sofa that she'd fallen in love with at first sight. The black-and-white floral curtains were pulled back, exposing the large picture window. Cynful was sleek and modern, yet still feminine, and Glory loved it with all her greedy little heart.

Hell, even the floors were nicer here, a gorgeous dark oak that had sold them all on the shop. And the new landlady, Mrs. H., made sure they had all the things they needed to feel safe, even at night. Hell, at least once a week she brought them lunch and just sat and chatted with them. She was the mother Glory wished she'd had, but never did.

Maybe she should change her last name from Walsh to H—

"Earth to Glory." Tabby sat in her favorite chair and propped her feet up on the distressed chest-slash-coffee table Glory had discovered at a secondhand shop. It had seen far better days, but with a little polish and some elbow grease it had become a thing of beauty despite its scars. "You're going to have to make a decision about Ryan."

Glory whimpered and tossed her head back. "Why? Why do I have to do anything?"

"Don't you feel *anything* for him?"

Cyn's serious tone caught her attention. "I do, but…"

"This is because he left, isn't it?"

Glory couldn't look at them. They must think she was crazy.

"Glory, honey. Ryan didn't leave you. He was—"

"Hunting the bad guy. I know." And no matter how many times they tried to tell her, her heart just wasn't hearing it. Every time she thought about being in the hospital, hurting and alone, with Ryan nowhere to be found, she wanted to scream and cry. She had, back in the hospital, crying out for Ryan while half out of it on pain meds and anesthetic.

Ryan never came.

"He went after that guy and tore him into dog kibble. Cut him some slack, okay?"

Glory shrugged. So what? Ryan had destroyed the man who'd nearly killed Glory, but he should have been with her. He was supposed to be her mate, not her avenger. Still, she could understand why everyone, including herself, was frustrated. She *liked* Ryan, but she just couldn't get past feeling abandoned. "It's...complicated."

"Maybe you should talk to someone."

Glory stared at Tabby, blinked at Mt. Doom (was it *bigger?*) and sighed. "You think I should have my head shrunk."

"You know I love you, Glory, but you're being a bitch." Cyn shrugged when Glory turned and glared at her. "My family is the one that took you in, remember? I know all about your abandonment issues, and Ryan didn't do that. He's here, every day, and he's not going to go anywhere."

Glory lay down with a sigh. She really needed a chaise like this in her apartment. It was so much nicer than the lumpy couch she had now. "I know that up here—" she pointed to her head, "—but not here." When she laid her hand on her heart, Tabby began to cry. It seemed she did that when the wind blew, when the bell jingled, hell, when the coffee pot turned off. The woman was trying to drown them all in salt water and pregnancy angst. "Aw hell. Not again."

The bell over the door jingled, and the deep voice of Alex "Bunny" Bunsun, Tabby's mate, rang through her like guilt in hammer form. "Why are you crying, sweetheart?"

Before they knew it Alex had Tabby in his lap, cuddling her close and cooing in her ear. It was revolting. Hell, he'd even sat her so the growth was against his chest.

Glory had the sick urge to poke at Tabby's head and see if the thing was bouncy like a ball.

Ugh. She really needed to get a life.

"Hey, pretty girl." Ryan squatted next to her chaise and brushed some of her powder-blue curls from her forehead. The hopeful expression on his face had her heart pounding in both fear and longing. God, she wanted what he was offering so badly, but the courage she thought she had disappeared whenever he turned those blazing sapphire eyes on her. "I brought ham and cheese subs."

At that, her stomach growled loud enough to startle a grizzly. "Spicy brown mustard?"

He nodded.

"Tomatoes and lettuce?"

He was smiling, watching her with all the wonder of a boy with his first love. "Would I bring you anything else?"

She reached with greedy hands toward the bag he was holding between his knees. "Gimme!"

He leaned over her, caging her with his body. "Say the word, and you can have that any time you want."

There was no doubt what he was talking about, since he was still holding the bag between his knees. She pushed him back and glared. "I want the ham, not the salami." Behind him, Cyn barked out a laugh. "Gimme."

Ryan chuckled, and oh God, what that low, seductive sound did to her. It was like feeling his joy feathering over her skin. "Here, you greedy little thing."

Glory took the bag and dashed off the chaise, heading for the back room. "Meat! Woo-hoo!"

Ryan's chuckles followed her the entire way.

CHAPTER TWO

Ryan watched the woman of his dreams run away from him yet again and laughed. God, she was so adorable it shattered him. Long, powder-blue curls, pale blue eyes, and a tongue that would make a harpy blanch; she was everything he'd ever wanted and more.

Too bad all she ever did was run away from him.

Too bad for *her* he would follow no matter how far she ran.

"Hi, Heather." He paused long enough to kiss his sweet little cousin on the forehead. The shy smile he got in return always made him want to protect her from the world. Thank God Julian's mate had taken a liking to her. Heather was blossoming at Cynful Tattoos, despite Eric Bunsun's objections. Eric was *very* protective of little Heather, and snarled at anyone who made her so much as frown.

Ryan followed Glory into the back room, laughing harder when he found her hunched over the unwrapped sandwich and muahaha'ing in her best evil overlord voice. "Do I get a sandwich?"

She glared at him. "Mine."

He shook his head and took his sandwich anyway, aware she wasn't going to try to keep it. The woman was insane, but she wasn't nearly as mean as she pretended to be. He pulled a bottle of water out of the mini fridge and sat across from her at the small table the girls had set up for their breaks. "So."

"Mm?" She had a mouth full of ham and cheese. A smidgeon of mustard was on her lip, and the urge to lick it away was nearly overwhelming.

"I want to take you out."

She blinked and swallowed. "Like a hit man?"

"Yup, because I'm a total Mafioso." Ryan did his best fake Italian accent, her little snort of amusement his reward. "No, SG. I want to go on a date."

She tilted her head in confusion, for once ignoring his nickname for her. He'd totally lied when he said it didn't stand for Super Grover. He liked his nuts right where they were. No, he'd agreed that it stood for Super Glory, and in return she let him get away with it. "Why?"

This time he was the one who was confused. "Huh?"

"Why do you want to go on a date?" She bit into her sandwich, her expression curious, almost wary.

How the hell to answer a question like that? *Because you're my whole world* didn't seem like something Glory wanted to hear. *You're my mate* probably wouldn't cut it either. So he decided to go with the simplest answer, the one he hoped would get her to say yes. "Because I want you." He held up his hand when she started to speak. "Not just in my bed, but in my life."

"Because I'm your mate."

He smiled, trying to convey what he was really saying. He'd known Glory for almost a year now, and he'd fallen for her, quirks and all. He couldn't imagine having a life without her in it, even if she chose not to accept him as her mate. "Because you're Glory."

Her cheeks turned bright red. "I'm not that great." She couldn't meet his eyes. "I have…issues."

"Want to tell me about them?" He put his hand over hers, surprised when she started. "Glory?"

She took a deep breath, obviously gathering herself together. "No. I don't want to tell you. Not yet, anyway."

That hurt. "Haven't I earned a little trust?"

The sandwich paused halfway to her mouth. "If you hadn't you wouldn't be back here with me." She bit into the ham and cheese with all the concentration she usually gave to her craft.

Glory was the piercer for Cynful Tattoos, and she took her job seriously. It might sound like a simple little job that didn't require much thought, but Glory was always looking for a way to improve not only her skills but her stock. She attended conventions held just for piercers to learn new techniques and was utterly dedicated to her craft. She kept abreast of all the safety and health regulations, and stayed on top of the latest trends. She'd had to learn anatomy to determine where to safely pierce, such as where saliva glands and ducts were, and where nerves ran so that she wouldn't do any permanent damage to her clients.

Ryan was in awe of her. She worked just as hard as he did at something she loved, and didn't let anyone give her crap for it.

Her own piercings were subtle. She had a pretty, glittery diamond nose stud, a delicate silver ring in her eyebrow, tiny silver rings up her right ear and another diamond stud he'd heard called a Monroe, right above her upper lip on the right side. As far as he was concerned each piercing only enhanced her beauty, made her more exotic. He wanted to lick each one, to strip her and see if she had any piercings in places he hadn't discovered yet. Did she sport studs in her nipples, or little hoops he could tug on? Were her labia pierced, or her clit? He shuddered with need just picturing her sweet pink flesh decorated with gold and silver.

Speaking of piercings, perhaps it was time he asked for one. "If you were going to pierce me, where would you do it?"

The grin she shot him was so full of evil he nearly backed up. "You sure you want me to answer that?"

"I'm serious." He sighed, not sure how to get through to her. It always felt like he took one step forward, but she'd take two steps back. "I want you to give me a piercing, but it will be my first one. What should I get?"

She sat back, her expression becoming serious, professional. "How adventurous are you feeling, and how will a piercing affect your work?"

"I'm pretty much stuck in the office, doing paperwork." He was the head accountant for Bunsun Exteriors, Pennsylvania branch. Thanks to Bunny, he didn't have to return to Oregon. When Bunny opened the Pennsylvania branch he'd brought Ryan in as the money man and head paper pusher. So far, business was slowly growing, partly on the reputation of Bunsun Exteriors and partly due to the hard work of Bunny, Ryan and Eric.

She studied him intensely.

He decided to push a little bit. "Pick something you'd like to look at."

She gave him that innocent look that always spelled trouble. "But, Ryan, they don't make a Chris Hemsworth piercing."

He growled, but she just laughed. "Think of something else, SG."

She grumbled a bit under her breath at the familiar nickname. Her head tilted left, then right, then left again, and all the while she just…stared. He squirmed under her gaze, wondering how she'd try and emasculate him *this* time. But instead she surprised him. "I think, considering what you do for a living, we should keep it simple. Do you want one ear done, or both?"

He was almost disappointed. He'd thought she'd suggest an eyebrow ring or a nipple piercing, though he'd probably balk at a Jacob's Ladder. "That's it? An ear piercing?"

She giggled, the sweetest sound he'd ever heard. He could listen to Glory's laughter for the rest of his life and never get tired of it. "You want a gauge? I can get one that looks like a tire rim."

"Those are the huge ear piercings, right?" That was one piercing he knew he didn't want. While he didn't mind the look on other people, it just wasn't him. "I think if I'm doing my ear we'll stick to a stud."

She made a face, and he wondered if he'd picked wrong. Maybe she'd been testing him, seeing how far he'd go to fit in with her life. "Any particular kind of stud?"

He shrugged. On this, he could be flexible. "You pick."

Glory bit her lip. "I…"

"You?"

"I have something. Wait here." She got up, her sandwich half finished, to root around in her piercing stores. She pulled out little drawers, rooting through the jewelry within them until she pulled something out with a satisfied "Ha! Found it." She held out the little stud by his eye, nodding in satisfaction. "It's a titanium stud with a London blue topaz. What do you think?"

She held out a stud much larger than he'd thought it would be. The dark metal made the blue of the gem stand out. It was unique, just like his mate. "I like it."

"It matches your hair and eyes." Her startled expression was quickly suppressed. She must not have meant to tell him that.

"I'll wear your stud with pride."

She rolled her eyes at him, but that delicious pink tone raced across her cheeks again. "It's not an engagement ring, Mr. Williams."

He kissed the fingers holding the stud. "Not yet, anyway."

She snatched her hand back, but he could tell she was wavering in her resolve not to go out with him. "I'm *so* charging you full price."

He grabbed her hand and held it between her own, the stud digging into both their palms. "Go out with me."

"Ryan…"

"Please. We'll make it a lunch date rather than a dinner date, something nice and casual." He put some of the desperation he'd been feeling for months behind the plea. "Please, Glory."

Her shoulders slumped. "I'm going to regret this."

"Yes?"

Those pale blue eyes were full of uncertainty. "Yes."

Ryan leapt from the table with a war cry. "She said yes!"

Immediately Glory was surrounded by her friends, all three women chattering a mile a minute. Ryan stumbled as Alex pounded him on the back. "Congratulations, cuz. How did you get her to agree?"

"I used the Williams charm."

"Oh," Alex drawled. "You dazzled her with bullshit."

"Exactly." Because if Glory thought Ryan was going to stop at a single date, she had another think coming.

***

Ryan didn't stay in the back for long. Oh, no. He had that look in his eye, the one that said he was up to something and Glory had better watch out. The last time he'd gotten that determined look he'd nearly ripped the head off of Cyn's ex-boyfriend, the one Glory had chosen to flirt with.

Glory pretended not to notice when Ryan pulled Tabby aside for a little chat. Too bad she didn't have that super-shifter hearing her friends now had, because she'd love to know why Tabby suddenly shot her a sly look before whispering in Ryan's ear.

This couldn't be good.

It got worse when Cyn joined them, also whispering in Ryan's ear. Ryan grinned at something Cyn said, laughing out loud when Tabby added a quiet remark that Glory barely heard.

So Glory pasted on her most innocent smile and strolled over to them. "What are you three talking about?"

"Uh…" Tabby shot Ryan a look chock full of guilt.

Ryan took hold of her hand. "I have to go home to Oregon for a week or so, and I was asking them to keep an eye on you."

Glory's blood ran cold. He was leaving her again. "Glory?"

She could barely hear him over the roaring in her ears. Her chest hurt, her hands and feet tingled. God. She hadn't had one of these in years, but she recognized all the signs. She had to calm down.

"Shit. What's happening?" Ryan's voice, so distant, was thick with fear.

She doubled over, unable to catch her breath, nausea racking her until she began to dry heave.

"Glory!"

She couldn't catch her breath, damn it.

"…panic attack…"

Spots danced before her eyes, blocking her vision. The edges went dark, and Glory knew she was about to pass out. Cyn and Tabby must be freaking the hell out.

"…lay her down…"

The voices of her friends barely registered, but Ryan's arms, his scent, enveloped her. Dizzy, she clung to his shoulders, barely aware he'd picked her up.

No. She had to leave, had to find a place that was safe. Ryan was leaving.

Leaving.

She needed to get away.

She began struggling violently, desperate to run, to flee from the knowledge that the man who was supposed to stay by her side, had *promised her* he wouldn't leave, was once again going away.

A deep hum shattered the fear, the notes off-key yet soothing, a masculine lullaby that slowly but surely chipped away at the edges of her terror. Glory blinked, the spots receding, her breath coming easier as that hum enveloped her in warmth. She could feel it moving inside her, soothing her pain, helping her find her center.

When she could focus enough to see past the panic, she realized she was firmly on Ryan's lap, being rocked like a child. He held her close, her head under his chin, her arms firmly around his waist. He was humming something that was probably a lullaby but sounded more like a cat with a hairball trying to purr.

"You okay, sugar?" Tabby was kneeling beside Ryan, her hand stroking Glory's curls.

Glory's breath was coming a bit easier now. "How long?" When Tabby frowned, she explained. "I lose my sense of time when..." She couldn't finish. She was just too embarrassed that this had happened again, especially after such a long period of time had passed since the last attack.

"When you have a panic attack." Cyn's no-nonsense tone was almost as soothing as Ryan's off-key hum.

"Yeah." There was no sense in denying it. She'd had panic attacks frequently when she first moved in with Cyn and her family. Cyn knew the signs of one, and had helped head one off while Glory was in the hospital. Hell, she'd helped calm Glory down when they'd met with the Halle Puma Alpha and Curana, Max and Emma Cannon, to discuss how to deal with the man who'd shot Glory.

Ryan hadn't been there, either.

"What happened?" Alex, his hand on Tabby's shoulder, was studying her closely. "I get you had a panic attack, but why? What set it off?"

Glory refused to answer. There was no need to share her shame.

"Ryan talked about leaving." Cyn sighed as Glory started to lose her breath again. "Glory, he's not going anywhere."

Glory flinched. She couldn't let Ryan know he was the reason she'd—

"I did this?" Ryan tucked his fingers under her chin and gently lifted her face to his. "Oh, sweetheart. I'm so sorry."

She struggled again to get out of his lap, but he held fast, refusing to let her go. "Let. Me. Go."

"No." He began rocking again, humming under his breath.

Damn it. Why did the sound of his voice, the way his chest vibrated against her cheek, soothe her so much? Not even her mother, who'd left soon after Hope disappeared and divorced her father in a bitter battle that left the family in ruins, had been able to calm her the way Ryan did.

"I won't leave you. I give you my word, Glory." Ryan's vow was made in a voice that could have chipped diamonds. "I'll stay here and get someone else to take care of the problem."

She took a deep breath, aware that Ryan understood what had set her off. Damn it, she didn't need to be even weaker in front of him. "I'm fine."

"Bullshit." Cyn scowled down at her, but Glory could see the concern. "Glory, you have an anxiety disorder. It's nothing to be ashamed of."

Yeah, right. Glory didn't see Cyn panicking every time Julian went somewhere.

Cyn growled. "Ryan, Glory's had episodes off and on for years. They're always triggered by the fear that she'll be abandoned."

"I'm *fine*." Glory was going to kill Cyn.

He tilted her face up again. "No. You're not. But I'm okay with that."

"Ryan…" She sighed, cuddling up against him. The sound of his heartbeat, the knowledge that he was right there, solid and real, began to destroy the last of the fear. "I'll be all right." She had to be. She'd gone through this before, and she'd live through it again.

Everyone left her eventually.

Everyone.

Her heart pounding, Glory shook her head. "I can't."

"Can't what, SG?"

Part of her was humiliated that she'd had an episode. The other part was so relieved he wasn't leaving she was almost giddy with it. "I can't do this. I need… I need to go."

The low, feral growl was barely audible, but it rumbled through his chest and shook her to the core. "You aren't going anywhere."

She risked looking up and found his normally blue eyes had gone dark brown. Fangs peeked over the edge of his bottom lip. Five-inch black claws scraped across her gauzy top, catching in the thin fibers. "Um. Down, boy."

He cocked an eyebrow at her. "I won't leave you alone."

Now she was going to panic for a whole other reason. "Don't make promises you can't keep."

"Watch me." His voice was low, gravelly. Ryan must be close to losing to his Bear.

"Calm down, Rye. She's fine, she's in your lap. It's a panic attack, nothing more." Alex helped Tabby to her feet. "Take her into the back room and get her some water."

Before she could protest Ryan was on his feet, Glory cradled in his arms as if she weighed nothing. He carted her into the back room, refusing to let her down when she struggled.

"Don't." The low warning was barely human.

She must have frightened him, more than she thought possible, because Ryan was right on the edge of changing. "Are you all right?"

He stared at her, his expression surprised. "I should be asking you that." A little bit of blue peeked out from the dark brown of his Bear's gaze. Ryan was gaining some control back. He leaned forward, holding her steady. "Grab a bottle of water?"

She did as asked, her hands shaking too badly to open it.

He sat at the break table, keeping her in his lap, and took it from her. He opened it and held the bottle to her lips. "Drink."

Taking a sip of water, Glory studied him from under her lashes. The brown was slowly seeping away as the shakes that had racked her body subsided. She cleared her throat and handed him back the water. "I told you. I have…issues."

"I noticed." He took a sip himself before recapping the bottle and placing it on the break table. "I want to know what happened, but not if it will set off another attack."

She bit her lip. Did she want to give him that much power over her?

"Please."

The pain, the plea in his voice, gave her the power to speak. He was practically begging to shoulder her pain. "Everyone leaves." The words came out in a rush, surprising her. She hadn't meant to say it quite that way.

Ryan's eyes went wide before closing. "Oh, shit. Your family."

"Hope disappeared, my mother left, my father took the rest of my family out of state and left me behind." The words wouldn't stop tumbling out of her mouth.

"Everyone leaves me. Brittany left when she found out what Tabby was."

Ryan pressed a soft kiss to her forehead. "I won't leave you, I swear."

"You already did."

Ryan froze. "What do you mean?"

She shrugged, clamping her lips shut before her diarrhea of the mouth took over again.

"The hospital?"

She huffed out a breath. Damn perceptive Bear. Wasn't she allowed to have any secrets?

"I didn't leave you voluntarily. You know that, right?"

She refused to look at him, and he didn't force the issue. Instead, he pressed her head against his chest again.

"The hospital staff wouldn't let me in."

She knew that, but it didn't matter. He should have waited for Julian or Dr. Howard instead of taking off. When she found out Ryan had gone missing she'd damn near lost it. To find out he'd disappeared voluntarily?

She'd been furious and terrified at the same time. The word *rogue* had been whispered when they thought she couldn't hear. From the sound of it, that wasn't a good thing to be labeled in the shifter world.

He rubbed his chin against the top of her head. "I will never leave you again."

"Ryan—"

"*Never.*" His tone was firm. "From now on, I'm stuck on you like glue."

Wonderful. Half of her was doing the Snoopy dance of happiness, while the other half was terrified out of its wits. "I told you not to make promises you can't keep."

"Sweetheart, I hate to tell you this, but now that my Bear knows about your abandonment problems I *can't* leave you alone, even if I want to." He sighed deeply. "We can't stand the thought of you hurting, let alone being the cause of it. So, please. Trust me when I say, you'll never truly be alone again."

Hell. She almost believed him. "Okay."

"I mean it."

"I know you do." Strangely enough, she did. The last of the panic began to recede, Glory relaxing in his embrace. "But you can't follow me into the ladies' room."

He chuckled. "Try and stop me."

She bit back a grin, refusing to acknowledge how right it felt to be cuddled up in his lap. "You're such an ass, Ryan."

Her sappy tone belied her words. He was getting to her, the big oaf, and if she wasn't careful she was going to fall in love with him.

Admit it. You're already in love with him.

"Your ass." When she glared up at him he kissed the tip of her nose. "Give me a chance to prove to you that not everyone leaves, all right?"

She bit her lip. "I keep telling myself that Cyn and Tabby are still here, but part of me believes even they'll go away eventually." God, she'd been terrified when her family up and left. The fight had been huge, the bruises her father had left behind a reminder of why it had been a good thing in the end.

But she missed her brother and sisters with a ferocity that would have shocked anyone who didn't know her well. Temp, Hope and Faith had been the only things that made living in the Walsh household bearable. When Hope disappeared, Glory had been devastated.

It was the first of many losses she'd suffered over the years. Her twin had never been found.

"Glory?"

"Hmm?"

"Tell me about Hope."

Glory winced. "Another time?"

30   www.danamariebell.com

He studied her for a long, uncomfortable minute before nodding. "I want to know. Maybe we can ask some of the shifters to help find out what happened to her."

For the first time in a long while Glory felt some hope. Why hadn't she thought of that? "You think they'd be willing to?"

Ryan smiled. "You're technically a member of the Halle Pride. I think Max and Emma would be willing to help you out."

Glory smiled. "Maybe it's not such a bad thing, having you stick around."

"Yup. I'm like Super Glue. You'll never get me off your skin."

He sounded far too happy about that. "You're crazy."

He hummed under his breath. "Leave everything to me. You worry about our date, and I'll worry about setting up a meeting with the Alpha and Curana. Deal?"

Jeez. She was going to regret this, she just knew it. But what else could she do? She kissed his chin, knowing that sooner or later she was going to give in to him. "Fine. Deal."

The soft, sweet kiss she received in return made her think that belonging to Ryan might not be such a bad thing after all.

CHAPTER THREE

"Changing your shirt again?"

Ryan snarled at Julian DuCharme, the Spirit Bear who'd mated Cyn. The man was smirking, his dark eyes sparkling with mischief. His long hair was tied back in a braid that Cyn would undoubtedly undo the moment she got her hands on it.

"It's like watching a sixteen-year-old girl get ready for a first date." Alex, bald and big and sweet as honey unless you pissed him off, grabbed a dark blue button-down shirt. "Here. It goes with your eyes." The asshole batted his lashes at Ryan and sighed. "You want me to do your hair?"

Julian began to laugh. "I get to do his nails."

"Fuck you both very much." Ryan slipped the shirt on, checking himself out in the mirror. He wanted to look perfect for Glory. She deserved to have a mate she could be proud to be seen with, and he was going to do whatever it took to give her that. Even…

He shuddered.

Go clothing shopping.

Ugh.

"Okay, pretty boy. Let's make you gorgeous." Julian grabbed a brush, laughing harder when Ryan swatted him. "Oh, come on. We can put barrettes in and everything."

Ryan thought about gutting them both, but at least his hands had stopped shaking. The two of them had stopped by, taken one look at his pale face and wide eyes and shoved him back into his apartment. They'd proceeded to try and get him to relax, but until he had Glory mated and marked, not much was going to accomplish that.

She'd scared the shit out of him earlier that day. Her panic attack, and the reason behind it, had left him with very little choice. He had to make sure she understood exactly what she was to him, and fast. Seeing her in pain, unable to breathe, unable to even think, had shaken him to the core.

He'd already called Eric, Bunny's brother and Ryan's cousin, and sent him back to deal with the work in Oregon. Ryan couldn't leave Glory, and Glory couldn't leave Cynful, so Ryan was staying in Halle. Eric was just as qualified as he was to handle the money aspect of the business, and since he would wind up inheriting Bunsun Exteriors along with Bunny, Ryan had no issue with Eric taking over the books.

But somehow, Ryan didn't think Eric would remain in Oregon for long. All the Bunsun-Williamses had fallen in love with the small Pennsylvania town. Ryan was positive they'd all wind up here in the end, taking Bunsun Exteriors' corporate offices from the West Coast and moving it to the East.

Ryan had no issue with that. The closer he was to Glory, the better.

"Seriously, though. You look good, you've got a great plan and Glory panics at the thought of you leaving. I think you're doing better than you thought you were." Bunny grabbed the picnic basket Ryan was planning to use for today's date and placed the wine he'd picked out and two plastic glasses inside. "If she cares enough about you to have a panic attack, then she might be closer to allowing you to mark her than we thought."

Dear God, Ryan hoped so. The mate dreams were exhausting him.

Julian handed Ryan his jacket. "Remember. Glory's a lot more delicate than she seems."

This time it was Ryan who laughed. "She's survived losing her family, her twin's disappearance, being shot at and almost killed. She's stronger than you think, Julian." Ryan slipped the jacket on and grabbed the basket. "Just because she's prone to panic attacks doesn't mean she's weak. My mate is a survivor." And no one could be prouder of their mate than Ryan was. Glory was *amazing*.

"I'm just saying, be careful with her. I don't want to have to explain to Cyn how my friend broke hers."

Ryan snorted as the three men left the apartment. Ryan still had to pick up the food and Glory. Checking his watch, he saw he still had plenty of time. "I'm not going to break her." He grinned evilly. "Well, not in a *bad* way."

Bunny shook his head. "Just do us a favor and make sure your mate is happy."

"Because if your mate is happy, our mates are happy." Julian climbed into his car. "And one more bit of advice. Clean your apartment before you bring her back here."

Ryan frowned. "What's wrong with my apartment?"

Bunny and Julian glanced at each other and shuddered. "Just do it."

"It's not that bad."

Both men stared at him.

"Really. My place in Oregon was way worse."

Julian cocked an eyebrow at him. "Did any of the intriguing new life forms you were breeding start to speak to you? And how did they feel about your leaving them alone?"

"Fine." Ryan sighed. "I'll run the vacuum before I bring her back."

Bunny shivered. "You might want to consider a flamethrower. I hear you can get one on eBay."

"Or Craigslist."

"Even better."

"Ha. Ha." Ryan climbed into the car, placing the empty picnic basket on the passenger side floor. He was going to do this up right, damn it. "I have to go pick up the food before I get Glory."

"Good luck." Bunny patted the hood of his car. "And remember what we said."

"Be good to Glory and fumigate my apartment."

Bunny and Julian both laughed as they said good-bye. Ryan made his way to the restaurant and picked up the food before heading over to the apartment Glory had once shared with Cyn and Tabby. Now that the girls were living with their mates in their homes, Glory was all alone. That was something Ryan hoped to fix, and soon. He was more than willing to do what Bunny had done and buy a home in the area, but first he had to mark his mate.

He pulled up in front of Glory's home on time and wiped his sweaty palms against his jeans. The guys were right. He *was* acting like a sixteen-year-old on his first date, but damn it. He'd waited so long for her to say yes to going out with him that he felt nervous as hell. What if the date was a flop? What if she decided he wasn't worth it?

He took a deep breath and got out of the car. There was only one way to find out, and that wasn't sitting in the car and hyperventilating.

Ryan knocked on Glory's door and waited. He knew the area around her apartment intimately, having stood guard over her both when Tabby was in danger and when the girls were being targeted by a madman. He scanned the area now, automatically looking for threats to his mate. Finding none, he turned back to her door just in time to see her open it.

His mouth watered at the sight of his mate. God, she looked edible. Jeans that were painted on, a wispy nothing of a top, and high-heeled boots combined with that cascade of blue hair, and he was ready to say fuck the picnic and, well, just fuck her. "You look incredible."

She grinned. "So do you." She waved him in. "Let me grab my coat and we can get out of here."

He was all for that. "I think you're going to like what I've got planned." And if things worked out the way he hoped, he'd love the aftermath.

"We'll see."

He didn't let her skepticism get to him. He understood now why she constantly pushed him away. He'd have to prove over and over that he wasn't going anywhere, but his mate was worth it. He'd show her however many times she needed that she'd never be alone again. "You ready?"

"Ready." She slid her arm through his and grabbed her purse. "Ryan?"

"Yeah?"

For just a moment, she looked terribly sad. "I'm sorry."

"For what?"

She locked her door before answering. "Do you know why none of my relationships have ever worked in the past?"

"Because you always leave before they do." She glanced at him, obviously startled, as he led her to his car. "It's not rocket science, SG."

She blew her curls out of her eyes as she settled in the passenger seat. "You're such a smart ass."

He laughed as he settled into the driver's seat. "Better a smart ass than a dumb ass."

She glanced at him sideways. "But first you have to be smart, or you're just an ass."

"Oh, ouch." He put his hand to his chest. "You wound me."

Laughing reluctantly, Glory put on her seat belt. "Do I smell Chinese food?"

"Yup."

"But I thought…" She trailed off, biting her lip.

"What?" *Oh, God. Don't tell me I screwed up on the first date.*

"Nothing." But she turned to look out the passenger side window rather than at him.

"I wanted us to be alone, so I arranged a surprise. Was I wrong?"

She looked back at him, her gaze speculative. "No, maybe not."

Thank fuck. Because he'd have to ditch the food in the nearest trash can if she'd said yes, and he really liked Kung Pao chicken. "Then let's get this party started."

The mysterious smile that crossed her face scared the shit out of him, but it was too late now. He just hoped things went the way he'd planned, because he didn't think he could survive it if his idea set him back to square one with her.

There was only one real place in town worthy of a first date: Noah's, the best restaurant in town. So that was what she dressed for, expecting spaghetti carbonara and good wine, despite the fact that he'd said the date would be casual.

So of course, that wasn't where Ryan had planned to take her, because Ryan rarely did what she expected. She should have known.

Hell. She should have worn sneakers.

"The park?" Glory shivered, glad she'd chosen to dress in her good black jeans and not the teeny skirt she'd originally intended. It was cold out, the sky that bright, pale blue that you only saw at the tail end of winter.

Ryan glanced down at her, amused. "You want to run into my family?"

Glory winced. The Bunsun-Williams clan was loud, boisterous and very much a part of Ryan's life. She'd watched Tabby and Cyn struggle with the overwhelming family. None of the girls were used to having that kind of loving dynamic in their lives, and the adjustment was an ongoing process that sometimes left them exhausted. The Bunsun-Williamses had "accidentally" intruded on more than one of Julian and Cyn's dates in the past. So perhaps having a picnic wasn't such a bad idea after all. "Good point."

"Just so you know, I can't cook." Ryan grinned. "I can't boil water without setting something on fire, so unless you can cook we'll be eating a hell of a lot of takeout."

Glory took the hand he offered when her heeled boots sunk into the grass. Spring was definitely coming if the ground had started to thaw enough for that. "You think so, huh?" He was assuming an awful lot if he thought she was going to cook for him.

He chuckled. "Ask Bunny about the time I tried to barbecue. He still screams like a little girl when I mention pork chops."

She helped him set up the blanket on the ground. "I thought barbecue was bred into the bone with guys, like football and setting farts on fire."

He stared at her for a moment. "Farts on fire?"

She shrugged. She'd seen more than one butt burn when her brother was younger.

"Yeah. Not this guy." He settled her on the blanket, taking a seat next to her. "I wasn't kidding when I said I set water on fire." He opened the basket and pulled out a bottle of wine. "My cousins played hockey with the leftovers."

She sputtered a laugh and began helping him unpack their dinner. The smell of Chinese food filled the air. She opened one of the boxes as he took the other. "Mm, General Tso's chicken. How'd you know that's my favorite?"

"A certain little Wolf told me." He handed her some chopsticks, using his own pair to dig out what smelled like Kung Pao chicken. "Dig in."

She did, moaning as the spicy-sweet flavor exploded on her tongue. "'S good."

He poured two glasses of wine, handing her one. "I want something from you." He laughed when she glared at him. "That too, but, no. I want you to ask me anything."

She blinked, confused. "Anything?"

He nodded, licking sauce off the end of his chopstick. "We've danced around each other quite a bit, but..." He sighed. "We haven't tried to get to know each other, not the way mates should."

Glory grimaced. Most of that was her fault. He'd been trying so hard to get close to her, even leaving her those presents, but she couldn't help the way she reacted to Ryan. The man scared the piss out of her. No one she'd ever met had ever held the power to hurt her quite so badly, but Ryan Williams could without even trying. Already she couldn't imagine him not bopping into the shop, smiling and chasing her around her piercing station.

What would she do if he left?

"No. Don't feel bad." He put his hand on hers, his blue eyes going brown for an instant as his Bear peeked out at her. "*Don't* feel bad. I should have known why you kept pushing me away."

"Oh really? Like I go around telling people I have abandonment issues." Glory rolled her eyes.

He used his chopsticks to pick up a bit of General Tso's and held it to her lips. "I still should have known."

"I hate to tell you this, but you aren't Super Bear." She laughed. "Hell, even Super Bear didn't know, okay?"

"Then I want to know. Tell me everything."

Glory sighed. "Wonderful first date topic. You really know how to show a girl a good time."

He froze, his expression stricken before it closed off. "You're right. We should keep things light—"

She covered his lips with her finger. "Damn it. Don't look like that." She pouted at him. "How long have we known each other?"

"Close to a year."

From the wary way he answered she was willing to bet he knew down to the day, but didn't want to seem like a stalker. Which he totally was. "You said you wanted me to ask you anything, but the truth is you want the same." He nodded, still wary. "Then do it. Ask. I'll tell you if you go too far."

"You mean it?"

"Have I ever said something I didn't mean?"

"I refuse to answer that on the grounds that I may be incinerated." He popped a bite of General Tso's in her mouth when she opened it to reply. "All right. Back and forth?"

She tilted her head. "You mean, I ask you something, then you ask me?"

"One for one, with the caveat that we can say no with no hard feelings."

She thought about that for a moment, but she couldn't see a downside. "That's fair."

He held out his hand. "It's a deal, then." She smiled and took his hand, ready to shake, but instead he tugged her forward and planted a soft kiss on her mouth. "Go ahead, sweetheart. Ask me something."

She licked her lips, the spice from his dinner mingling with the sweetness of hers. "Um." Her brain had completely blanked out at the touch of his lips.

He gave her that smug, knowing smile that made her want to beat him with a sledgehammer...or ride him like a pony. She hadn't decided yet. "What's wrong? Bear got your tongue?"

The sledgehammer was winning. "What's it like having to call Alex boss? You know—" she leaned in closer and ran her finger down his arm, "—having to do *every little thing* he tells you to."

"Do I want to know what's going through your head, or should I just assume it's dirty and try not to picture it?" He shuddered when she wagged her brows. "Ugh. Really?" He grimaced. "I'd rather…" His gaze went dreamy. "Oh. Cyn is *your* boss. Can I picture—"

She hit him. Hard.

"All righty then." Ryan rubbed his chest absently, ignoring Glory as she shook the pain out of her hand. His chest was a lot harder than she'd thought. "First off, I don't call Bunny boss. I call his dad boss, remember? Bunny doesn't own the business. Besides, odds are good it will be Eric who becomes the owner of Bunsun Exteriors. Bunny wants to run the East Coast operations, but our home base is still in Oregon." He picked up her sore hand and kissed it.

"But didn't Alex say they might be moving it here?"

Ryan nodded. "Yeah, but I don't know if the whole business will, or just the family."

"I can't see one going without the other." She took another bite of food.

"True. Maybe they will move out here, but either way Alex and I will be staying here, where you and Cyn are." He smiled. "My turn. Tell me about your family."

"I have two sisters and a brother. Hope disappeared when I was sixteen. Temperance is my older brother—"

"Temperance? Poor bastard. Who names their son that?"

"My asshole dad, who wanted us all named after virtues. Faith is my younger sister. She should be about Heather's age."

"Speaking of which, Heather is working out, right? She's been really happy coming into the shop."

Glory grinned. "That kid is going to own her own shop someday. She's really good, Ryan, and she's scary-smart. I'm glad Cyn offered her a job."

"Me too, no matter what Eric says. I've never seen her so happy before, and she's coming out of her shell a little more every day." He kissed her hand again. "Thank you for that."

She blushed. "I haven't done anything."

"You've done more than you know." He picked up his carton and began eating again. "Your turn."

She bit her lip and asked the one thing that she'd always wondered about. "Why me?"

"Besides the fact that your scent fills my head, your voice sends shivers down my spine and your smile makes the sun shine?"

"I…guess." Oh, he was *good*.

Ryan kissed her again. "I like you, more than you know. You're funny, brave, smart and beautiful and you're not afraid to fight for your loved ones. You're not perfect—" for a second she almost felt insulted, "—but I like your quirks just as much as your strengths."

"Fine." She bit her lip, unbearably touched. "You get a second date."

Ryan just smiled and fed her another bite of food.

"Oh, I've been meaning to thank you."

"For what?" Ryan was watching her, his blue eyes blending with the brown of his Bear.

"The presents."

Ryan's stillness frightened her, but his question terrified her. "What presents?"

Glory took a deep breath. "Shit. You didn't leave me champagne and roses this morning, did you?"

"No." And his blue eyes were now completely brown, fangs peeking out from under his lip. "I didn't."

"Then who did?" Because now she was creeped the hell out. Someone had been watching her closely enough to figure out what her favorite things were without her knowing about it.

Worse, her shifter boyfriend, who was constantly around her apartment, hadn't noticed.

CHAPTER FOUR

Ryan opened the front door of his apartment the next morning and stopped dead in his tracks. "Shit."

Bunny held up a sack of donuts. "Good morning, Ryan."

No one should look that fucking cheerful that early in the morning. Ryan wanted to maul him just for the grin.

Julian breezed past him holding a huge box of coffee. "Good morning, lover boy."

Ryan whimpered. Not him, too. Julian might live only because he had the coffee.

"So." Bunny's grin got impossibly wider. "How'd it go?"

"Yeah, did you express your undying love?" Julian put his hand to his chest and fluttered his lashes.

There was not enough coffee in the world. "Hell. You're going to make me talk about my feelings, aren't you?"

Bunny started setting out the donuts while Julian poured three cups of coffee. "Yup. We might even curl our hair and wax our legs."

Ryan whimpered and shut the door. "Can't I just go to work?"

"Nope." Bunny handed him a jelly-filled donut. "Spill."

"Yeah, did you mate her?" Julian's wicked expression would have looked more adult if he didn't have a ring of powdered sugar around his mouth.

Nothing says "I'm sexy" like appearing as if you've just blown the Stay Puft Marshmallow Man. "No." He'd walked her to her door like a gentleman, refusing to give in to the howling of his Bear. He'd sat outside her apartment building, guarding her until the wee hours of the morning. He hadn't scented anything strange around her apartment, but that didn't mean whoever had left those presents wasn't around. "But she told me I'm getting a second date."

"Huh. For Glory that's practically a proposal of marriage." Julian fixed his coffee, adding enough sugar to send a six-year-old into orbit. "So things went well?"

Ryan took his cup and his donut and sat his ass on the sofa. If the two wanted to discuss his love life he was going to be comfortable, damn it. "Sort of." When the two shot him concerned glances he told them about the gifts someone had been leaving his mate. "We think someone's been watching her for a while now. They know her tastes, and I'm willing to bet that they know now that she's living alone."

"Shit." Bunny clapped Ryan's shoulder. "You need us to guard her?"

Julian shrugged, his expression unhappy. "I've got some free time."

Ryan winced in sympathy. Julian hadn't found a new job since Dr. Howard's practice had shut down. The man was a registered nurse, but his gift as a Kermode prevented him from working in the hospital. The other doctors in town weren't hiring at the moment, which meant Julian was SOL in Halle. He was even thinking of taking work outside Halle, just so his work visa wouldn't get revoked. If that happened, he risked deportation back to Canada. Hell, Ryan was about to suggest he get a job at the local college campus. It would be something, at least. "Thanks, and yeah. Any help you can give would be good."

Bunny squeezed his shoulder before letting go. "As far as the date went, did you round any bases?"

Ryan stared at Bunny. "Really?"

"What?" That innocent look on Bunny's face was as out of place as whiskers on a rock. "When are you going to claim her?""I thought I'd get to second base first." Ryan grinned at his cousin as Bunny settled on the sofa next to him.

"Good. Tabby wants this settled. She says Glory's panic attack scared her, and when Tabby is frightened I'm one unhappy Bunny." Bunny growled. "And if Glory has a stalker, Tabby is going to be *very* unhappy."

"I swear, our mates are trouble magnets." Julian sipped his coffee with an unhappy sigh.

"It could be worse."

"How?"

"They could be Rangers fans." When the other two stared at him blankly, he changed the subject. "We're going to try and find out what happened to Hope."

Julian settled on the overstuffed recliner Ryan loved napping in. "I can contact Gabe, see if he's willing to help us look into her disappearance. We should tell him about the stuff someone's been leaving for Glory as well."

"You think they're connected?" Bunny scowled.

"We *just* decided to look into Hope's disappearance. Glory says the presents have been showing up for a few weeks now, and from the looks of things the asshole's been watching her, learning what she likes."

Both men cursed, but Julian summed up his feelings perfectly. "We need to find this guy and rip his head off. I'm tired of our mates being in danger."

"It could truly be a secret admirer, someone who simply wants to make an impression."

Bunny could be right, but Ryan wasn't so sure. "We can ask the girls if anything odd has gone on around the shop, but we all know the answer to that one."

All three men grimaced. Sometimes it seemed like nothing normal ever happened around their girls.

Ryan sighed. "We should talk to Emma and Max Cannon. Since Glory and Hope were human when she disappeared, we might need their approval to borrow Gabe for the investigation."

Bunny shook his head. "I don't think so, *because* they were human. This would fall under Gabe's job as sheriff of Halle, not as a Hunter or even the Second. There shouldn't be any conflict, so I'd go straight to him with this."

"I agree." Julian leaned forward, impatiently brushing a lock of his waist-length black hair behind his ear. "This isn't shifter business, but human. So his human authority would be ascendant. Besides, Max declared all three girls under his protection. He'd probably give his permission anyway, so the point is moot."

Ryan had to admit they were probably right. "Then I'll call him and ask him to meet us at Cynful. Glory can talk to him, explain what happened all those years ago."

"And Gabe might even have the original missing person's report on file, since she disappeared here in Halle." Julian grinned. "Cyn will be willing to give you any help you need."

"Tabby too, though I've already told her to take it easy. I don't want her risking the baby."

"Thanks, guys. I don't think they'll be in any danger, but whatever we find, Glory will need her friends and family around her."

Julian pulled out his cell phone. "Want me to call Gabe and have him meet us there?"

"Not a bad idea. I'll call Glory and let her know what's up." Ryan pulled out his own cell phone and punched in the number for Cynful.

"Good morning, Cynful Tattoos, Cyn speaking. How may I help… Oh. It's you."

"And good morning to you too, sunshine."

Cyn grunted.

"Are we still decaffeinated?"

She grunted again.

"Julian's here with coffee."

"I hate you so much right now. Tabby vomits if she even smells coffee." Cyn whimpered. "I'm *dying* here."

Ryan didn't laugh. "Listen, the guys and I are heading over with Gabe."

"Why? What's wrong?"

That overprotective instinct of Cyn's had kicked into high gear. She suddenly sounded wide awake and vaguely growly, her Bear ready to defend her friends.

"It's okay. I promised Glory we'd look into Hope's disappearance, so we thought we'd meet with Gabe at Cynful where Glory feels most comfortable."

"Oh." Cyn sighed, the sound relieved. "Good idea. Come on over, and bring herbal tea."

Ryan started to laugh. "Can you sound any more disgusted?"

"Hate. You." And Cyn hung up before he could answer, not that he could. He was laughing too hard.

Julian was clipping his phone back to his belt when Ryan hung up. "Gabe says he'll be there in an hour."

Ryan stood, putting a lid on his coffee. Tabby might not be able to stand the smell, but Ryan wasn't giving up his early morning love. "Your mate wants to kill us for our caffeine."

Julian sighed, but it was anything but sad. "Yeah. She's mean like that."

Bunny shrugged on his jacket and grabbed his coffee. "C'mon. I'll need you both to suck some breath mints before we go in the shop."

Julian's expression turned instantly concerned. "It's that bad?" When Bunny nodded glumly, Julian frowned. "Do you want me to check her out?"

As Bears, each of them had the power to heal, both themselves and others. But where Bunny and Ryan could only heal minor wounds, aches and illnesses, Julian, as a Spirit Bear, had powers neither of them could truly comprehend. He could take someone on the brink of death and drag them back to life, but the cost to him was horrific. He'd nearly died twice, once when saving Jamie Howard when Jamie's mate was killed, and again when saving Cyn after she'd been shot by Tabby's ex-Alpha. If anyone could help Tabby with her morning sickness and her aversion to coffee, it would be him.

But Bunny shook his head. "Nah. Her OB/GYN said this was normal. It'll pass once the baby's born, if not sooner." With Jamie Howard no longer practicing medicine, Tabby had been forced to go to a human gynecologist. Luckily, shifter pregnancies followed human ones. A baby would pop out, not a cub, so they were safe there. Still, just to be safe, Julian was monitoring her pregnancy almost as closely as Bunny was.

"If you're sure." Julian tugged on his own coat.

Ryan headed for the front door, donut and coffee in hand. "If you value your lives you'll bring those donuts."

Laughing as the two Bears scrambled for the donuts, Ryan headed out to his car, eager to see his mate.

"Rye?"

"Hmm?"

Bunny frowned. "If we stay in Halle…?"

Ryan nodded. "I'll work with you."

Bunny relaxed, his natural, easy-going smile gracing his face. "Good."

"You were seriously worried about that?" Ryan shook his head. "Chloe's out here, Glory's out here. You're out here. Of course I'm staying. Asshole."

"Thanks. Buttmunch."

Julian walked past them snickering. "I do not want to know if you're kissing cousins."

Rolling his eyes, Ryan slipped into his car. "Meet you at Cynful."

"Will do. And Ryan?" Bunny squeezed his shoulder reassuringly. "It's going to be all right, no matter what we find."

"I know. Because I'll be there for her, no matter what."

"Exactly."

***

When Ryan said he was going to do something, he sure as hell did it. Glory watched as Gabriel Anderson, the Halle sheriff and one of the local Pumas, stepped into Cynful Tattoos with a file folder in his hand and a determined air. The man filled out a uniform like no one else, his broad shoulders and piercing blue eyes giving her more than one wet dream before Ryan came to town.

But the sheriff was utterly devoted to his wife, Sarah, a sweet woman who worked in the local high school, and Ryan…

Well, Ryan had given her more than wet dreams.

He was standing there, arms crossed, blue eyes sharp, his dark hair tousled like he hadn't gotten the chance to brush it before leaving his apartment that morning. His breath had smelled suspiciously like orange breath mints when his lips had grazed hers.

"Hey, Glory. I hear you want to talk to me." The sheriff held out his hand, looking surprised when she hugged him. He'd helped save Cyn, and been instrumental in giving Tabby a home. As far as Glory was concerned, he was family.

"Gabe." She pressed a kiss to his cheek, enjoying the blush that highlighted his face. The man was adorable, and Sarah was a lucky woman. "Did Ryan fill you in?"

"Ah. Yes." He fumbled the papers he'd been holding in his hands. "You want me to reopen the case into your missing twin." And that quickly, the blushing man turned into the no-nonsense sheriff. "It won't be easy. It seems like the investigator seriously dropped the ball on this one." He shook his head. "I have to contact the old sheriff and see what he knows about it."

"Was he…?" Glory held up her hands, making claws of her fingers, and snarled, pulling her upper lip back from her teeth.

"You're cute." Gabe grinned and patted her on the head. "Yes, Sheriff Giordano was a shifter."

Why did that last name sound familiar?

Gabe must have understood her confused expression. "The old sheriff was the father of Dr. Adrian Giordano."

She'd been around the Pumas enough now to know that Adrian Giordano was one of the rulers of the Pride. The Alpha and Curana led the pride, with their Betas, Simon and Becky Holt. Then there was the Marshal, Dr. Giordano, who ruled over the physical well-being of the Pride. He was the one who saw to it that all of them were safe and controlled any enforcers needed to protect them all. His Second was Gabe.

Gabe's mate, Sarah, was the Omega, a woman who could sense the emotional well-being of the Pride and, in some cases, manipulate their emotions, calming ongoing feuds or shoring up a Puma's flagging self-esteem. Tabby had told her once that Sarah had walked up to Alex and stopped him from going into a rage when he discovered that Tabby had nearly been raped. Glory had seen Alex and Ryan shifted. She knew how large and angry the Grizzlies could be.

And Sarah had tamed the beast to her hand. That was one scary power…and one awful responsibility. Glory was glad Bears didn't have Omegas. She'd hate to think that she might accidentally wind up wielding power over someone else's emotions when her own were such a roller-coaster. Glory knew she had no business messing in someone else's head.

"All right." Gabe led Ryan and Glory into the back room. Cyn and Tabby would watch the shop while Glory answered Gabe's questions. Gabe set the file folder on the break table and took a seat. "Tell me what you remember."

Glory sat across from him, not surprised when Ryan took the seat next to her. She took a deep breath and began. "When my sister and I were sixteen, she disappeared."

Gabe nodded and opened up his notebook. "Go on. She went to the library on…" He opened the file folder and took a quick look through the papers there. "August twenty-sixth."

"Yeah." Glory twirled some of her hair around her finger. It helped calm her, the powder-blue curls so unlike her twin's pale blonde hair. "I didn't want to go. I wanted to go shopping with Cyn. So Hope left without me, and my father wasn't happy about it."

"She went alone?"

"Yes. We had a huge argument about it. My mother was still married to my father at that time, and tried to intervene, but we'd learned by then that she didn't have any real power over us. It was my father who held it all."

"He was abusive toward you."

"He would beat us, but no one believed us when we tried to tell them what he was doing. He was a man of the cloth, a preacher. No one wanted to believe he was abusing his children."

"No one except Cyn and her mother, who took you in when your family abandoned you."

"Mrs. Reyes is more my mom than my biological parent ever was." Glory grinned, hoping they didn't see through the sharpness to the pain. "And Cyn is more a nagging dad."

"I heard that!"

Glory rolled her eyes. Cyn's hearing had gotten super-scary-good recently, ever since her mate had claimed her and turned her into a Kodiak. "Good!" she bellowed back.

Ryan stuck his finger in his ear with a wince.

Grinning, Gabe shook his head at her. "All right. So you go shopping with Cyn—"

"Nope. I never made it. My dad got a hold of me and grounded me."

Gabe's brows rose as he flipped through the papers again. "The notes here say you went out with Cyn."

"That's what my father told the officer."

Gabe's gaze hardened. "What did *you* tell the officer?"

"The officer never spoke to me."

Gabe swore under his breath. "He was a member of your father's congregation."

"Sorry, Gabe." She hoped the man had retired by now, but if not, Gabe might have to sanction a seasoned officer for not speaking to a possible witness. "If it helps, I think he told the officer that I was too traumatized by Hope's disappearance to speak."

"What was the truth?" Ryan's voice was dangerously soft.

"I was black and blue." Glory tugged on her curl. "Look, my father was very good at making me seem like the bad child, the wild one who needed to be punished constantly. He hated that I was friends with Cyn, that I wanted a tattoo or my ears pierced. I wasn't godly enough to be his child, and he made sure I was the example the others didn't want to live up to. Even Hope couldn't stop him from taking things out on me, and he adored her."

Gabe's jaw clenched. "You were identical?"

Glory nodded. "She always dressed the way he wanted and wore her hair the way he wanted, to keep him from hurting her."

"Do you think he did other things to her?"

God, how many times had she asked herself that over the last few years? "I don't know. She was always quiet, withdrawn, but it got worse as we grew older. I just thought she was trying to stay off my dad's radar."

"Do you think your father had anything to do with her disappearance?"

She shrugged. "He lost his mind when we couldn't find her. I've never seen him that angry. And he blamed me, like he'd hoped I would be the one taken and not her."

Gabe tapped his pen against the table, his expression grim. "Is it possible that what happened to her was meant for you?"

She hated to do it, but she nodded. "Yes. If my father was the one behind it, then yes."

"All right. Walk me through everything you remember before she disappeared, the day she went to the library, and the days afterward."

Glory nudged Ryan. "Can you get me some water? This is going to take a while."

Ryan softly kissed her forehead. "I'm here for you, sweetheart."

"You shouldn't be." She closed her eyes. God, why did she keep trying to push him away? She was such a masochist.

"But I am, and I'm not going anywhere." He got up and grabbed a bottle of water out of the mini fridge. "Go on. Tell him what he needs to know."

She opened the bottle and took a sip before obeying Ryan's request. "Before she left, everything seemed normal." She snorted. "Normal for us, anyway. We all went to school, we all came home and did our homework. We hung out with our friends and gossiped about boys."

"Your brother and sisters acted normally?"

"Before Hope went missing? Sure. Temp tried to keep the peace between us, but even he couldn't keep our dad off us if he decided we needed to be punished." She fiddled with the bottle cap, refusing to look at Gabe. "Temp was nothing like our dad. He was the one who did all the dad things, like making sure we got to school on time and lecturing us about boys." She smiled wistfully. "And he doted on Faith."

"Your youngest sister."

Glory bit her lip. "I hope…" Ryan took hold of her hand, and only then did she realize how badly she was trembling. "I hope Temp kept our dad off her."

"Why didn't your mother gain custody?"

Glory finally looked at Gabe. "Because doormats don't get anything but stepped on."

Gabe nodded once. "All right. Everything was normal right up until Hope went to the library. That day, did any of your family react oddly? Was there anything strange, anything out of place?"

Glory tried hard to remember the details of that day, but everything up until the moment they all realized Hope wasn't coming home was a blur. "I spent the day in my room, bruised and sulking. Temp brought me lunch and Faith tried singing to me through the door before my father screamed at her to stop. Dinner came and went, but Hope didn't come home."

"Then what?"

"The cops came and took a statement from my dad. They declared her missing because she was a minor, and they wanted to get her face out to the surrounding police precincts. But they never found her."

"Your father left town when you were eighteen and left you behind."

Glory hated thinking about that time. She'd been left in the cold with the clothes on her back, beaten black and blue and with five dollars in her wallet. Thank God for Mrs. Reyes, and thank God for Cyn, because otherwise Glory would have been homeless. "Yeah."

"The years in between must have been hard."

Ryan was still holding her hand, but at that he glared at Gabe. "I'd imagine so, if her dad blamed her for her sister's disappearance."

Gabe sighed. "I have to know this stuff, Ryan. The family is the first place we look when a child goes missing, even a teenager like Hope."

"It's okay, Ryan." Glory leaned her head against his arm briefly. "I'm okay."

He huffed out a breath, but it didn't sound quite human.

Glory ignored him. "My dad became vicious to all of us, but especially me. My mother ran, just disappeared one night while we were sleeping."

Gabe's brows rose. "Disappeared."

"We got post cards from her. I think she's in Phoenix."

Gabe made a note. "Temp?"

"Stuck around, mostly for me and Faith." She sighed. "Faith is eighteen. With any luck, they're both free of my dad."

"I'm going to try and find them, see what they know."

"I have no idea where they went when they left Halle. My dad didn't exactly care if I could get a hold of them or not."

Gabe's smile was cold. "Then I will *make* him care."

Ryan's smile was just as vicious as Gabe's. She had the feeling that if Pastor Walsh ever returned to Halle, he'd be the victim of a bear mauling, and she found she couldn't care less. Any love she'd once had for her father had long since been beaten out of her.

"Good."

CHAPTER FIVE

Ryan managed to catch Gabe before he got too far from Cynful Tattoos. He needed to catch the sheriff before he climbed into his patrol car. "Hey, I wanted to talk to you."

Gabe stopped at the door of his car and eyed him for a moment before sighing. "You want to help in the hunt."

Ryan nodded. "Wouldn't you, if it was your mate's sister who was missing?"

"Fuck yeah." Gabe jerked his head toward Frank's Diner. "Let's grab some coffee and chat."

"Thanks, Gabe." Ryan would have tried to go it alone, but he had Glory to think about now. He couldn't allow her to think that he'd left even for a second, not until she got it through her head that Ryan would rather cut off important body parts than leave her.

The two men entered the diner, and Ryan grimaced. The new waitress was a perky brunette with a big smile and bigger tits, but he much preferred the one who'd been forced by circumstances beyond her control to quit. His baby sister, Chloe, had loved working here and at the veterinarian's clinic where she hoped to someday become a vet. Those dreams, like this job, were gone now, lost to a brutal beating that had nearly killed her and left her with problem hands and a speech impediment. Chloe had only survived thanks to the intervention of Bunny and Julian, something Ryan would never forget.

The waitress seated them far enough away from the rest of the diners that Gabe and Ryan could enjoy a private discussion. Gabe must use this place often for quiet chats. It was the place he'd first questioned Bunny when they'd arrived in Halle, and was one of the most popular eateries in the town.

They ordered coffee, and waited until the waitress was out of earshot. "All right." Gabe folded his hands on the table. "Talk to me."

"I want to be involved in the hunt for Hope."

"You think Glory is in danger?"

"If we poke the hornet's nest, something might come out to sting her." Ryan wasn't going to let his mate hurt.

"Agreed, but—"

Ryan held up his hand. "You're in charge. I'm not stupid. I'm not a law enforcement officer or a Hunter, so I'm leaving it up to you."

"But you could be."

Ryan's brows rose. "I'm no Hunter."

"Your instincts are good. You could be in law enforcement."

Ryan started to laugh. "I'm an accountant."

"Yet you managed to track that rogue Alpha all on your own."

Ryan's laughter cut off, his eyes shifting to his Bear's. Whenever he thought about what that son of a bitch ex-Alpha had done to his mate he wanted to rip him to shreds all over again. "I wasn't tracking him because he was Tabby's stalker."

"I know." Gabe's voice hardened. "That doesn't mean you won't be an asset on this case."

Ryan's eyes returned to their normal human blue, his Bear backing down instantly. Ryan's Bear was calmed by the anger in Gabe's voice. Gabe had been just as outraged over the pain Glory suffered as Ryan had been, and the knowledge that a Hunter agreed with him soothed his beast.

Hunters were a group of men and women sanctioned by the shifter Senate to hunt rogue shifters down. Rogues threatened the fabric of shifter society, either by almost outing their existence to the humans around them or by going after other shifters. The man who'd hurt his mate had been rogue, hurting the people around Tabby in order to hurt her. More often than not, a Hunter would be forced to kill the rogue in question. If the ex-Alpha hadn't been rogue, Ryan would have been labeled a rogue himself for killing him. Instead, the Hunter had approved the kill, and had made sure the Senate had no room for complaint.

"Glory's also been getting presents left on her doorstep."

Gabe's brows rose. "Oh, really?"

"I didn't scent anything around, but we know some shifters are good at masking their scents."

"A Fox?"

"Or another shifter who's learned how to hunt."

Gabe snarled. "A rogue Hunter."

This time it was Ryan who was shocked. "Your Hunter instincts are going off."

Gabe nodded. "Which is one of the reasons why I'm not fighting you on this. Something isn't right. There have been too many attacks on the girls, and the whole Gary thing still isn't completely resolved."

"Still?" Tabby's stalker had almost raped her in the woods. Twice. He was lucky to still be alive. Hell, if it had been Ryan, he wouldn't be. But the Alpha had ordered Bunny to stand down, to allow the shifter Senate to dispense justice to Gary. "He still hasn't told you who his Alpha is?"

"No. He's kept his mouth shut and his head down. He'll do time for what he tried to do to Tabby, but that's it."

"Shit."

"Add in Hope's disappearance and the presents on Glory's doorstep and I'm worried."

Ryan's skin crawled. "You think Hope was attacked by a shifter?"

"Yes."

Ryan took a deep, calming breath. His Grizzly was pacing under his skin, restless to confront the danger to his mate and eliminate it. "Talk to me, Gabe. Tell me what you're thinking."

Gabe waited until the waitress finished pouring their coffee, ordering one of the breakfast specials when she was done. Ryan, not one to pass up a meal, also ordered. "I don't have any concrete evidence, but my Hunter senses are tingling. Gary still hasn't told us who he was working for, and his friends aren't talking either. Then there was the attack on Cyn, where Tabby scented an unknown cat who wasn't a Puma. I've also heard rumors that there's a group of shifters that are attacking cross-breeds like your sister."

"How does this tie in to Hope's disappearance? The Walsh family knew nothing of shifters before Tabby appeared on the scene." And how was Chloe involved in all of this? She'd been jumped back before Bunny claimed Tabby and almost died from her wounds.

"I know. So I have to wonder. Does this tie in to Tabby or Glory?"

Ryan didn't understand. "Tabby was kicked out of her Pack when she was fifteen."

"And Hope disappeared when she was sixteen."

"You think Tabby's old Alpha was somehow involved? Could her attacker have been a member of his Pack?"

"I…" Gabe growled. "I just don't know. I don't have enough to go on. Something just isn't right about all of this, and I can't figure it out, damn it." He ran his fingers through his hair. "I'm thinking of calling in back-up."

"Who?" Hunters didn't work a territory alone. There had to be at least two other Hunters in the area, but Ryan had no clue who they might be.

"James Barnwell, aka Barney. The man who trained me. He's a pain in the ass and nearly lost me my mate, but he's the best Hunter I know. Maybe he can help me figure this shit out."

"Anything that helps keep my mate safe is fine by me."

"I'd rather we did this on our own. If I call in Barney he'll try and take over. He won't think twice about separating you from Glory if he thinks it will protect her."

"That will never happen. Glory has issues with abandonment. If I walk away, even for her own good, I'll lose her forever. I won't let that happen."

Gabe grinned. "Good. Fight him on that. I should have, and I'll regret that I didn't for the rest of my life."

Their breakfasts arrived, and both men were quiet as they dug into their meal. After a few moments of nothing but shoveling food into their faces, Ryan broke the silence. "What do you need me to do?"

"For now, do what you've been doing. Stay as close as you can to Glory and, if possible, claim her as quickly as you can. Being a Grizzly, she'll be better able to protect herself if my instincts are right and this *is* a rogue shifter."

Pfft. Like Ryan needed to be told to stick close to his mate. "I planned on doing that anyway."

"I'm going to dig into the case a bit more. The notes the cop took on the case are sketchy at best. I need to have a long talk with him, see if he noticed anything odd when he was questioning Pastor Walsh."

"We should try and find Pastor Walsh as well. Maybe get a hold of Glory's siblings, Temp and Faith. Maybe they know something."

"Good idea. I'll also need the presents that were left for Glory. Maybe there will be a scent or a clue we can follow up on."

"I'll talk to her, have her send them to you."

"The fewer people who touch them the better. Maybe I can have Sarah take a look at them as well, see if she can sense anything. If the presents are innocent, like Alex believes, then that will be one worry off our shoulders."

Ryan relaxed. Sarah's powers were scary-strong. If there was any evil intention behind the presents, the Halle Puma Omega would sense it. "Thanks, Gabe. You have no idea how much I appreciate this."

"Anything to keep our mates safe."

"Agreed." And the two men finished their breakfast in perfect accord.

***

The day after her meeting with Gabe, Glory opened her front door to find another gift lying on her doorstep. But this one was different from the others.

This one scared her to death.

Glory bent down and picked up the single dead rose, careful of the vicious thorns still on the stem. The note tied around it was written on yellowed paper. Only one word was written on the note.

Whore.

Glory shuddered, glancing around involuntarily. What if he was watching her right now? Whoever he was, he must have seen her going on her date with Ryan. Why else would he have written that kind of note?

Glory carried the rose inside and put it in a box with the rest of the gifts. She was heading to the police station to see Gabe. Maybe the sheriff could find something useful on the—

Glory jumped as the doorbell rang. Her heart pounding, she tiptoed to the front door and peeked out the peephole.

Ryan. Oh, thank God.

She opened the front door and threw herself into his arms. "Ryan."

He hugged her tightly, the feel of him easing her fears. She wasn't alone, and that knowledge filled her with the strength to pull away from him.

Worry was clearly etched on his face. "What happened?"

"I got another present."

Worry turned to fury. "Let me see." He nudged her into the apartment and shut the door, still holding her tightly against him. Together, they walked to where she'd gathered the gifts together.

"There." She showed him the note and the dead rose, but he didn't touch them.

Brown seeped into the midnight blue of his eyes. "Let's go see Gabe."

She wasn't fooled by his calm tone. Ryan was pissed. He still hadn't let go of her, and if she was honest with herself, having him so close made her feel much safer. "Good idea."

Ryan picked up the box and, his arm still around her, led her out to his motorcycle. She carefully placed the box in the motorcycle's tail box and pulled on the helmet Ryan handed her. He'd bought it especially for her. The custom black helmet was decorated with a yin-yang symbol done in dark and powder blue, the exact color of Ryan and Glory's eyes. Ryan's helmet was plain black, but both helmets had built-in communicators that allowed them to speak to one another even while roaring down the highway.

Ryan didn't waste any time in getting them to the police station. Glory's legs were shaking by the time he parked, her nerves over the gifts and Ryan's admittedly justified anger making her want to puke. She gathered the box out of the tail box with trembling hands.

Before she could start toward the station Ryan's arm was around her waist, steadying her. "It's all right," he cooed in her ear. "I'm here."

She blew out a deep breath, trying to control her jitters. She had nothing to fear here, not while Ryan watched over her. Especially not with Gabe right in the building. "Okay."

Ryan guided her into the building, careful not to touch the box she cradled close to her chest. He led her over to the front desk, calmly asked for Sheriff Anderson, and the two of them were led right back to Gabe's office.

Gabe greeted them both with a smile and some coffee. He closed his office door and gestured toward two seats in front of his utilitarian metal desk. "Those the gifts Ryan told me about?"

Glory nodded and placed the box on Gabe's desk. "I got another one this morning." She held up the dead rose and the note.

"Shit." Gabe leaned close, closing his eyes and sniffing deeply. "I can smell…something, but it's so faint I can't tell what it is. It's not you or Ryan." He picked through the rest of the box, sniffing each note, each gift. "That scent is on all of them."

"So you have it." Ryan's hands were clenched. "You can hunt that scent."

"If I smell it, I'll know it's our stalker." Gabe held up the note with the word *Whore* on it. "And this alone tells me that's what we're dealing with."

"Any idea whether or not it really is a shifter?"

Gabe took another deep whiff. "I think so, but it's so faint that I can't tell what kind." His gaze was somber. "I don't want to scare you, but something about this is making my Spidey senses tingle. I want Ryan to stay with you until this is over."

The satisfaction that radiated off of Ryan was off the charts. "I can live with that."

Glory wasn't so sure, but she understood the safety concerns. "Ryan still has to work."

"And so do you. Talk to Cyn. Tell her you need to work when Ryan is, and that you need to be off when he is, at least until we catch this guy. I'm pretty sure she'll understand."

Of course Cyn would understand, but the scared rabbit that lived in Glory's heart didn't. If she lived with Ryan, she was that much closer to getting that bunny ripped out and eaten. "Any news on Hope?"

Gabe pushed a file folder across his desk. "I've talked to the officer who took your father's statement. While he filed a missing person's report, because Hope was sixteen he'd felt she'd left voluntarily. He did examine the route your sister tended to take and found no signs of a struggle, no witnesses who said she was kidnapped. So for better or worse, he marked her as a runaway."

"My sister hated our life but she wouldn't have left us behind." They'd had plans, damn it. "We were going to go to college together, maybe try and get Faith out from under my dad's thumb before he hurt her too badly."

"Did anyone else know of your plans?"

"Only Temp. If we didn't get out, he was going to take Faith and run. But with Hope's disappearance our father clamped down on us. We couldn't breathe without him knowing." Still, she prayed once they left that Temp had found the means to get Faith away from their father. Faith deserved so much more than Hope and Glory had found. She'd been sweet and innocent the last time Glory saw her, and she prayed that hadn't changed.

"Any scents would be long gone. We have no witnesses, no physical evidence, just a missing girl and, years later, a stalker." Gabe's eyes widened. "Were you and Hope *identical* twins?"

"Yes, why?" Glory jerked. "You think he's after me because of Hope. But that makes no sense. Hope disappeared years ago."

"It's possible he stalked her first."

"Hope never said anything about feeling uneasy or someone following her." The shakes were back, hardcore. Some sick asshole who might have hurt her sister might now be after her.

Ryan took hold of her hand. "If it was a shifter stalking her she never would have noticed him."

"Or her. God knows we've had our share of crazy females in this town." Gabe tapped his pen against the file folder, his expression pensive. "I wouldn't rule out the possibility that if it's the person who took Hope, he's only targeted you now because he's lost her somehow."

Chills ran down Glory's spine. "You're saying she may have been alive and held by a maniac all this time?"

The look on Gabe's face said it all. "And if he's come after you…"

"Hope is dead." Glory scowled and hoped that for once someone would believe her. No one else except Cyn ever had. Most had told her that, at best, it was wishful thinking, and, at worst, she was trying to hurt her parents. "See, that was always something that bothered me. You know twins have a bond, right?" Gabe nodded and Ryan squeezed her hand. "I've always believed Hope was alive. It was one of the reasons my father beat me so hard." Ryan's snarl interrupted her, and this time she was the one to squeeze his hand, comforting him. "I never once sensed she was dead."

"And now? Do you sense anything at all?"

Glory shook her head, relieved. She should have known Gabe would believe her, considering his mate's special abilities. "I still don't think she's *dead.*

It's...strange. At one time I would have said she was alive and well. Now, the bond is weak but it's still there. Maybe she's in a hospital or in a coma or something?"

"If she is, we'll find her." Ryan kissed her cheek. "Do you have a picture of her when she was younger? If we send it to local hospitals we might find something."

Glory smiled at Ryan, her heart pounding. She hadn't been this happy since Tabby met Bunny. "You believe me?"

"Of course." He sounded almost insulted.

Glory kissed his cheek, the faint hint of whiskers tickling her lips. "Thank you, Ryan."

He lifted her hand and kissed it. "Nothing to thank me for. You're my mate."

She was slowly starting to understand what that meant. For the first time in a very long time, Glory felt like someone had her back.

The fact that her someone was a Grizzly who'd proven he was willing to kill for her only made her feel safer.

Glory blew out a breath. "My father kicked me out with the clothes on my back and the money in my wallet. I had nothing when I moved in with Cyn and her mother, not even a photo of my family." She bit her lip. "But I can find a wig in my natural hair color. If I do that, we can take a picture of me and put it out there. I haven't changed *that* much."

"Why not Photoshop your hair blonde?"

Glory rolled her eyes at him. "Do you have the program? It's expensive, and unless you know what you're doing with it you wind up with something crappy."

"Our police artist still sketches on paper so we haven't bothered to invest in it. But doing a picture is a good idea. It should show how Hope has aged, unless..." Gabe grimaced.

"Unless something horrific happened and disfigured her." Ryan tugged Glory close. "I want to find this fucker and end him before he hurts Glory."

"He's a shifter. You'd be within shifter law to kill him if he threatens your mate. But let me try to find him first. This might not be the first time he's done this." Gabe leaned back in his chair, the squeak startling her. "I've put in a call to Barney. He should be joining us within the week."

Next to her Ryan relaxed. Even the brown left his eyes. "You trust him?"

Gabe nodded. "He's an asshole, but he's an effective one. With his help we'll have this wrapped up in no time." Gabe grinned. "I should warn you, though. Barney is…unusual."

"How so?"

"I'll let you figure it out when you meet him." Gabe stood and held out his hand. "If you two think of anything else, give me a call. And Glory, once you have that photo, email it to me. I'll get it out as quickly as I can."

"Thanks, Gabe." Instead of shaking his hand she moved around his desk to give him a hug. Surprisingly, her aggressive Bear didn't growl. "Tell Sarah I said hi."

"I will." Gabe hugged her back. "She says she's thinking of getting a tattoo."

"I can have Heather draw her up something. That girl has mad skills."

"I think she'd like that."

Gabe let her go, and Ryan nudged her aside so he could do his own bro-hug with Gabe. "Thanks, man."

"You're welcome." Gabe pointed toward the door. "Now, go get me that picture while I prepare for Barney's arrival."

Ryan put his arm around her waist. "I'll take her to work and talk to Cyn and the others. Hell, I'll call in the whole fucking clan for this. Glory will never be alone if we can help it."

"And your crazy family might just keep her stalker from winning."

Glory groaned. It looked like the Bunsun-Williams clan would be converging on her en masse.

And secretly, part of her loved the thought. Ryan's family was a blast. An annoying, poking-in-your-life, loud-and-proud blast. And some of the few people who didn't make Glory feel like a freak of nature.

But instead of letting Ryan know that she actually adored his family, she sniffed. "I guess if we have to."

Ryan hugged her tighter to his side. "We have to."

Glory sighed. It was going to be a fun couple of weeks.

CHAPTER SIX

Ryan escorted his mate into Cynful Tattoos, his senses on high alert. He very much doubted her stalker was sitting in Frank's Diner eating pancakes and eggs. He was willing to bet his right arm the son of a bitch was watching them as they entered Glory's place of business. He sniffed the air, hoping to catch that elusive scent Gabe had pointed out to him on Glory's gifts.

Nothing. Not a single scent was out of place. Ryan gritted his teeth. He wanted to know who the son of a bitch was so he could make sure the shifter knew Ryan's mate was protected. But images tumbled through his mind, each one more horrific than the last. What if he'd gotten close to the girls? If he was hiding in plain sight, it would be easy to figure out Glory's likes and dislikes. He could be the mailman, the guy who'd installed the security system, even the pizza delivery guy.

Worse, what if he was a client? What if Glory had pierced him, laying her soft hands on his skin? Ryan could understand why one touch from his mate would make someone obsessed. Ryan was dying to feel her caress him, to direct all her passion on him. It would be amazing to feel that focus taking him over.

Ryan's Bear was beginning to push harder than ever. They needed to claim their mate, make her one with them.

First he had to figure out how to get her to agree to the mating bite, and soon. But the thought of frightening her was abhorrent. He couldn't force the bite on her, no matter how badly he wanted to. He needed her to accept what was going to happen between them or it would be a violation of everything he believed a mating should be.

"Glory!" Tabby hurled herself into Glory's arm, nearly knocking his tiny mate onto her ass. "What happened?"

Ryan left the girls to chat, drawing Bunny's attention. He pulled him into the corner of the shop. "I need you to gather the family."

Bunny's eyes glazed over, his Bear peeking out. "Is Tabby in danger?"

Ever since Tabby had gotten pregnant Bunny had been insanely overprotective. But if it got the family out to protect Glory, he'd sacrifice Bunny's peace of mind in a heartbeat. "I'm praying not."

That was all it took. Bunny was on his cell phone in an instant, calling in the troops. Knowing how the family reacted to threats, Ryan had no doubt they'd be converging on Halle within a day, even the ones in Oregon.

"Smart move." Julian peeked out from behind the curtain hiding the employee area. "Your cousins can watch over Glory when you can't. I mean, you have to sleep some time."

With any luck, he'd be sleeping in Glory's bed from now on. He caught Glory's quick glance before she turned back to her friends. The flush on her cheeks had him wondering what she'd been thinking about. "Who said anything about sleeping?"

"Hey." Bunny stepped between Julian and Ryan. "Mom and Dad are making arrangements. The family will gather at Ryan's apartment tomorrow night."

Since tomorrow was Sunday and they all had it off, it made sense. "Shit. I have to clean."

"Clean what?" Glory wrapped herself around his arm and he couldn't have been happier.

"My apartment."

"Uh. I'm not helping with that." Bunny held up his hands and backed slowly away. "The last time I did something tried to bite me."

"It's not *that* bad." A few pizza boxes here and there, some dishes in the sink. Nothing to cause Bunny to shudder in horror. Like his cousin had never left a few glasses lying around.

"Oh, it is." Julian smirked as he leaned against the doorjamb. "Trust me on that one."

Ryan glared at Julian. "Since when did you become a domestic goddess?"

"Since my mate will skin me if I don't pick up after myself." Now it was Julian's turn to shudder. "She threatens to withhold video games."

Ryan blinked. God, the man was weird.

Glory glared up at him. "Your apartment is dirty?" She smacked him in the stomach. "And your family is coming?"

Ryan smiled weakly. He was going to kill Julian and Bunny for getting him into trouble with his mate. "Have I mentioned that you're cute?"

Glory rolled her eyes. "Girls?"

"I'm in." Cyn grinned as Julian tugged her close. "I have got to see what frightened Bunny."

"I'm in too." Tabby literally bounced in place. "I've already cleaned our place so many times the polish is going to come off the granite."

"You're nesting, Tabby." Cyn shrugged. "It's normal."

"I'm a Wolf. We don't *nest*." Tabby sniffed in disgust. "We make a den."

Bunny snarled and tugged Tabby behind him. "You're not going anywhere near Ryan's apartment. It might eat the baby."

Ryan rolled his eyes. "It's not *that* bad."

Bunny stared at him. "It's a petri dish for a mad scientist."

"Now I'm *definitely* going." Tabby tickled Bunny's side, the big man squirming away from her until she was able to maneuver herself in front of him. "When do we start?"

"Tonight after work, if you're willing." Ryan was beyond grateful. He hated cleaning. "I'll pay for pizza, beer and baby-appropriate soda."

Bunny shook his head. "I'm telling you. You're all going to get eaten."

Tabby pouted at him. "You're going to let me go alone?"

"Uh…" Bunny, his expression panicked, backed up a step.

Tabby batted big, brown eyes at her mate. "You'll come with me, won't you?"

Ryan bit back a laugh. Bunny never could resist the Puppy Eyes of Death, and Tabby was a master at them.

Bunny glared at Ryan. "If my baby comes out mutated I'm blaming you."

"It's not that bad!" Geez. So maybe he should buy a vacuum on the way home. Maybe then they'd get off his case.

"I'll go get the hazmat suits." Bunny was grumbling to himself as he left the shop, sending Julian into a fit of laughter.

"Cyn? Do you know where we can get a blonde wig?"

Ryan turned his attention away from Bunny's antics and toward his mate. "We're going to do it now?"

Cyn, who was shooing a still-laughing Julian behind the curtain, paused. "What?"

"Since Hope and I are identical twins, Gabe thought if we slapped a blonde wig on me and took a picture we could send it to area hospitals and police stations."

"So they'd have an idea of what Hope looks like now." Cyn smiled approvingly. "Good idea. Let me see what I can dig up."

"Thanks. I don't want to use one of those brassy Halloween wigs. I want to get as close to my natural color as possible."

Tabby settled into one of the turquoise chairs. "Do you even remember what that is? Or do you have to grab a mirror and drop your panties?"

"Aw, Tabby. Would you like some coffee?" Glory smiled sweetly at Tabby as the Wolf gagged. "Extra cream, extra sugar?"

Tabby gagged again. "I hate you so much."

Glory blew Tabby a kiss. "The feeling is mutual."

Ryan had to smile. She might have lost her biological family, but his mate had made one hell of a new one in her friends. Even if they were crazy as hell.

***

"Y'all have *got* to see this."

Glory followed Cyn into the bathroom. Considering what else they'd found she wouldn't be surprised to see an alien reading the newspaper. So far she'd found a box with what she thought might be pizza in it. Or a fuzzy new life form. She wasn't sure. Oh, and the jar of peanut butter that had been sitting in a coat pocket since the dawn of time. The peanut butter was so hard the spoon was permanently cemented into the jar. And did they even make that brand anymore? And why was it in a coat pocket from his high-school days? He had to have packed the coat, moved it to Halle, and then unpacked it, all without removing the jar.

And she didn't think she'd ever forget what they'd found in the crockpot. Glory shuddered. At least now they knew why it had been duct taped shut. She was pretty sure the fuzzy stuff inside had tried to smack the shit out of her.

The carpet, which they'd thought was a speckled brown and beige, was actually pale beige once they vacuumed it.

And who the fuck didn't own a vacuum? Seriously? They'd had to pick one up and put it together, sitting on the sofa because none of them wanted to risk the floor. Bunny had actually snarled at Tabby when she started to lower herself onto the carpet.

The kitchen counters were sticky, the sink full of dishes, and worst of all, the entire place smelled like man-socks.

The place was filthy. No wonder Bunny didn't want Tabby here. The good news was, with a little elbow grease, it would be just fine. Ryan, for the most part, put things back in their places. He just didn't bother to clean the surfaces.

Glory peered warily into the corner of the tub where she'd put the experiment in creating a new form of life. That crockpot was going straight to the apartment building's Dumpster. There was no way in hell she was risking unsealing the beast again. And Ryan was the one who was going to carry it there. The Grizzly *might* be safe from the rampaging fungus.

And she was never, *ever* watching John Carpenter's *Prince of Darkness* ever again. The scene where the cylinder opened and spewed liquid Satan all over the place kept replaying in her mind every time she thought of opening the Crockpot of Hell.

"What is that?" Cyn tapped a sad, brown piece of foliage sitting on Ryan's toilet tank. It broke apart with an audible crunch, drifting down in a sad, brown powder.

"An air fern, I think." Tabby swallowed hard.

Glory stared at it in disbelief. "Don't they live on nothing but air?"

Tabby nodded, obviously too horrified to even speak.

Cyn lifted the toilet seat with the air of someone who was about to find a dead body in their freezer. When it was up they reared back.

"What…what is that?"

"Dear God, please let it be dead."

Tabby gagged behind her hand.

"I didn't realize Bears shed so much." Cyn tilted her head. "Either that or Ryan has a thing for fuzzy toilet seats."

Tabby was a little green around the gills. "That's not *Bear* hairs. That's…" She slapped her hand back over her mouth.

"Ugh." Cyn stomped out in disgust, muttering profanities in Spanish.

"That's *revolting*." Glory took a step back, ready to bolt after Cyn. The man was simply not that cute.

"Not my mate, pregnant, see ya!" Tabby slammed out of the bathroom. "Free! I'm free!"

"Bitches." Glory stared at the travesty of a bathroom and gritted her teeth. Ryan was *so* dead when he got back.

It took the three of them hours to get the apartment ready for Ryan's family, but it sparkled when they were done. The rug had to be not only vacuumed but shampooed before Glory was satisfied she'd gotten everything out of it. The toilet, tub and tile in the bathroom gleamed like new, and the kitchen, while dated, was as clean as beige laminate could ever look. Hell, they hadn't even realized the place had a dishwasher until Tabby went to take care of the dishes Ryan had left in the sink. The leather sofa and recliner no longer stank of Cheetos and feet, and Ryan's bedroom was neat as a pin, with fresh sheets. By the time they were done, even picky Cyn was satisfied with the place.

Glory sighed as she stared around the apartment, realizing something she should have been willing to acknowledge a long time ago.

It had to be love. No one cleaned a toilet that furry without adoring the man who'd fuzzed it. But that didn't mean she wasn't going to kick his ass when he came home.

It was nearly midnight before the men got back. Alex, Julian and Ryan slipped into the apartment, looking guilty as hell.

Ryan, his expression wary, held out a bag of what smelled like her favorite tacos. "Glory? We're back. I brought you—"

Glory went on the attack, swinging a roll of paper towels like a ninja sword. She proceeded to beat him to within an inch of his quilted, two-ply life, while Alex and Julian just stood there and laughed.

When she was panting, sweating and ready to collapse, Cyn stepped forward. She held up her own fresh roll of paper towels. "My turn."

She then proceeded to attack Julian, hitting much harder than Glory could. "Ow! What did I do?"

"You left me. You *left me here*. Do you know what was in that crockpot? *Do you?*" Cyn got in an especially good hit, half of the roll unraveling to pool on the newly cleaned carpet.

Alex was laughing so hard he started crying. Tabby tapped her roll against her palm. "You're next, sugar."

Suddenly Alex wasn't laughing so hard. He held out his own bag, the scent of cinnamon pastries strong. "I love you."

Tabby bopped him over the head, then stole the bag. "Forgiven."

"Hey, I get some of those too." Glory grabbed for the cinnamon goodness, only to come up short when Tabby dashed into the kitchenette. "You're pretty fast for a whale."

Tabby poked her head around the corner. "I may be a whale, but I'm a whale with a bag full of fresh churros, bitch."

"Gimme." Cyn grabbed the bag of tacos and led the way to Ryan's small dinette set. "I'm starving. Let's eat."

Glory collapsed onto one of the dining chairs and grabbed her share of tacos and nachos. "Star. Ving."

"Mm-hmm." Cyn already had a mouth full of taco, an expression of bliss on her face. "So good."

Ryan placed a glass of soda in front of Glory, pressing a kiss to her head. "Thank you, by the way." She growled at him, and he laughed. "Only SG could have gotten this place to look this good so quickly."

Glory sniffed. "You're taking the crockpot out to the Dumpster."

He stared at her, looking confused. "Why? It still works, doesn't it?" When she threatened him with the beat-up roll of paper towels again he held up his hands. "Okay, okay! I'll toss it after dinner. But you're helping me pick a new one."

"Only if you promise not to duct tape it shut again."

Bunny choked. "Geez, you still have that? How long ago did we make that chili?"

Ryan frowned thoughtfully. "In college?"

"That's disgusting." Glory almost put her taco down. Almost. They were *really* good tacos.

"I was planning on cleaning it." Ryan actually had the balls to look hurt.

"I told you to get that flamethrower." Julian moaned as he bit into his own taco.

Glory shook her head. That wasn't strong enough. "I think the life form inside would survive a little fire. No, that calls for something more drastic."

"Blast it into space." Tabby came back into the room smelling suspiciously like cinnamon. She settled on Alex's lap and pulled one of his tacos toward her.

"Nah. I'm afraid if we do that, it will take over some planet, make slaves of the indigenous species and come back here with an armada and revenge in mind." Glory waved her hand. "I think we need to consider sinking it into the sea."

"With our luck it would float to the Bermuda Triangle and mutate further." Cyn laughed. "It could become the Triangle's Nessie."

"Really. It's not that bad." Ryan grabbed another taco. "I think it can be saved."

"Oh, sugar, no." Tabby patted his shoulder. "That stuff is way too evil. It will never come to Jesus."

Laughter erupted as Tabby calmly bit into her taco with a smug smile.

"Seriously, though. I think it needs a hazardous waste container."

"Fine. I'll carry it to the Dumpster after dinner." Ryan gathered up the empty taco wrappers and carried them to the trashcan. "Wait a minute."

"What?" Glory got up to see what he was staring at.

Ryan was looking down, but Glory couldn't see anything strange. At least she didn't until Ryan exclaimed, "Whoa. The carpet is *beige?*"

Three sets of paper towel rolls hit him in the head at the same time.

CHAPTER SEVEN

Ryan woke the next morning to a strange sound in his living room. Slipping from between the sheets, he padded silently to the bedroom door.

"Take that, asshole."

Someone had broken into his apartment and was in his living room, playing...video games?

"Ha! I love it when their heads explode." Suddenly the door was pushed open, knocking Ryan back a step. Whoever it was, the man was *huge*. "You coming out or not?"

Ryan blinked. "Who the fuck are you?"

The blond man had to be at least six foot eight, easily, and he smelled strongly of Bear. His gray eyes twinkled merrily under his cowboy hat. "I'm James Barnwell, but you can call me Barney."

"Shit." Ryan immediately relaxed, remembering that this was the Hunter Gabe had sent for. "That was fast."

Barney winked. "Most of the Hunters I train only call me on the hard cases. You a hard case, Ryan?"

"Ask me that after I've had coffee." Ryan stumbled back into his bedroom to the sound of Barney's laughter.

"I brought breakfast sandwiches with me."

"I hope you brought enough for the clan." Ryan tugged on a T-shirt and jeans, foregoing shoes. He wasn't planning on going anywhere. Cyn and Julian had taken Glory home with them when Glory refused to spend the night at Ryan's.

Ryan was going to work on that. If she wanted him to move in with her, he'd be packed up and ready in a nanosecond. He wasn't attached to this apartment. He had no trouble leaving it for Glory's far more eclectic, colorful place.

"Clan?" Barney leaned against the doorjamb, watching him dress.

Ryan didn't get any skeevy vibes off the guy. He seemed to be watching Ryan like a bug under a microscope, studying the way he moved and reacted. Well, Gabe had warned him Barney was a strange one. "My family is coming today."

"The Bunsuns, Williamses and Allens?" Barney whistled and glanced back toward Ryan's tiny living room. "I think you need more seats."

Ryan barked out a laugh as he headed into the bathroom. "You think?" He began brushing his teeth.

"You're surprisingly easy with me being in your apartment."

Ryan spit into the sink. "You're here to protect my mate and Gabe vouches for you. That's good enough for me."

"Hmph." Ryan turned to find Barney walking around his bedroom, studying his belongings. "You should be more cautious. For all you know I *am* your mate's stalker." Before Ryan could react, Barney was across the room, his arm around Ryan's throat. Ryan's air was cut off as Barney squeezed. "I could kill you before you could—"

Barney screeched as Ryan's five-inch Grizzly claws sank into his balls. He let Ryan go immediately, cupping himself with a shocked expression.

"Before I could what?" Ryan's Bear was close to the surface. He suspected the Hunter was simply trying to teach him a lesson, but it was one Ryan didn't need to learn. He knew Barney wasn't there to hurt Glory, but damn if his attitude wasn't pissing Ryan's Bear the hell off. "You might want to think twice before pulling that shit on me again. Got it?"

Barney took a deep breath and closed his eyes. Ryan could sense the healing spiral all Bears danced when healing. The damage he'd inflicted on the Hunter was slowly being repaired. "Got it," Barney wheezed. As he slowly straightened, his expression turned speculative. "Have you ever considered Hunter training?"

"Fuck no." Ryan laughed and moved past Barney. His family would be here soon, and Ryan had to make sure everything was ready. "I'm not Hunter material."

"Mm-hm." Barney flopped onto Ryan's sofa and picked up the controller. "I think you'll find that you're wrong on that."

Ryan froze, his hand on the refrigerator door. "You're kidding me."

"Nope." Barney sighed wearily. "And I have to wonder. If an Oregon Bear with Hunter potential has moved into Gabe's area, in Gabe's backyard even, what the hell is going to happen around here?"

"What do you mean?" Ryan pulled open the door and grabbed the bottle of orange juice.

"These things happen for a reason. Always. The powers that be arranged for you to come here."

Ryan snorted. "That's because my mate is in Halle."

"Uh-huh." Barney's tone was skeptical. "I think there's more to it than that."

The last thing Ryan needed was to become a Hunter. He had enough on his plate, what with Glory's missing sister, her stalker and her refusal to let him worship her. "Yeah. You believe what you want to. My only concern is my family and my mate."

Barney began firing on the zombies on the screen. "Thanks. I will."

Ryan shook his head as he poured himself some juice.

"You knew it was a shifter."

Ryan's hand jerked, spilling juice on his newly cleaned counter top. "How did you know that?"

"You also knew it had something to do with Hope Walsh's disappearance." The sound of rapid gunfire almost drowned out Barney's voice.

"And?" Ryan began making coffee.

"We need you."

"Who is we?" Ryan's hands were shaking.

"The Senate."

Shit had just gotten real if he'd caught the attention of the shifter Senate already. "You really think I'm some kind of proto-Hunter?"

Barney turned and stared over the top of the sofa at Ryan. "Proto-Hunter?" He burst out laughing. "Oh, I like that."

"I'm an accountant, for fuck's sake. Gabe's the one in law enforcement." Hell, even Bunny would make a better Hunter than Ryan. The man had self-control down to a science now, but he was still a fierce warrior when he needed to be.

"You went on a Hunt already, Ryan." Barney paused the game again. "You found the bad guy and administered justice."

"He shot my mate and was going to kill her best friend."

Barney sighed. "What do you think Hunters do, Ryan? We take down rogue shifters. And like Alphas and Betas and Marshals, they're born, not made. I can't *make* you a Hunter, Ryan. I can only train you, because you already *are* one."

Something in Ryan shifted. His Bear was listening intently, even as his human half denied what the other Hunter was saying.

Wait. Did I just think of Barney as the other Hunter? Shit. It couldn't be. Ryan had never intended to become something so lofty as a Hunter. He'd been content working for Bunsun Exteriors.

"You'd be surprised how little your life will change. You'll still have your job and your place in your family group." Barney grinned. "Hell, maybe I'll be nice and stay in Halle to train you rather than take you home."

"I won't leave my mate."

"Did I ask you to?"

Ryan snorted. "Gabe warned me about you."

"Nag, nag, nag. Gabe needs to get over himself. I trained him the way the Senate needed me to. But with you, I can make my own decisions."

Ryan poured two cups of coffee. "Then your decision had better be to remain in Halle, because otherwise I won't become a Hunter."

When Barney tried to stare him down, Ryan kept his gaze steady. He didn't give a flying fuck about Barney and what he wanted from Ryan. All he cared about was fulfilling his promise to never leave his mate.

"Fine. We'll play this your way, Ryan. Just be aware, I'll do what's best for you *and* your mate whether you like it or not."

Ryan snarled. "You won't separate us."

Barney smiled, turned back to the television and unpaused the game. "We'll see."

***

"I can't believe what you guys have done with this place." Chloe Williams, Ryan's little sister, was leaning against the wall in Ryan's bedroom, where Glory was getting ready to have her picture taken for Gabe's hunt for Hope. She was watching them closely as Cyn adjusted Glory's wig. "I mean, who knew he had a *beige* carpet?"

"Ugh. Don't remind me." Glory fluffed out the blonde wig Cyn had managed to dig up. It was as close as they could get to her natural hair color. "How do I look?"

She stuck her tongue out at her blonde image. Blech. She *hated* the pale blonde locks she'd been born with. They were so blah, not like her pretty powder blue, or the violet she'd sported in college.

Maybe it was time to go back to that pale lavender color? While she loved the blue, it *was* getting a little old. She'd had it for almost two years now.

Or maybe… Maybe a deep, vampiric red? Her pale skin would really stand out then. And she'd always wanted to be a redhead.

"It looks fine, Glory." Cyn carefully brushed bangs over Glory's forehead. "You look just like you did in high school. Bitch."

"Just because some of us got wrinkly and old…" Glory laughed when Cyn growled. "You know you're hot."

"Damn straight." Cyn sniffed. "You know…"

"What?"

Cyn put the brush down. "Have you thought about changing your hair color? It's been a while, hasn't it? And I know how you get bored with it after a while."

"Oh! Go a darker blue, like midnight blue or something. You'd look cunning." Chloe picked up the camera she'd offered to use to take the pictures for Gabe, fumbling with it when her damaged hand wouldn't close completely around it. "Yarn it."

Glory smiled at the pretty Fox with the short, pixie-cut red hair. Chloe, Ryan's sister, was still recovering from the near-fatal beating she'd taken the night Alex claimed Tabby. She still had trouble using one of her hands, and her words got seriously mixed up at times, but she was still the same sweet girl who'd once been a waitress at Frank's diner. Her dreams of becoming a veterinarian had been shattered, but she still hoped to work with animals in some capacity. The double-tailed kitsune, or fox spirit, she'd had inked on her shoulder was a symbol of her acceptance of her new life. "I was thinking vampire red."

Chloe, Cyn and Tabby, who'd just waddled into the bedroom, all stared at her.

"I think I'd look good!"

"I don't know. I'm not sure you have the skin tone for red." Chloe leaned down and put her head against Glory's, making sure her red hair was against Glory's skin. "What do you guys think?"

"I think her skin matches yours. The red could work, but I kinda love the blue." Tabby tapped her fingers against her thigh. "What about a rich purple?"

Glory fluffed the blonde wig, trying to make it look less…boring. "I used to do my hair lavender."

Tabby's eyes went wide. "Ooh. We could totally do different colors."

Glory sat up straighter. "Purple, blue, red—or maybe pink, if we're doing pastels—and a little green?"

"It would be a lot of work." But Cyn had that gleam in her eye, the one that said she was already plotting out how to do it without turning Glory into an Easter egg. "If we cut in some layers we could add a different color to each one."

Glory winced. "No. No cutting my hair." She loved her waist-length curls just the way they were. "But…we could frame out my face better." The blonde bangs were giving her ideas. "We could give me bangs, I suppose."

"That could work. Do the area around your face in teal, maybe, then—" The sound of the doorbell interrupted Chloe. "Shut. Let me make sure Ryan's got the door." Chloe left the room, her expression irritated. "It's Julian!"

Cyn, who'd been puttering around Ryan's bedroom, instantly went on alert. "I'd better go see how he is. He was talking about visiting the hospital this morning." And she was gone, her concern for her lover overcoming everything else.

And she had reason to be worried. Hospitals were the bane of a Kermode Bear. His urge to heal could drive him to literally kill himself for the sake of someone else. If Julian was visiting the hospital, it meant nothing good, especially for him and Cyn.

"I guess we head out there." Tabby patted her belly. "Ready to get your picture taken?"

Glory shrugged. "As ready as I'll ever be." She couldn't wait to get the wig back off. The thing itched.

"Glory?" Ryan poked his head into his bedroom. "My parents will be here soon. Did you want anything from Frank's? They're bringing burgers and fries."

He didn't even bat an eye at the blonde wig. "What do you think about rainbows?"

"I like your hair blue. Burger?"

She rolled her eyes. Of *course* he'd known why she asked. Ryan was uncannily in tune with her. It was one of the things that kept freaking her out. "Get me the usual. Oh, and a chocolate shake." He turned to leave the room. "Oh! And some of that apple pie." She bit her lip. "Make that cherry."

"Two double-bacon cheeseburgers, hold the mayo, a basket of fries, a chocolate shake, a slice of apple and a slice of cherry. Got it."

"Two?" But Ryan was gone, already holding a phone to his ear and giving her food order. "I'm not eating two burgers. And I'm certainly not eating two things of pie."

"Sounds like my kind of lunch." Tabby licked her lips. "I hope Alex got my order."

"That's because you're a pig." Glory patted her hips. "Some of us have to keep our girlish figures."

"I hate you, heifer."

"Same to you, Miss Piggy." Glory slid her arm through Tabby's, taking a deep breath. "What a way to meet the in-laws, huh?"

Tabby giggled. "Tell me about it. Remember when I met them all? Chloe was in the hospital and Alex had already marked me. *And* I was Outcast." She shook her head. "It still amazes me how easily they all accepted me." She took hold of Glory's hand and began dragging Glory through the bedroom door. "Trust me. They're going to *love* you."

"On a ciabatta roll with Dijon mustard, maybe." When Tabby started laughing, Glory shrugged. "What? I'm an acquired taste."

"You certainly are." Ryan gently tugged Glory away from Tabby and faced the people in the room. "This is Glory. Glory, that's Raymond and Stacey Allen. They're the parents of Heather, Keith and Tiffany."

The two waved hello. Raymond had his children's flaming red hair while Stacey had the Williams smile.

Ray actually got up and gave her a hug. "Thanks for giving Heather a job. How is she working out, really?"

"Dad!" Heather, her cheeks flaming red, hid her face in her hands.

"She's good, but you'd do better asking Tabby and Cyn. She's a tattoo artist, not a piercer like me."

"Ah. I'll do that, then." Raymond settled back down next to his wife, chatting quietly with her.

"Aunt Stacey and my father are twins." Ryan grinned as he pointed toward the next older couple. "You know Aunt Barb and Uncle Will."

The Bunsuns both came and gave her a hug, knocking her wig askew. "It's good to see you and Ryan working things out." Barbara Bunsun gave her a sharp, toothy smile. "We want all our kids to be happy."

Will pulled his wife away. "Settle down, tiger. I think Glory's well on the way to accepting Ryan."

The doorbell rang again, and Will opened it to allow in…

Whoa. *Big.* The guy quietly greeted Will, then made his way to Ryan. "So this is your mate?" A strange, *huge* blond man walked up to her, eyeing her up and down. "She's teeny. Forget the roll, I don't think she'd fit on a cracker."

"Heard that, did you?" Ryan laughed.

"Uh, Ryan?" Glory took a step back, surprised when her over-protective Bear didn't get in this guy's face.

The one who did, the one who surprised them all, was Chloe. She got between the giant man and Glory and snarled. "Leave her alone."

The huge man's expression gentled. "You're Chloe Williams."

Chloe nodded, but didn't move.

The man bowed deeply. "The spirits send their regards."

One of the people in the room gasped, but Glory couldn't see who it was.

"Thanks. I think." Chloe dropped her arms, her stance relaxing. "Who are you again?"

"James Barnwell, but you can call me Barney." The massive blond straightened up. "I'm the Hunter Gabe warned you about."

"You're going to help us find the shifter who's been stalking me?" Glory wasn't too sure about this. The guy looked like a cowboy, had the attitude of a New Yorker and spoke with an authority she'd only seen in Gabe Anderson and Max Cannon.

"Yup. I..." Barney sniffed, then frowned. "Uh. Excuse me for a moment." He tilted his hat back and stared around the room, finally settling his gaze on Heather. "Crap."

Heather tilted her head, a smile slowly rounding her lips. "Hello to you too."

"Fuck me with the rotating pineapple attachment."
Barney took a step toward Heather, who got up from her
seat and started toward the huge Bear.

"That might hurt." Heather's smile was turning into a
frown. She crossed her arms over her chest as Barney
sighed. "Is there a problem?"

"That's what I want to know." Ryan put himself
between Heather and Barney. "What's going on?"

Barney waved a hand toward Heather. "She's my
mate."

He sounded as happy as a man told he needed a
prostate exam. "Is that a problem?"

Barney grimaced. "Not a problem, per se." He put his
hand on Heather's head. "She'll need climbing gear to
check out my knees, though."

Heather snarled. "I'm not that short."

Barney patted her head. "You're an Oompa Loompa."

"A what?" Glory had to bite back her laughter.

"You know. Short."

"But she's not orange." Ryan sounded confused.

"Are you kidding?" Barney picked up a lock of
Heather's hair. "See?"

Heather snarled and snapped at Barney's hand.

He abruptly let her hair go. "My, what sharp fangs
you've got."

"The better to bite your—" Heather glanced over at
her parents, "—behind with."

Barney laughed. "You're cute." He patted her head
again. "I bet your Hobbit hole is filled with ponies and
rainbows."

Heather snarled again and sat next to her mother,
ignoring the Bear completely.

Ryan's front door blew open and two more people
entered. A man who looked a lot like Stacey Allen, down
to the dark hair and blue eyes, was followed by a tiny
redhead who bore a striking resemblance to Raymond

Allen. The man stopped short, several bags that smelled of meaty goodness in his hands. He stared at Barney, who merely stared back. "Whoa. Honey? I think we need to order some pizzas."

"What are you... Oh. You must be Barney." The small redhead held out her hand. "Laura Williams, Ryan and Chloe's mother."

"Charmed." Barney kissed the back of Laura's hand, ignoring the growl that erupted from Steven's throat. "You have two very interesting children."

At that, Laura bristled. "Really?"

Barney laughed. "I'm a Hunter, ma'am." He patted her hand gently. "And so is your son."

All eyes in the room turned to Ryan. His own rolled. "I'm still not sure I believe him."

"Keep telling yourself that, Ryan." Barney settled on the sofa next to Aunt Stacey. "But we both know what you were born to be."

"Can we just get the pictures done and figure out how to keep Glory safe?" Ryan pulled out one of the dinette chairs and settled Glory into it. "Where's the camera?"

Chloe handed it over. "Here. Want me to take the picture?"

"I've got it. Thanks, sis." He held the camera up. "Say cheese." He snapped off a few shots, then checked the images on the camera's tiny screen. "Looks good. What do you think?"

He turned the camera so Glory could see. "They work. Now we just need to email them to Gabe and he can send them out."

"I'll take care of it after lunch." Ryan and his mother began distributing the food.

"Have you heard from Jim Woods recently?" Ryan's mother caressed her daughter's short hair.

"Nope. He's avoiding me like the vague." Chloe sighed, the burger Ryan had put in front of her remaining untouched. "I understand why, but that doesn't mean it doesn't flirt."

Glory had begun to notice something. The more upset Chloe was, the worse her speech became. Words became mixed up, exchanged for others that rhymed but did not hold the same meaning. "Maybe we can do something about that? I mean, why is he staying away from you?"

"My age. He thinks I'm too rung for him."

"You're twenty-three. That's not too young."

"I know that. You know that. Explain it to Dr. Woods." Chloe slowly unwrapped her burger. "And he probably still thinks I'm carrying a torch for Abe."

"Who's Abe?"

Chloe winced. Because of her brain injury, she didn't notice when she misspoke. Most of her family seemed determined not to point out the mistakes, and normally Glory wouldn't have. She wouldn't do anything to hurt the fragile Fox's feelings. "G-abe."

"Oh." Glory smiled her thanks as Ryan handed her one of the bacon cheeseburgers. "Maybe you should hunt him down and bite the shit out of him."

The older shifters clapped, while the younger ones shook their heads at her. But it was Ryan who put it into perspective. "Should I do that to you too?"

Glory, the burger halfway to her mouth, grimaced. "You're right. Forget I said anything."

"I thought so." But Ryan pulled his chair closer to hers, sharing one of the huge baskets of fries. "As much as it pains me to say it, Jim deserves the same courtesy I've given you."

For the first time since he'd shown up Julian piped in. "But if he doesn't accept the mating soon…"

Every shifter in the room grinned as Alex flexed his fingers. "His ass gets bit."

Steven clapped his hands. "All right, people. Enough about Jim Woods. He'll be dealt with, I promise."

"Dad."

Chloe's warning tone was ignored as her father continued. "For now, we need to figure out how to keep Ryan's mate safe. We'll handle Jim later."

Everyone in the room, including Cyn, stared at Glory. She now knew what the juicy rabbit felt like just before the wolf pounced. "Uh. Hi?"

Steven Williams smiled warmly. "Don't worry. We're just going to watch over you twenty-four seven." His blue eyes turned dark brown. "We're not going to allow you to get hurt."

"Are we even sure it's a shifter who's been stalking her? It could be a human." Stacey moaned as she bit into her burger. "God, it's going to be worth it moving here just for these."

"It's decided, then?" Alex had relaxed, settling on Ryan's recliner, his mate in his lap. He was feeding bits of burger to Tabby, who accepted them happily. "We're definitely moving here?"

Will Bunsun nodded. "Eric will be going back and forth to oversee the transfer, but Bunsun Exteriors' main office will be moving here. We've got enough of a presence on the East Coast to justify the move, and we all agree we want to be near you guys. Eric will be moving here as well. We'll leave the West Coast operations up to one of your other cousins. Probably Keith."

Heather shook her head. "Nope. Both Keith and Tiff want to move with the rest of us. You'll have to find someone else." She shot a quick glance at Barney. "And it won't be me, either. I like it here."

Barney's brows rose at her sharp tone. "Like I have a say in it."

"You're right. You don't."

"'Cause I can't fit in a Hobbit hole."

Heather yipped, a canine sound that had Barney laughing. "Asshole."

"Heather, language." Stacey's tone was more amused than angry. "Call him buttmunch."

Heather smirked at Barney. "Buttmunch."

"You're just cranky because you missed elevensies. You should eat something." Barney ducked as Heather swiped a claw-tipped hand at him. He shook his finger at her. "Temper, temper."

Laura exchanged a look with Stacey, who shrugged. They both looked like they were trying not to laugh. "It's decided, then. Glory will move in with Ryan—"

Glory blinked, distracted by the slap-fight going on between Heather and Barney. Heather seemed to be winning, most likely because Barney was unwilling to use his strength against his teeny mate. "I will?"

Ryan's mother smiled serenely. "Yes. You will. Because if you don't, we'll move in with you." She ignored Glory's protest and continued. "We'll take turns guarding Cynful Tattoos. Whoever isn't working has a shift, so she's with one of us at all times."

Will shrugged. "Works for me."

"I like it." Ray smiled warmly at all three girls equally.

"As long as Ryan's mate is safe, I'm willing." Steven had the same stubborn look his son got sometimes. There would be no changing his mind on the issue of her safety.

Chloe patted Glory's leg. "Welcome to my hell."

Glory whimpered. "But the crockpot is still here."

Chloe smacked her brother upside the head. "Seriously?"

Ryan shrugged and took another bite of burger. "I'll clean it before she moves in."

"I'll clean it." Laura headed for Ryan's kitchen. It wasn't long before she shrieked. "Ryan David Williams! Get your ass in here *now*!"

Ryan gulped and got his ass in there.

Glory pulled the French fry basket closer as she listened to Laura bully her son into killing the alien life form. "So. Who's helping me move?"

CHAPTER EIGHT

Glory yawned, stretching out on the huge bed. She'd had the best night's sleep in quite a while, and the last thing she wanted to do was wake up.

"I hate you so much right now."

Glory bit her lip to keep from laughing. Poor Ryan. He sounded miserable. "Aw, did the big, bad Bear have a bad night?"

Ryan grumbled under his breath as he shuffled into the bathroom. "I need a bigger couch."

"You driving me to work?" Glory scrambled out of bed and stretched again.

"If I can get my back to unkink, sure." Ryan poked his head around the door. "I'm sleeping in my bed tonight."

"I don't think so, Goldilocks." She began unbraiding her hair. She rarely slept without it braided and always regretted it when she forgot. The tangles could take hours to undo.

"I do think so, baby bear." He shut the bathroom door, and she heard the sound of water running.

"Hmph." Glory got dressed, choosing one of her soft, wispy outfits in pale pink. She added some jingling bangles on her wrists and one of her ankles before pulling on her ballet flats. Now all she needed to do was her hair and makeup, and she was ready for her day.

If Ryan would ever get out of the bathroom, that was.

Glory pounded on the door. "Are you done yet?"

She barely heard his answering grunt.

"Fine." She left the bedroom and headed straight for his kitchen, making herself a cup of coffee.

Soon the scent of the brew filled the apartment. Ryan lumbered out of the bedroom, his shirt half tucked into his jeans and his feet bare, his morning scruff darkening his jaw. He whimpered as she picked up her mug and took a sip.

Glory gave him her most innocent look and took another sip. "What?"

"Evil woman." Ryan picked her up like she weighed nothing, kissed her and set her gently aside.

The man was good for her ego. He didn't even wince at her combination of morning and coffee breath.

"I'm going to go do my hair and makeup. Make me another cup, please?"

Another grunt, but she was pretty sure Ryan would do as she asked. She headed back into the bedroom and did her normal morning routine, getting ready quickly so her coffee would be nice and hot. By the time she got back into the kitchen, Ryan had his shirt tucked in and shoes on. He was leaning against the counter, his eyes closed, sipping at his coffee with a blissful expression.

"Food?"

He pointed toward the fridge. Almost afraid to see what was in there, she opened the door.

Inside was a barren wasteland of nothingness. She glared over the door at him. "Where?"

He opened his eyes. "Check the bottom drawer."

"For what? Tumbleweeds?" But she opened the bottom drawer, surprised to find it full of fruit. "Okay." She was used to something a little more substantial in the mornings, but she supposed she could make this work until she dragged him grocery shopping.

She made two quick fruit salads, scarfing hers down when she saw the time. "Hurry up, baby bear. We've gotta go or I'll be late for work." She took his cup and hers to the sink, rinsing them and their bowls out before setting them in the dishwasher.

Ryan grabbed both their jackets and Glory's purse while she rinsed their dishes. "We can pick up some breakfast sandwiches on the way in for Cyn and Tabby."

"Cyn's working this morning. Tabby has the night shift with Heather, so I'll take Tabby's sandwich." She was still starving. A woman could not live on fruit salad alone, after all. She grabbed her coat and followed him out the door. "Are you planning on hanging out at the shop all day?"

"I have to go get some work done, so my parents said they'd be in around ten." Ryan yawned. "Why do you have to go in so early?"

"It's eight thirty. What time do you usually head in?"

"I've been meaning to ask you. You guys are open until eleven, so why do you go in so early?"

Glory gave him her best innocent look. "Business meetings."

Ryan snickered. "Is that what you call your good morning gossip session?"

"Actually, Mr. Accountant, we do the books, discuss the clients for the week, take inventory, do the orders for ink, needles, jewelry, go over the latest trends, decide if we're doing any of the cons this year—"

"Okay, geez. I didn't realize you guys did so much in the mornings."

"We really need another piercer too." Glory yawned. Some days it felt like she never left Cynful.

Ryan pulled out of the parking lot and onto the street. "I telecommute so I don't start until nine. And since we're now on East Coast time while the main office is on West Coast, I usually don't start until noon."

"That's going to change now that the business is moving here."

He shrugged. "I can handle it." He shot her a steamy glance. "You're worth it."

Glory squirmed and cleared her throat. "If you say so."

"I do."

It didn't take long to stop off at a local fast food place to pick up some breakfast, and they were pulling up in front of Cynful Tattoos before the sandwiches had cooled. Ryan and Glory made their way to the front of the building, smiling and waving at Cyn through the plate glass window.

"Good morning!"

"Morning, guys." Cyn stopped polishing the glass on the countertop long enough to sniff appreciatively. "Egg, ham and cheese?"

"Would we bring you anything else?"

"God, I love you." Cyn reached for the bag and pulled out her sandwiches. "I'm starving. Super Bear decided to work with Alex today."

"He still worried about deportation?" Ryan settled down on the gray chaise and pulled his own sandwiches out, handing the bag to Glory when he was done.

"Yes, even though Gabe and Max both reassured him that the Senate was working on keeping him in the States." She sighed. "We're thinking of pushing up the wedding."

"Don't do that." Glory ripped open the wrapper. "Give yourselves the wedding you want."

"If it means getting Julian his green card, I'll marry him tomorrow."

"If the Senate doesn't come through or if they take too long, then yeah." Ryan threw away an empty wrapper and grabbed his second sandwich. "I would move up the wedding. But wait another month or two before you decide, okay? You can always do a courthouse wedding, and then hold your dream ceremony later on."

The girls both stared at him. "Thought about this a lot, have you?"

He shrugged. "Julian's family."

And that was it as far as Ryan Williams was concerned. Julian was family, and the Bunsun-Williams clan would back him one hundred percent.

"Then let's not worry about it until all this other shit is taken care of." Cyn gathered her empty wrappers and tossed them in the trash. "We need to get ready to open. Take the trash out for me? I'll start setting everything out for the day."

Glory crumpled up her empty wrapper. "Will do."

"We can't keep an eye on you if you go out back to the trash bin." Ryan scowled. "I'll take the trash out. Cyn can keep an eye on you right here."

Glory rolled her eyes. "Fine." Glory picked up the glass cleaner. "I'll just do the windows, okay?"

Ryan relaxed. "Thanks, sweetheart." Ryan stole a brief kiss before gathering up the wastebaskets behind the counter and by the chaise.

Glory began cleaning the plate window, trying to ignore the way her lips tingled. She was getting used to those stealthy, sweet brushes of his mouth against hers. She wanted more, though. Deeper and longer, and that both scared and excited her. If she allowed Ryan the type of kiss they both seemed to crave, she doubted it would stop there. Ryan would take her, mark her and make her like he was.

Was she ready for that?

She watched out of the corner of her eye as Ryan headed into the break room. The way his jeans cupped his ass...

Woof. Glory was going to have to use her handful of paper towels to clean up the drool.

"I think that window is clean." The amusement in Cyn's voice caught her attention.

Glory rolled her eyes. "I can't get this hand print off. I think it's outside." It wasn't uncommon. People leaned against the huge window all the time. Some of them were trying to get a better look at the flash—or tattoo art—in the window. Some were fixing something with their shoes, or just needed a second to rest while shopping. "I'm going to head out front and clean it."

Cyn frowned, but really, there wasn't anything she could say. Glory would be on a main street, in broad daylight, with other shops open all around them. There might not be any place safer. "All right…"

Glory rolled her eyes. "I'm not going to be mauled by a shifter right on the street, Cyn. Besides, you're right here. I think, Miss Kodiak, you can protect me. Right?"

"Just stay where I can see you, and everything should be fine. I don't want to have to explain to Ryan how I lost his mate." Cyn folded her arms across her chest. "And I don't want you hurt again on my watch."

"It wasn't your fault that I got shot, Cyn."

Cyn sniffed. "I know that."

"Bullshit."

Cyn huffed. "Just go clean the window."

Glory was shaking her head as she stepped out of the front door of the shop. No matter how much she tried to reassure Cyn, the woman still felt like it was her responsibility that Glory had been shot by a madman. None of them had expected a sniper would take shots at them. That was the kind of thing that happened in the movies, not real life.

"Glory Walsh?"

Glory started to turn, to answer the man who'd spoken her name, but before she could she was yanked back against a hard chest. A sharp pain pierced her neck as the man bit down, and Glory screamed.

Cyn came barreling out of the door with a roar, but it was too late. The man was gone, running down the street as Glory collapsed to the pavement, bleeding and crying.

Ryan must have heard Glory scream, because he came careening out of the alley with his claws extended. He started to give chase to the man.

"Ryan!"

He ignored Cyn's shout, continuing down the street. If he got his hands on the man, Glory doubted the guy would survive.

"Ryan," Glory gasped as Cyn pressed the paper towels she'd planned on using on the window to her neck. "Ryan, please." Her vision was going dim.

Ryan stopped running. She barely noticed the inhuman roar that seemed to rip its way out of him, but he was coming back, running as fast toward her as he had after the bad guy. His blue eyes were totally brown when he knelt at her side. "Glory." He stared at the bite mark on her shoulder and hissed. "Son of a fucking bitch."

Together, Cyn and Ryan helped her into the shop, holding her up when she nearly fainted from the pain. "I'm sorry, sweetheart. So sorry."

"Not your fault." She thought she'd be safe. For fuck's sake, it was right out on the street, in broad daylight. There were people all around.

But apparently crazy dickheads didn't care about being caught.

"Shit." Ryan sounded furious, but she could barely see him. Her vision was wavering in and out of focus. "He gave her a changing bite."

What? Was that why she felt like her veins were running with ice? Her hands trembled, her breathing coming in short gasps.

"Glory?"

The roaring in her ears, the pain in her chest, her hands and feet tingling, could only mean one thing. Glory was having another panic attack.

Spots danced before her eyes and Glory knew she was about to pass out.

But then Ryan's arms, his scent, enveloped her. He began to hum, the same lullaby that had broken through her panic the last time, and she began to calm as he rocked her gently.

Ryan sniffed the bite mark the stranger had given her and snarled. "I need to bite you. I need to try and overcome the mark that god-damn Wolf placed on you."

"You're sure it was a Wolf?"

Ryan nodded, answering Cyn. "I'm positive. I can smell him in the bite." His hold was gentle, but his voice was furious. "I'm sorry, sweetheart. This isn't the way I'd planned on claiming you."

Glory opened her mouth to give him permission. Better Ryan than the man who'd possibly killed her sister. But before she could respond he'd already bitten down.

Ryan's fangs sank beneath her skin, the sensation completely different from what she'd felt when the stranger had bitten her. Glory gasped as intense pleasure flooded her being, the best orgasm she'd ever fucking had tearing her apart. She clung to him as the pleasure went on and on, the pain of the previous bite subsumed under the bliss Ryan gave her.

Why the fuck had she waited so long? If she'd known it would feel like this she would have let him bite her months ago.

His teeth pulled free, and Glory mourned their loss. She wanted that sensation again and again. "Ryan." Her voice was breathless, needy.

"I'm sorry, Cyn. I need…" Ryan's voice was almost as bad.

"Damn it." Cyn sighed. "Try not to scare off the customers."

What customers? And what was Cyn—

Whoa. Glory clung to Ryan as her Bear lifted her in his arms. "I need you," he whispered as he nuzzled the top of her head.

"Mm-hmm." Glory could barely think, but she had the feeling that she was about to be mauled by her Bear.

She could hardly wait.

***

Ryan couldn't believe he was about to fuck his mate for the first time in the break room of her shop, but thanks to the son of a bitch who'd tried to change her he had no choice. Neither of them would be completely satisfied until Ryan sank inside her and finished marking her. The need to make her come again was riding him hard, urging him to just take her where they stood.

Thank God she'd worn one of her soft, gauzy skirts. He could lift it up, rip off her panties and pleasure them both with ease.

But first, he had to make sure his mate's legs could hold her up. She'd scared the piss out of him when she collapsed. Ryan opened his senses to the healing spiral, dancing down it to make sure Glory wasn't hurting.

He smiled as he sensed the touch of Cyn. Apparently she'd healed Glory even as Ryan marked her, making sure that Glory wouldn't suffer any more than she already had. Ryan would have to make sure to thank Cyn for that, though he had the feeling she wouldn't accept it. He knew how much Cyn loved both Glory and Tabby, how protective she felt toward both of them. She'd be furious with herself over the fact that Glory had gotten hurt again.

He pulled out of the healing spiral and placed his precious burden on the break table. "Let me love on you, Glory."

She shivered, her pupils blown. The effects of the mating bite must still be with her. Good. It meant she'd be far more open to fucking him than she might have been otherwise.

God, he hated that this was forced on her. He'd be apologizing for the rest of his life, but the thought of Glory bearing even a trace of that fucker's mark on her made him want to roar with rage.

Instead, he would try and make this the best, or at least the hottest, experience of her life. The Wolf—that's what he'd scented before Glory called him back—wasn't going to win.

Ryan licked his lips as he reached under Glory's skirt, pulling her panties off and dropping them on the floor. "Lean back on your elbows, sweetheart."

Glory whimpered, but obeyed. "Jesus, Ryan. I can't believe we're doing this here."

"You'll never be able to come into the shop again without thinking of me." And that's just how Ryan wanted it. Fuck the strange Wolf. Glory would remember today as the day they'd mated if it killed him.

Ryan carefully pushed the hem of her skirt up until the thin material bunched at her waist, exposing the blonde fuzz that covered her pussy. He was ready to whine like a child, desperate for a taste of candy.

Glory slowly spread her legs. "Rye?"

He stroked her legs, trying to calm her shivering. "Shh." He brushed his tongue over her clit, smiling when she gasped and lifted her hips. "Let me taste you. I've been dying for you." The mate dreams weren't enough, never had been, and now that he had her spread out like a buffet Ryan planned on gorging himself.

Glory lay back on the table, her legs dangling over the edge. She cupped her small breasts through her shirt, her thumbs circling over the nipples.

"Are you wearing a bra?"

Glory grinned secretively and spread her legs wider.

"Shit." Ryan pressed his mouth to her pussy and began eating his mate out. He alternated fucking her with his tongue and sucking on her clit, delighted when she began to softly moan. The knowledge that he was bringing his mate to orgasm thrilled him and soothed him at the same time. He needed to make her come, preferably more than once, before he took his own pleasure. So Ryan concentrated on the spots that made her moan the loudest, took note of the ones that made her softly sigh, and mixed it up, waiting for the moment when she'd quiver in ecstasy beneath his touch.

Her hands slipped beneath her shirt and pushed it up, revealing that his hunch was right. His mate wasn't wearing a bra, her small breasts allowing her to get away with it. He wanted one of them in his mouth almost as badly as he wanted her to come.

Soon. Soon he'd be pounding into her, one of her breasts sucked into his mouth, listening to her scream as her pussy pulsed around him.

But first, he was going to make her shudder on his tongue.

Her breath was coming in needy gasps, her thighs quivering as he pressed her legs apart, refusing to allow her to close them. He wanted, needed, full access to her quivering hole.

With a whimpering cry Glory came, her back arching, her blue hair spilling around her. He could barely stop himself from spilling in his jeans at the sight, his gorgeous, fairy-like mate finding her satisfaction at his hands.

"More. Oh, fuck, Ryan. Give me more."

"Tongue or cock, sweetheart?" He wiped his hand across his lips, her juices sweet on his tongue. He was willing to do either, but eventually he would sink into her warm depths.

She pressed the palm of her hand against her clit, one of her fingers sinking deep inside her.

Ryan watched, entranced, as she fucked herself, rubbing her clit at the same time. But he couldn't stop himself from touching, stroking her soft, pale skin, tangling in the pale curls at the juncture of her thighs. Before too long his finger joined hers inside her.

Her blue eyes were glued to his face, her free hand stroking over his chest, tugging at his shirt.

He began lifting the edge of the shirt with his free hand. "You want this off?"

She whimpered and nodded.

Ryan whipped the shirt over his head, dropping it beside her panties. Her free hand immediately went to his chest, her fingers bringing his nipples to stinging life.

Ryan brushed her hand off her pussy and lifted her legs over his shoulders. He bent and once more took her clit in his mouth, sucking on it strongly. His fingers entered her, fucking her in time to the strokes of his tongue.

"Oh. Oh, Ryan. Yes, right there." Glory's hips rose and fell, her thighs clamping down around his head.

Ryan could feel it, the quivering wetness of her, and knew she was close. He wanted to drive her over the edge one more time before sinking into her. He'd ride her, thrust against that amazing ass, cup her breasts through her shirt and finally, finally sink his fangs into her once more.

Glory grabbed hold of his head and Ryan stilled everything but his tongue. Within seconds she was crying out, her legs tightening around his head as the orgasm tore through her.

Ryan kept up a gentle sucking until her legs relaxed. "Think you can stand?"

"Uh-huh."

"Good." Because Ryan had a fantasy that involved her lying against the break table, her ass in the air, his cock in her pussy, and damn it if he wasn't going to make it come true.

He helped her off the table and pulled off her shirt, revealing her pretty pink nipples. He sucked one into his mouth, enjoying her soft moans as he brought it to a stiff peak. "Bend over the table, sweetheart. Let me have you."

Glory complied. "Make it good, Ryan."

He chuckled, aware how raspy it sounded. God, even now she was pushy. "Yes, ma'am."

"Damn straight." But her ass went up, her legs spread, and Ryan was completely lost.

Grabbing her hips, Ryan slid inside her, groaning at the feel of her tight, wet heat. Slowly he began to move inside her. "This good?"

"Faster."

Ryan refused to go any faster until he knew for certain her knees would hold her. "No."

Glory growled and reached behind her, slapping his hip as hard as she could. "Faster."

Ryan laughed. "Yes, ma'am."

Glory started to laugh, but it was abruptly cut off as Ryan gave her what she'd been demanding. He began pounding into her, the sound of their flesh slapping together filling the room.

"Oh, yes, fuck yes." Glory began to thrust back, meeting him move for move. "Do it, Ryan. Fuck me hard."

She was going to be the death of him. Ryan grabbed her hips and began to really fuck his mate, thrusting so hard she was moving jerkily against the table. He could see her breasts bouncing, the hard tips rubbing the table top. Her hair, that mass of wild blue curls he loved so much, brushed against him with every thrust. She felt so good, so tight, Ryan never wanted to leave. He wanted to stay buried inside her for the rest of his days.

She grabbed hold of the edge of the break table, steadying herself against his thrusts. "Yes, yes, yes," she chanted, inflaming him further. His mate was a talker, and he loved it.

"Tell me. Tell me it's good."

"Fuck, so good." Glory moaned, going on her tiptoes. "I need it. I need, Ryan."

"Bare your neck, sweetheart."

She lifted her hair away from her neck. Her blue eyes were glazed, the red mark left by his teeth stark against her pale skin. He'd healed the Wolf's bite as he'd claimed her, leaving nothing but his own mark behind.

She was so beautiful, so fierce, his tiny mate. He could feel himself near to coming, ready to spill inside her.

Lightning fast he struck, sinking his fangs into her neck.

Glory shrieked, spasming around him so hard he thought his dick would be ripped off. The tight spasms of her orgasm forced his own, and Ryan spilled inside his mate, blind with ecstasy. It felt like it went on and on, the pleasure wringing him dry as Glory cried out his name.

When it was over Ryan tried to hold himself up, tried to keep from collapsing on his tiny mate. "Fuck."

Glory giggled, the sound breathless. "Let's go again."

Ryan lost the battle, collapsing on top of her with a laugh. "Give me a minute, SG."

She patted his hip. "Take your time, son. Take your time. I'm just gonna rest here with a pole up my—"

"You couldn't wait, could you?" Julian's amused voice floated over him, startling them both to silence. "You just *had* to do it on the table where I eat my lunch." Julian tsk'd. "There's not enough antibacterial cleaner in the world."

Ryan froze, aware his bare ass was facing the curtain that separated the main part of Cynful Tattoos from the break room. He was giving Julian one hell of a view, his jeans barely to his knees, his cock still sunk in his mate's pretty pussy. "What can I say? I was hungry."

This time, when Glory smacked him, he just laughed.

CHAPTER NINE

Glory could not believe she'd had sex in the break room. What the hell had she been thinking?

She shot a glance toward Ryan, who was filling his parents in on the attack against her. He winked at her when he caught her staring, his expression unbearably happy.

Oh, right. I was thinking of getting me a piece of that.

God, the man knew what he was doing. She hadn't taken so much pleasure from another person in... In...

Ever.

Glory huffed out a sigh. He was going to be insufferable now. No doubt his couch surfing days were over too. He'd crawl into bed with her tonight, and from the way her body tingled she wouldn't exactly be kicking him out again. Hell, she probably wouldn't complain too much if he left entire sandwiches in the bed, let alone crumbs.

No way in hell would she admit to him how good he was. He had a fat enough head already.

"Hey." Glory turned as Cyn put an arm around her shoulders. "You okay?"

"I'm fine." When Cyn's eyes narrowed suspiciously, Glory laughed. "No, seriously. I'm okay."

"You think Ryan managed to overcome the mark the other shifter put on you?"

"You tell me, oh Sniff Master. What do I smell like?"

Cyn took a deep whiff of Glory's neck, tickling her. "You smell like Glory." She stared at Glory for a moment before bellowing for Julian. "Super Bear? Come sniff Glory and see if she's going to be Bear or Wolf, will ya?"

Glory felt her cheeks flaming with embarrassment as Julian sauntered toward them and took a deep whiff. "I can't tell. Right now I smell Ryan more than anything." He smirked, but there was a hint of silver in his eyes and hair. The Kermode was either healing her, or had recently done some healing, the mark of his power plain to see. "I can't imagine why."

Glory rolled her eyes. "Can I help it if Ryan went all cave-Bear on me?"

Julian patted her head. "Don't worry. It won't be long before we know which one will win out. Your scent should change soon." He smiled. "But I'm willing to bet Ryan's bite will overcome the other, simply because it's a mating bite as well as a changing one. It will be stronger than any other bite you could receive."

"So you're pretty sure I'll be a Bear." Glory was strangely relieved. As much as she loved Tabby, the thought of becoming just like her attacker had made her feel sick.

"I do, but we'll know for sure by the end of tomorrow. Either way, it should be a few days before you change for the first time."

"And when that time comes you'll listen to what we have to say. The last thing you want to do is change in the middle of the shop." Ryan tugged her close, kissing her with a possession he hadn't shown before. "I have to go to work."

He sounded so cute and pouty. "Then go already."

"Listen to what my parents say. They'll keep you safe."

"We need to call Gabe and let him know what happened." Julian was already dialing the phone. "We should have done that while you were, um, making sure Glory wasn't hurt too badly."

"Yup. He checked my tonsils with his tongue." Among other things, the thought of which made her blush furiously.

The man was seriously talented. Just the thought of a repeat performance had her squirming in her seat.

Ryan laughed. "What can I say? I like playing doctor." He cuddled Glory close. "Want me to take your temperature?"

He grunted when she jammed her elbow into his stomach. "Go to work."

"Yes, SG." He cupped her chin, his expression serious. "Listen to my parents."

"I will." The last thing she wanted was to be attacked again by the psycho. "Ryan?"

"Hmm?"

"Should I go get a rabies shot?"

"No."

She used her best puppy eyes on him. "But I don't know where that guy's been." Honestly, she didn't want Ryan to go. She felt safer when he was hovering over her. It didn't matter how nice, how fiercely protective his parents were.

They weren't him, and already the beginnings of panic began to fill her. She took a deep breath, trying to get her raging emotions under control.

Ryan growled. "Maybe Bunny can work without me today."

"Ryan?" His father, Steve, came over and studied them both. "If you're going, you need to head out."

Glory continued her deep breathing. She'd be okay. She really didn't need Ryan. Cyn would keep her safe.

"Is Glory all right, son?"

"Panic attack." Ryan picked her up, cradling her close. "Calm down, sweetheart. I telecommute, remember?"

"Going to use your amazing psychic powers to dig holes?" Glory closed her eyes and breathed deep. Was it her imagination, or did Ryan smell really good?

"Damn. You figured out my super power."

Glory giggled.

"Seriously. I think Bunny will understand if you need me to stay here. I'm pretty sure I can keep the books from your shop." Ryan kissed her forehead. "Say the word and I'm on your Internet, not checking out porn at all."

She laughed again. God. She really didn't want to force him to stay, but the thought of being in the shop without him? Chills raced up and down her spine. Her arms were quickly covered in goose bumps. She was pretty sure her hair was standing on end. "I'll be all right."

"Bullshit." Julian was crouching in front of her, his eyes totally gray. A thick strand of silver appeared right over his temple. "You are very far from okay." She felt a tingling sensation as Julian used his Kermode powers to calm her racing heart. "I think you need to stay, Ryan."

"Why is this happening? I thought I was over this." Glory leaned back against Ryan, his strength becoming her own. "I hadn't had a panic attack in years, and now I'm getting them all the time."

Julian shared a concerned look with Ryan. "When you stopped having them, you went into 'remission'." Julian took hold of her hand. "Have you ever seen a psychologist for your panic attacks?"

She shook her head. "No."

"That's why. For some reason, the fear of the panic attacks receded, sending the disorder into remission. The recent attacks on Tabby, Cyn and yourself, plus the stress of moving the business and finding out there are shifters, *plus* the stress of finding your mate, have all combined to bring them back. It isn't your fear of being left that's causing all this. It's your fear of change."

Glory blinked. "What? That makes no sense."

"It started when Hope disappeared, continued through your family's abandonment of you. No one has truly left you this time. You're not alone, not ever. And part of you knows that, but the panic disorder doesn't distinguish between true changes and what's happening now."

"I know that." She clutched Julian's hand. "Ryan won't leave me. I know nothing's *really* changed."

"But your heart and your head are at odds. Tabby mated Alex and moved out of your apartment." Ryan placed his finger over her lip when she tried to speak. "Then Cyn moved in with Julian. Then the shop got moved."

"And last night I moved in with you. So it's all about change, good or bad." It made sense, in a twisted sort of way.

"Mm-hm." Ryan stroked her hair. "No one's saying that what you're feeling isn't legitimate. You've been through a hell of a lot, sweetheart. It's a testament to how strong you are that you haven't lost your mind for real."

"And the panic attacks can be controlled, just like any phobic reaction." Julian was smiling, but his eyes were still silver.

She glared at them equally. "So you guys are saying I'm crazy."

"No. You're coping with crazy. There's a difference." Ryan tugged her hand out of Julian's, stroking her fingers soothingly. The sensation of Ryan's power washing over her was different, more jagged and not as strong as Julian's. "This is something you may overcome with time, or something that will occasionally hit you for the rest of your life. The important thing is knowing what causes it and trying to overcome the fear that triggers it."

"That's it?"

"That's it." Ryan kissed the top of her head. "And for now, at least, I telecommute from here. If it keeps the panic attacks at bay, it will be worth it."

"But we still need to address the phobia, and for that we need an expert."

"Then we find one. But for now?" Glory smiled as Ryan's arms tightened around her. "I'm not going anywhere."

And he didn't, not for the whole day. He stayed out of the way, peeking in on them every now and then to make sure the asshole who'd bitten her hadn't returned.

Ryan claimed he had a whiff of the guy now, and if he caught even a smidgeon of his scent anywhere near Glory the asshole was going to suffer a Bear mauling.

He also told her it was the same scent that had been on the gifts she'd found outside her apartment.

That didn't creep her out the tiniest bit.

Nope. Not at all.

Deep breaths, Glory. Deep breaths.

Ryan sauntered out to the front of the shop, stopping to check out the piercing jewelry. Ryan was pleased with the dark earring she'd picked for him. Maybe he was considering getting something else done as well.

Some people loved getting piercings, while others simply did their ears and nothing else. She was beginning to think Ryan might be in that first category. Maybe he would let her pick his next piercing again. Maybe she'd do one of his nipples? She didn't think he was ready for a Prince Albert or a guiche, but a pretty gold ring in his nipple for her to play with?

Yum.

The bell over the door jangled, catching Glory's attention.

A white-blond, blue-eyed man walked in and took a quick look around. She gasped, the stranger all too familiar to her.

He took a look around, his gaze glancing off both Cyn and Glory before whipping back to Glory. "Glory? Is that you?"

Glory collapsed into one of the turquoise chairs, her hands clenching on the arms. It couldn't be, but it was. "Temp?"

The man's smile was huge, his blue eyes, so much like Glory's, sparkling with happiness and tears. "Damn, girl. You look good."

Glory covered her mouth, her own blue eyes huge. "Oh. My. God."

The bell jangled again, and another pale blonde walked in. This one was tiny and feminine, a younger, slightly taller version of Glory. "You found her, Temp?"

"Faith?" Glory was shaking, her voice weak with shock. She stood and took a step closer to her baby sister, a sister she'd never thought to see again.

"Glory!" Faith rocketed forward, throwing herself into Glory's arms. "It's really you."

"Oh my God." Glory began to breathe erratically as Faith sobbed in her arms. "How?"

Temp watched the two women hugging, silent tears streaking down his cheeks. "It's so good to see you again." He moved forward far more cautiously than his sister had, watching Glory as if she might collapse at any moment.

Ryan crossed the room to her side, putting his hand on her shoulder. "Easy, sweetheart."

Her breathing evened out as Ryan's power poured into her, soothing her. "Rye? This is my family."

"I know, sweetheart."

For some strange reason, Ryan saying that made everything real. Glory began to cry, finally embracing her siblings. Ryan watched over them all, making sure she remained calm. The three of them murmured to each other, soothing words of how they'd missed one another and loved each other.

Faith stroked Glory's hair. "I like the blue."

Glory's laugh was watery. "I was thinking of going back to lavender."

Ryan growled. "I like the blue too."

Temp pulled way from the girls, shooting Ryan a distrustful look. "Who are you?"

"I'm Glory's fiancé." Ryan took hold of one of Glory's hands, reminding her that he was right there, that it was all right to lean on him. "Name's Ryan Williams." He held out his free hand.

"Temperance Walsh. Nice to meet you." Temp relaxed, shaking Ryan's hand. "I was hoping Glory would find someone."

"She found us." Cyn, ever protective of her friends, also put herself between Temp and Glory, much to Julian's obvious dismay. The man made an abortive gesture toward Cyn, but they both knew if it came to a fight between Temp and Cyn, the Kodiak would whoop the human's ass with ease. "Why are you here?"

Temp looked taken aback. "Faith turned eighteen last month. We've been traveling back toward Halle ever since we escaped my dad."

Cyn didn't look convinced, but Glory stood and took a step toward her brother, clinging to Ryan's hand. She might not want to admit it, but she needed his strength right now. Faith still had her arm around Glory's waist, clinging to her older sister as if she never wanted to let go. Glory let her, but kept her gaze on Temp. He was the strongest of them, had always been so. "Where is Dad?"

Temp shrugged. "Last we saw he was in some little town in Washington, preaching fire and brimstone as always. He's been traveling a lot, doing tent revivals, keeping us under observation. It…wasn't easy getting away."

"We're sorry to barge in on you like this, but we just found out where you were." Faith was hugging Glory tightly again. She couldn't seem to take her hands off her. "Some nice ladies over at Wallflowers told us to come here when we started asking around."

"Hell, we were just happy you were still in town." Temp ran his fingers through his hair, something he did often if the ragged mess was anything to go by. "But we didn't know where else to start, so we came back here, hoping you'd have told Cyn where you were going."

Cyn visibly relaxed at the mention of Wallflowers. Neither Emma Cannon nor Becky Holt, the Curana and Beta mate of the Puma Pride, would send someone to Glory they thought was a threat to the Cynful girls. "You met Emma?"

Temp grinned. "She's small, but she's mighty."

"She grilled us for an hour before she'd tell us where to find you." Faith's hopeful gaze hadn't once left her sister. "How have you been?"

"I've…been." Glory took another step toward Temp. "Cyn's family took me in."

Temp grimaced. "I wish I'd been able to stop him from throwing you out, but the way he beat you, I thought…" Temp sighed, touching Glory's cheek. "I don't know what I thought. I'm so sorry, kiddo. I wish I could have stayed with you, kept you safe."

"I know." Temp had done everything in his power to protect her, but their father was big and mean, and Temp had his own share of scars to deal with.

"You thought she'd be better off without us." Faith put her hand on her brother's arm. "You couldn't protect her anymore, and you told me you thought Dad was going to kill her."

Temp shrugged uncomfortably. "I didn't manage to protect any of you as well as I would have liked."

Glory winced. "He went after Faith?"

Temp grimaced. "Not as badly as he went after you, but yes."

This time it was Faith who looked uncomfortable. "I don't think I have nearly as many scars as you do."

"Scars? You have scars?" Ryan put his arm around his mate, tucking her close to him and dislodging Faith.

"All of us do, Rye." Glory shrugged. "Some of us just have deeper ones."

Temp winced, his shoulders moving uncomfortably. "I stopped as much of it as I could, but it was never enough. I was never enough."

"You did what you could, Temp." Glory smiled at her brother. "Don't ever think I wasn't grateful, because I was."

"Yeah. I knew why you left with Dad, Temp. I always knew." Glory stepped forward, away from Ryan, and allowed her siblings to embrace her again. "I really missed you guys." Damn it. She hated crying. She always wound up looking like she'd spent a week in Margaritaville.

"We missed you too, squirt." Temp held her tightly, only letting go when Glory pushed. Faith took his place, her embrace lasting longer than her brother's.

Glory took a step back, and Ryan pulled her close again. "Will Dad come after you?"

"He might." Faith visibly shivered.

Temp grinned savagely. "But if he does, he'll have to deal with all of us now."

Faith grimaced. "All except Hope."

Glory leaned into Ryan's embrace. "About Hope. We've decided to search for her."

"Really?" Temp grinned again, looking relieved. "Thank you, God. We were hoping you'd want to."

"Alive or dead, we want her home." Faith smiled sweetly.

Glory returned her sister's smile. Faith was gentle, sweet and far from capable of defending herself. She'd have to make sure the clan knew to keep an eye on her baby sister. Maybe she'd introduce her to Heather. She had the feeling the two girls would find they had a lot in common. The way Heather was coming out of her shell, perhaps she could help Faith. And with Barney watching over Heather, it would be an added layer of defense for her.

"Good. We've got the sheriff, Gabe Anderson, on our side." Glory pulled away from Ryan again and led her siblings to the little seating area, settling down once more in her favorite chair. "I don't suppose you know anything that could help us find her?"

"Well…" Faith shot a glance at her brother, who nodded. "There was this strange man who was following Hope."

Glory frowned. "Hope never mentioned anything about a stranger to me." But Hope had become strangely quiet during those last couple of months. Had she been hiding something from Glory?

Temp nodded. "She didn't want to tell anyone about it. She thought it was just a guy who came and went to the library the same way we all did."

"But Hope said she got creepy feelings off him, so she told Dad about it. Temp overheard it, but I didn't find out about it until recently."

"Dad told her there was nothing to worry about, that it was probably her imagination, so she let it go. You remember how he indulged her. She probably trusted his word that everything would be all right." Temp growled. "The way he would look at her… Sometimes I wonder, but I like to think my father wasn't a fucking pedophile."

Faith put her hand on his leg. "Dad never touched me in…*that* way."

Glory sighed. "Or me."

"Good." Ryan settled on the arm of her chair, his hand on her shoulder once more. "If your father had touched you I'd be forced to hunt him down and rip off his arms."

Glory blinked. "Down, baby bear. Daddy Dearest has a lot to answer for, but not that."

"I'm not so sure." Temp exchanged a glance with Ryan that sent chills down her spine. "The way he acted around Hope? Tell me it never crossed your mind that he finally snapped and did something to her, then killed her to cover it up."

"I think…" Glory shook her head. If she was wrong, she was giving her siblings false hope. But, if she was right… "I think Hope is alive. There's something inside, where we were connected, that tells me she's still somewhere on this earth. When I tried to tell Dad I could still feel her, he beat me pretty badly."

Ryan growled, but coughed it back when Temp and Faith shot him curious glances.

"Then why didn't she come home?" Temp leaned forward, resting his elbows on his knees and clasping his hands together. "You think she's being held captive? That maybe Dad didn't do anything to her?"

Glory didn't want to give what they'd learned away. She doubted either of her siblings knew anything about shifters, and for now that's how it needed to stay. "It's possible. We won't know for sure until we find some clues." She'd have to figure out a way to keep them out of the loop until the rogue Wolf was found and dealt with. She'd talk to Ryan about it later, once Temp and Faith were gone.

Temp studied them all for a moment, his gaze lingering longest on Ryan. "Whatever you need, sis. Whatever you need, you just ask."

"What I need is my sister back, one way or the other. What I'm going to *get* is a caramel macchiato once I send Ryan to the coffee shop." Glory grinned up at Ryan, aware it was a pale imitation of her usual expression.

Ryan sighed. "The things I do for love."

She patted his knee. "Extra whip, dear."

Ryan laughed, even as her siblings looked utterly confused. "Of course. Would you have anything else?"

She sighed and kissed his cheek, more grateful to him than he could ever know. "Nope."

CHAPTER TEN

Ryan hadn't felt entirely comfortable leaving Glory with Cyn, but one look at the Kodiak and he'd known she'd defend Glory to the death. She couldn't be in better hands, unless they were his own.

Still, he found himself hurrying back. It just seemed way too convenient to him, Temp and Faith showing up just as they began searching for Hope. He couldn't help but wonder how much of their tale was true, and how much made up. He very much doubted that Reverend Walsh had let his last two children go without a fight.

If their father had sent them, then Ryan wasn't sure what he'd do. Glory would be crushed to discover her siblings were working against her, but Ryan couldn't allow even a hint of a threat to his mate. It was bad enough she'd been attacked when he'd been right there with her.

He'd have to see if the apples were as rotten as the tree they'd fallen from.

Maybe he could get Gabe to look into their backgrounds, especially Temp. As the oldest, he was the one who had the best chance of getting Faith away from an abusive parent, yet he'd chosen to stay in a toxic environment. Why? Why hadn't he brought proof to the authorities that Reverend Walsh was an unfit father? As abusive as the good reverend was, Ryan had no doubt he'd abused either Temp or Faith, or both. With two of his daughters and his wife gone, he would have needed a direction for his rage, and Faith was both female and, young as she'd been, highly vulnerable.

Could Temp have taken part in the abuse?

Ryan shook his head and ordered the coffees. No. Glory seemed to think Temp had tried to protect them from their father. She truly believed he'd only gone with Reverend Walsh to take care of their youngest sister. She'd had no problem filling Ryan in on the abuse her father had heaped on her. He doubted she would have held back if her brother was the same.

No, she would have told him. And Temp would have died the moment he stepped foot inside Glory's shop.

Ryan paid for the coffees and headed for the door. He was still planning on looking into Temp's background. It was possible Glory was wrong about her brother, and if so it was Ryan's duty to discover the truth and keep Glory safe.

Ryan turned the corner from the coffee shop to Cynful, when something hit him so hard in the back he stumbled and fell to his knees, the crack of metal on flesh shocking in the midst of the small-town shops. It reminded him of the aluminum bats he used to play baseball with when he was a kid.

Shit. Someone's trying to kill me. Ryan rolled to the side, trying to get to his feet before the fucker hit him again.

The bat cracked down on his shoulder, numbing his hand. Ryan cried out at the pain, aware something had just broken inside him. His Bear roared in fury, ready to bust out of Ryan's skin and kill the son of a bitch before he could take Ryan down.

Snarling, he pushed himself up with his good hand, ready to castrate whoever it was who'd decided to play ball with his head. Ryan got a glimpse of bright blue eyes behind a dark ski mask before the bat swung again, catching him in the cheek. He fell onto his back, dazed, his face hurting almost as much as his shoulder.

Ryan grinned savagely up at his attacker, allowing his fangs to show. "My turn."

Before Ryan could climb to his feet a loud scream sounded. Someone had seen the fight, and Ryan had no doubts the cops were being called. "Fuck."

The man took off, knocking people aside in his bid for freedom. But he left an important clue behind, one Ryan would use to catch his ass.

He smelled faintly of Wolf. The same one who'd bitten his mate.

Ryan was going to rip the man limb from limb when he caught him.

Rolling to his side, Ryan barely managed to sit up before a stranger knelt at his side, holding him still. "Are you all right?"

Ryan nodded, trying not to vomit as the pain bit into him with savage teeth. "Yeah. Asshole got away, though."

"I saw. I'm going to call an ambulance." The stranger, a well-dressed man who looked, and smelled, vaguely familiar, pulled out a cell phone. He was obviously Puma, but Ryan wasn't sure if he was part of the local Pride or associated with the college. "Stay calm and try not to move."

"Good plan." Because the little bit of movement Ryan had attempted made his vision black out. Ryan tried to focus, to go down the spiral path and heal himself, but the dizzying pain made concentration almost impossible. "I think the shoulder's broken. Maybe my cheekbone."

"Shit." The man paused before dialing. "I'm going to go out on a limb here and say you're one of the Bears that moved into town recently."

Ryan nodded. "You?"

"I'm Pride." He started to hold out his hand and grimaced. "Grayson Howard."

"Shit. Jamie's brother?" He didn't think the man even lived in Halle. Had he moved here because of the death of his brother's mate?

Jamie Howard, once the local doctor and a respected member of the Puma Pride, had become a severely damaged recluse. Grayson had been one of the people to warn them that they must keep both Julian and Cyn away from Jamie at all times. The doctor blamed both of them for saving his life when his mate died. Now the once happy-go-lucky man was a broken, icy shell who refused even his Alpha's order to appear before the Pride.

Ryan had heard that Gabe was keeping an eye on the situation. Ryan wondered if maybe he should do the same too. Gray's eyes were bloodshot, the skin around them sunken and dark. It was obvious he hadn't gotten much sleep recently. The urge to check on Jamie Howard, see exactly how far the man had fallen, was riding him despite the pain.

"Yeah. Small world, huh?" Gray stared at the phone for a moment before closing his eyes. "Want me to call Julian DuCharme, or an ambulance?"

"Julian. Please." If Glory found out he'd been attacked, hurt, she'd flip her lid. She might even have another panic attack. He couldn't risk it. "Please."

The sound of sirens interrupted them. "Someone else must have called." Gray stood, then smiled down at Ryan. "It's not an ambulance. It's Sheriff Anderson."

Ryan immediately relaxed. Gabe would understand what was going on. He hoped.

"Dude."

Ryan closed his eyes and whined. He recognized that voice.

"What the hell happened to you?"

"Hell, Barney. Where the fuck where you five minutes ago?" Ryan glared up at the Hunter.

Barney held up something wrapped in paper. "Bagel." He took a bite, crouching down beside Ryan. He tsk'd, touching Ryan's cheek with a surprisingly gentle touch. "That looks like it hurts."

Ryan flipped him off. "The bad guy got away."

"I see that." Barney sniffed deeply. "Got his scent, though."

"Goodie for you." Ryan leaned against the brick wall of the store he'd been attacked in front of and tried to concentrate on not puking.

"Hang in there. Julian's on his way." Grayson nodded. Ryan hadn't even realized he'd called.

"Hmm." Barney grabbed the back of Ryan's shirt and tugged him out of the flow of pedestrians. "Is he now? There's a man I'd like to have little a chat with."

Ryan groaned as his arm hit the bricks of one of the storefronts. "Damn it, Barney."

"Sorry."

"If you fuck with Julian you're in for a nasty surprise. And his mate has a hell of a bite."

Barney actually laughed as he parked Ryan at the mouth of an alley. "She's tiny. I can take her."

Ryan just stared at him. "If believing that helps you sleep at night." He shifted restlessly, groaning as a fresh wave of agony rolled through him. "Where's Julian again?" Ryan still couldn't focus long enough to go into the healing spiral or he'd try and take the edge off himself, and Barney had shown no inclination to help him other than to drag him out of traffic.

What a pal. Ryan couldn't wait to be trained by him. *Not.*

"He'll be here shortly." Gray held out his hand to Barney. "Grayson Howard."

"James Barnwell." Barney took Gray's hand and grinned. "Call me Barney."

"Okay, Ryan." Ryan jumped. When the fuck had Gabe gotten there? He must be in worse condition than he thought if he hadn't noticed the sheriff making his way toward them. Gabe knelt next to him, scowling at something. Possibly Barney. Ryan had the feeling the man inspired a shit ton of scowls. Hell, he'd managed to piss off Heather. That usually took an act of God. "Tell me what happened."

"Was coming back from getting Glory coffee when I was jumped. Asshole used an aluminum bat, tried to take my head off." The pain was becoming unbearable. Ryan could barely breathe through it. He filled his lungs in shallow pants. It felt like his head was going to explode, and the thought of moving his shoulder at all made him swallow thickly. "He had on a ski mask, so I didn't get a good look. He seemed maybe your height, maybe a little thinner in the chest and shoulders, but I was on the ground so it's difficult to tell for sure. Oh, and I caught sight of blue eyes through the ski mask. And he smelled of Wolf."

"That's it? That's all you got?"

Ryan shot Barney a look that bordered on loathing. "I was too busy trying to keep my head from becoming a piñata to catch his name and address, asshole." He turned his attention back to Gabe. "It was the same one who bit Glory."

"Bit Glory?" Gabe snarled, the sound pure cat. "When did that happen?"

Shit. What with Ryan claiming Glory and Temp and Faith arriving, they'd forgotten to call Gabe. "Glory went out front to clean the windows and got jumped by a Wolf. The same damn Wolf that just tried to hit a home run with my skull."

"Where were you when she got attacked?"

Ryan sighed. "Taking out the trash. I thought, hell we *all* thought, she'd be safe in front of the store in broad fucking daylight."

"We've got ourselves someone who's not afraid of the consequences." Barney's hat was so low on his forehead Ryan couldn't see his eyes. "Something's changed for him. All of a sudden he's attacking both you and Glory. Why?"

"He used a changing bite on her, but he couldn't claim her because—"

"She's not his mate." Gabe sighed. "This is so fucked up."

"Tell me about it."

"Barney." Gabe pointed toward Ryan's injuries.

"Pfft. He needs to learn to take care of himself in the field or he's never gonna make it." Barney pushed back his hat, crossed his arms over his chest and attempted to stare down Gabe.

Gabe snarled, but before the two Hunters could truly get into a pissing match, a very welcome figure spoke from behind Barney with an authority Ryan had only heard once before, when he'd nearly gone feral in a dance club full of humans. "Move, Boo-Boo. I've got this."

With a startled look, Barney moved.

Julian stepped into the alley and knelt next to Ryan, his black hair turning pure silver, his deep brown eyes going gray. "Hey, Rye. Glory's going to be pissed when she sees you've dropped her coffee."

Ryan sighed in relief as Julian's power washed over him, dulling the pain. "I'll get her another." Warmth washed over him in gentle waves, his bones realigning, the damage healed to a degree Ryan could not have done on his own. He shuddered as the pain finally ceased completely. "Thanks."

Julian's eyes opened, the silver fading once more to brown. Only a single silver line remained to mar his long dark hair. "You're welcome. What happened?"

"Got jumped by a dude with a baseball bat and a grudge."

Julian's brows rose. "Hope's captor?"

"Or the good Reverend Walsh." Ryan wasn't taking bets yet. As far as he was concerned, it was still fifty-fifty. For all he knew Glory's parent *was* a shifter. Her inability to scent it wouldn't be a surprise, and if the man had been changed after his children were born it would explain why they were all human.

Julian helped Ryan to his feet, rotating Ryan's arm and grunting in satisfaction. "It healed well."

Ryan tested his arm and his face with his own healing powers. They were nowhere near as strong as Julian's, but he could still heal in the same manner.

But where Ryan could seamlessly heal a paper cut or a small wound, Julian could take a brutal beating and make it almost disappear. Ryan couldn't detect anything had ever happened to him beyond the long-healed break in his arm from childhood. "You're good."

"I am." Julian buffed his nails on his shirt. "Make sure you point that out to my mate."

Ryan laughed. "I'll do that."

"Unless Reverend Walsh is a shifter, I doubt he's the man who attacked both you and Glory." Gabe sniffed deeply. "It's faint, but it's there, and most definitely Wolf."

Ryan exchanged a glance with Julian. "We have to call Alpha Lowell." A rogue Wolf was in the area. The Poconos Pack Alpha, Richard Lowell, would definitely want to know about it.

"Um, excuse me?" Barney tapped Ryan on the shoulder, his gaze still glued to Julian. "Why did I just obey your friend?"

Ryan grinned. "Because of his freaky shaman powers."

Barney grunted. "Okay. Anyone want to explain that to me?"

"Nope."

Barney growled.

Gabe laughed. "Man, I love the fact that I know something you don't."

"Asshole." Barney blocked the entrance to the alleyway. "Someone explain this to me. Now."

Julian rolled his eyes, then captured Barney's gaze. "*Move*."

Barney moved, his eyes wide and startled. But damn if the Hunter didn't make sure Julian and Ryan had plenty of room to get past him.

"Let's go, Ryan."

Ryan went, ignoring Gabe's laughter and Barney's sputtering.

"That guy needs an enema."

Ryan nodded his agreement. For someone who seemed so laid back, James Barnwell was wound really tight. "Or a good, hard—"

Just as Ryan made the very explicit gesture Barney caught up to them. "Wait!" Barney stared at Julian intently as he walked beside them. "Seriously. How the fuck did you do that?"

"One of the reasons Kermode stay separate from all of you is our ability to get other shifters to obey us." Julian eyed Barney. "Doesn't your Senate teach you *anything*?"

Barney shrugged. "Apparently not." He adjusted his hat. "So it's like an Alpha voice or something?"

"Not quite." Julian made a face. "Alphas, I've found, can usually shrug it off."

"So you don't have the same powers as the Leo." Barney seemed strangely relieved.

"No, thank fuck." Julian shivered. "Could you imagine?" He turned toward the coffee shop instead of Cynful Tattoos. "I feel the need for caffeine."

"You know, that's something to think about." Ryan frowned, trying to chase the elusive thought that had just occurred to him.

"Coffee?" Barney seemed to be getting more and more confused.

"No." God, this guy was slow. "The Leo is a white Lion. Kermode are white Black Bears."

"And rare as fuck. There aren't many of us left."

"There aren't many Polar Bear shifters that I'm aware of either. And they're as elusive as the Kermode." Barney shook his head. "Three hunters and a Kermode all in the same town. *Something* is about to go down. I just wish I knew what."

Ryan bit his tongue. The Hunter did *not* need to know there was one other white shifter in the area, one who didn't seem to have any strange powers at all. At least, none she'd discovered yet. Chloe's secret would remain just that until Ryan knew more about why she'd gone from a red Fox to a white one. "I hope it waits its damn turn. We have enough shit going down right now. We don't need some mysterious whatever turning up to fuck things up further."

"Amen, brother." Julian nodded his head. "Preach it."

"You guys are crazy. I like that about you." Barney grinned. "I'm going to try and hunt that Wolf's scent down." Barney stopped just outside the coffee shop. "I'll call you if I find anything." And with a final, weird glance in Julian's direction the Hunter took off for parts unknown, his cowboy hat still pushed back and his long brown duster flapping around his legs.

"Someone's lovin' the drama." Julian opened the coffee shop door with a smirk.

Ryan smiled. "Then he's definitely come to the right town."

CHAPTER ELEVEN

Glory watched closely as Julian, Ryan and that Barney guy all trooped into Cynful Tattoos with grim expressions. They took one look at her and immediately had guilt stamped all over them. What the hell could have happened while Ryan was out getting coffee? The coffee shop was only three blocks away, and as far as she knew Ryan wasn't the one the Wolf was after.

But it was obvious *something* had happened from the quick glance all three exchanged. She crossed her arms over her chest and glared at them. "Okay, guys. Spill. What happened?"

Both Julian and Ryan exchanged a startled glance, but Barney merely flopped into a chair with a nonchalance that didn't fool her for a moment. "I'm thinking of getting a tattoo."

"Good." Cyn, who'd just come out of the back room, grinned at the Hunter. "Come with me and we'll hook you up."

Barney, reluctance written all over his face, followed Cyn to her station. She bet the man would have something inked on his skin before the end of the day.

Barney would learn not to lie to Cyn. It just wasn't worth it.

Glory kept most of her attention on Julian and Ryan. One of them would crack and she'd know what had gone on. "Well?"

Julian patted Ryan's arm. "I love you, man, but you're on your own." He then carried his two coffee cups over to Cyn, handing one to her with a quick kiss and a whispered word that had Cyn glancing sharply over at Ryan.

"Rye."

Ryan sighed. "Don't freak."

Like *that* was going to calm her down. "Rye," she growled, startled at how deep her voice sounded.

"I'm fine. You can see that."

"So something did happen." God, she got that he was trying to keep her calm and all, but this dancing around shit was getting on her nerves.

He stared at her for a moment before answering. "I was attacked on the way back from the coffee shop."

Glory's blood ran cold. Her arms fell to her sides as her breath caught in her throat. "Are you hurt?"

"No. Julian took care of it."

Julian. He'd needed *Julian's* healing powers. That meant it had been bad, right? Because she knew from Alex that all Bears could heal minor wounds like other people breathed. "Rye?"

"I'm fine, SG. I swear it." Before she realized it he was in front of her, holding her hand, anchoring her before the panic could take her over. "I'm here, safe and sound, but he got away. Even better, Barney and Gabe got his scent." Ryan sighed and took hold of her arms, rubbing up and down. The soothing motion frightened her even more. "It was the same Wolf that attacked you."

Glory took a deep breath. Something inside her stirred, angered by the thought that Ryan had been injured. How *dare* someone lay a hand on her man? How dare someone try and take him away from her?

She was going to…

Her fingers twitched, itched in a strange way.

She was going to rip into the man who'd thought Ryan could be taken from her.

"Whoa." Ryan stroked her cheek. "Your eyes changed."

She blinked. What? "You mean like yours do?"

He nodded, looking unbearably pleased with himself. "And you definitely smell like Bear now."

Oh, thank fuck. If Tabby had bitten her, that would have been one thing. She loved Tabby like a sister and would have been proud to be her Pack mate.

Being changed against her will, forced to call the psycho who'd possibly stolen her sister, her Pack mate? That would have sucked big time.

Still, Glory wasn't finding it easy to let go of her anger. "I want to find the guy who hurt you and shove his nuts up his anus."

Ryan choked on a laugh. "Down, SG. Your claws are showing."

Glory looked down at her hands. Sure enough, her claws were visible. They weren't quite the five-inch monsters Ryan sported, but they were close. "Holy shit."

Ryan hugged her. "It's fine, Glory. This is what's supposed to happen." He chuckled again. "But I think you're going to change fast, just like Cyn did."

"Wonderful." Just what she needed on top of everything else. A big, furry ass.

"Look on the bright side. You'll be able to open the pickle jar all by yourself now." Ryan laughed as she smacked his arm and curled his fingers around her claws, hiding them from general sight. "Where'd your brother and sister go?"

"They left soon after you did. Temp said something about going back to their hotel to get some rest."

"Did he?"

She didn't like the speculation in Ryan's voice, but she couldn't blame him. He was attacked right after Temp and Faith left. It would be natural to suspect the new element in their lives.

But Ryan hadn't seen the way Temp had looked at her or the gratitude in Faith's eyes when she'd returned her sister's embrace. The two of them really wanted a life that included Glory.

And the dread she'd seen on their faces whenever their father was mentioned was all too familiar. Ryan didn't know what it was like to fear a parent, to know what it was like to realize that the person who was supposed to protect you was the one you needed protection from. But Glory did, and so did Temp and Faith.

If they were acting, they were damn good at it.

"Barney is going after the guy who did this." Ryan's embrace tightened. "And so will I."

"What? No." The guy had already hurt Ryan once.

"Listen. You know Gabe is a Hunter, right?" Ryan let go, cupping her face in his hands. "Remember what Barney said when we met with my family?" She nodded reluctantly. "Barney swears I'm one too."

She studied his expression, the determination on his face. The man was stubborn. If he truly believed he was a Hunter, nothing she said or did would deter him from becoming just that. "Do you think you are?"

Ryan reluctantly nodded. "Yeah. I think I am."

She blew out a breath. "What does that mean? Because Gabe and Sarah were separated for months while he trained." And if Ryan left for months to be trained, Glory would damn well be going with him.

"Don't worry so much. I'm not leaving. I told him he could shove it up his ass if he tried to get me to go."

Glory immediately relaxed. As stubborn as he was, Ryan would put his word to her above anything Barney wanted. Ryan wasn't going anywhere. "Good."

"But that doesn't mean I'm not going to train, and train hard. If I'm going to be a Hunter, I'm going to need to learn everything Barney and Gabe can teach me."

"As long as you come home safe at night, that's fine by me."

She squirmed in his grasp when she realized what she'd just said. Damn it. Why did she keep stripping herself bare in front of him? She might as well tattoo *Ryan's* on her ass, because now the shifter had to be aware he owned it.

Glory wasn't willing to admit out loud what else the Bear owned. Not yet, anyway. Let him work a little harder before she admitted to him how she really felt.

The satisfaction in his gaze wasn't making it any better. She had the bad feeling he was already aware just how much Glory was willing to give up for him. "That's a promise I intend to keep, sweetheart." Ryan kissed her, holding her with a possessiveness that should have had her fighting to get free.

Instead, she sank into his embrace, giving as good as she got. Because damn it, if her ass belonged to Ryan, then Ryan's belonged to her.

And it was about time she laid her own claim on the man who'd knocked her off her feet.

***

Ryan had refused to leave the shop, even to return home long enough to get his laptop. He sat in Tabby's empty station, watching like a hawk every single customer who entered, sniffing the air to make sure there wasn't anything odd about any of them. It was almost closing time, and he'd stayed right there the whole day.

Glory would never admit it, but just having him around calmed her. Knowing he was right there where she could keep an eye on him had soothed that strange feeling of *other* inside her. She'd been shaken to the core, more by the attack on him than on herself.

It had been unexpected, the rage that had filled her at the thought of Ryan so badly hurt he needed Super Bear's special touch. And until they caught the fucker who'd hurt him, she was going to insist he bring his laptop to the shop with him. Between Tabby, Cyn and Glory, Ryan would be safe.

She snorted, amused at the direction her thoughts had gone in. The man was the size of a small country. She was pretty sure if she told Ryan why she wanted him here, in her sight, he'd laugh his majestic ass off at her.

Either that or she'd find herself bent over the break room table again. She shivered. She wasn't sure if she wanted a repeat performance or not. The fact that she'd done him on there was going to fuel her fantasies for years, but the look on Julian's face had embarrassed the hell out of her.

Ryan fucked like a god, and that bite? Her cheeks flushed as she remembered how wonderful that bite had felt. Glory was looking forward to a repeat of *that* performance. She'd had some pretty decent sex in her life, but Ryan's bite took it to a whole other level.

I've developed a new kink, and its name is Ryan Williams.

Just as Glory was getting ready to close her station, the bell over the door jangled. A familiar voice called out, "Ryan?"

Glory grinned. Chloe had been coming around more often, getting out of her postage-sized apartment, much to her brother's relief. They were all thrilled that Chloe felt well enough to try and get out more. She'd tired so easily in the early days of her healing. Hell, she still tired quicker than Glory liked. "Hi, Chloe."

Chloe squeed and hugged her. "Congratulations!"

"Huh?" Glory returned the hug.

"You're mated. That means we're sisters!"

Glory shouldn't be surprised that the Fox could scent that on her, but she was. "I didn't know you could sense that."

"You smell of each other." Chloe looked genuinely happy for her as she pulled back. "You're good for him, you know? Most women bore him pretty quickly, but not you." Chloe waggled her brows. "Keep him on his toes."

Glory eyed him sideways, almost grinning when she saw him pale. "Has a lot of girlfriends in his past, does he?"

Chloe started to laugh. "Cheerleaders were all over him in high school. And in college? A couple of sorority sisters got into a fistfight in the student center."

"Chloe!" Ryan whined.

"What? Should I tell her about all those bored housewives watching you when you were working the landscaping part of the business?" Chloe leaned in and whispered loud enough for all of them to hear. "The late-night phone calls kept waking me up. The best one was the lady plumber who kept offering to check his pipe for leaks."

Glory didn't know whether to laugh or snarl, but the decision was taken out of her hands when Ryan abruptly stood and covered his sister's mouth. "Ixnay on my ipes-pay."

Glory lost it. "Let me guess. You trimmed her bush?"

Ryan turned bright red. "I did not."

"I think he raked her leaves." Chloe was giggling behind her hand.

"You suck." Ryan took hold of his sister's head and pushed her gently away. "Little sisters just suck."

Chloe was laughing so hard she could barely breathe. "P-planted his tree in her garden."

"I did not!" Ryan threw his hands in the air. "She was hairier than I am!"

Glory collapsed into her station chair, laughing so hard her stomach hurt.

Suddenly Ryan turned on his sister with a scowl. "Did you walk here alone?"

Chloe, still laughing, nodded.

Ryan growled. "It's not safe to be walking alone at night."

Chloe stilled, then sighed. "I'm okay, big brother. I'm not nearly as fired as I used to be, and I'm using all my Foxy ways to stay safe."

"Foxy ways?" Glory watched the interaction between brother and sister with a smile. The love between the two was obvious, and it did her heart good to see it. She wanted that back with her own brother, that teasing camaraderie they'd had out of their father's sight. "What does that mean?"

"Foxes are adept at hiding themselves. We can puzzle our scent to the point where we almost smell human. Pumas, whose animal counterparts are solitary in the wild, asked for the gift of the Pride, giving them the same advantages Wolves and Lions have."

It was strange, the way Chloe's speech problems seemed to come and go, but Glory was beginning to understand them a little. It seemed the more nervous Chloe was, the worse her speech became. But when she was comfortable and at ease with the people around her, the strange little quirks disappeared almost completely.

"Lions? How many types of shifters are there?" She'd gotten some of this from Tabby, but hearing it from another perspective might help her understand it better.

"Lions, Tigers, Bears, Wolves, Jaguars, Cheetahs… Name a predatory mammal and odds are good there either are, or were, shifters of that race."

"Wereorcas."

Chloe stopped. "Or not. I don't think there were ever Orcas, were there?"

Ryan shrugged. "Don't ask me, I have no idea."

"Huh. So what gifts do the others have?" Glory settled on the chaise, smiling as Chloe took a seat next to her.

"Lions have the ability to command other shifters, making them the rulers of the shifter world. The Leo, the one who tools us all, is always a white Lion." Ryan watched his sister and Glory on the chaise with a strange half smile on his face. He looked utterly content that they were there. Glory bet his protective personality was purring over the fact that the two people he considered his to protect were both safely in his sight. "I haven't met a Tiger personally, but I understand they're fierce warriors who have a half-man, half-Tiger form."

Whoa. That sounded massively cool. "Like a werewolf, but in cat form?"

"Exactly. Then there's Cheetahs, who are super fast."

Glory remembered that there were Cheetahs. One of them had broken Cyn's jaw. "Yeah. Are they all assholes?"

Chloe choked on a laugh.

Ryan shrugged. "No more than any other shifter species. Hyenas are very resistant to poisons and diseases, Lynxes are even better than Foxes at hiding their presence. Coyotes can tell if you're lying to them or not, Jaguars can bite through almost anything... Man, there are a couple of other species, but I don't know any of them personally. I'm not even sure I could find a Hyena or a Jaguar, honestly."

This was a lot of information to take in. "You said the Lions were the kings of the shifter world." How cool was that? "So it really is all about Simba?"

Chloe started laughing. "Do not ever call a Lion Simba or Nala. They fate that shit."

Ryan ignored them both. "The Senate rules us much like Congress or Parliament rules the humans, creating and enacting laws and watching over the shifters. They're the ones who send out Hunters to take down rogues." Ryan leaned forward. "When we're around humans, we discuss Packs, Prides and the Senate as if we're talking about a business. The Senate actually runs a legal corporation headed by the Leo, a charitable organization that's mostly concerned with the conservation of endangered species."

"The foundation only accepts donations from shifters, so they don't really fall under federal scrutiny. They keep it small, but they do a lot of good. The Wildlife Conservation Foundation is helping to repopulate the wolves in Yellowstone National Park and gives big cats born in the U.S. a safe environment to live in." Chloe's enthusiasm was apparent. Her face lit up as she discussed the foundation. "I'd hoped to work for them one day as a pet." Chloe's expression turned glum.

Ryan ruffled his sister's hair. "We'll figure out a way for you to work with animals again, Chloe. Trust me on that."

She shrugged, but her smile was stronger. Chloe was nothing if not resilient. Glory had no doubt the family would figure out a way for Chloe to live out at least part of her dream.

"So Barney works for the Senate and the Leo."

"Mostly the Senate, yeah, though I have no doubt if the Leo called on him he'd answer in a heartbeat. And so will I once I'm fully trained."

Glory took a good, deep breath. There was the faintest hint of that strange something she'd come to associate with shifters, and it was coming from Chloe. "What's that smell?" She leaned closer to Chloe, sniffing near the other woman. She was the source of the odd, faint scent. "Is that what a Fox smells like?" It was so faint it was barely perceptible, and it disappeared altogether as she leaned closer to Chloe.

Chloe looked startled. "Wow. You're scenting things already?" She smirked at her brother. "She's gonna be strong, Ryan."

"Yes, she is." And he couldn't sound any prouder of that fact. His arm wrapped around her waist and tugged her off the chaise and onto his lap. "She *is* SG, after all."

"Which stands for Super Glory, of course." She elbowed him in the stomach.

"Of course," he grunted.

Chloe just shook her head at them. "You two are nauseatingly cute." Glory stuck her tongue out at Chloe, who laughed. "Want to go grab a bite to eat? I'm carving."

Glory was slowly getting used to the random switches in Chloe's words. "I think we can do that. Ryan?"

He nodded. "We can walk you home after if you like."

"I like." Chloe snapped her fingers. "Can you hold on for a sec? I want to talk to Cyn about getting another tattoo."

Ryan frowned. "Are you sure?"

"Mm-hm. I even know what I want."

"What are you thinking of getting?"

"An open window." Chloe pulled a wrinkled, folded picture out of her pocket. "See, a lot of doors have closed for me."

Glory clapped. "But when a door closes—"

"Somewhere a window opens." Chloe grinned. "I knew you'd get it."

"Show the pic to Heather too." The part-timer had come in after lunch to work the evening shift. "I bet she can really make it shine."

Chloe nodded and, while Glory finished closing her station, chatted with Cyn and Heather about exactly what she wanted.

"I like seeing her smile." Ryan watched his sister with an indulgent smile. "I like even more that she's looking at the positive again."

"I'm betting she's plotting how to get Jim Woods to mate with her." Glory didn't understand how anyone could turn down the cute, bubbly Fox. Even with the odd quirks her injuries had given her, she rarely let herself get down. Only when she was exhausted could you tell that her mate's absence weighed on her. The veterinarian Chloe had fallen for before she'd been attacked was playing hard to get. "She still looks tired, though."

Ryan nodded. "I think that's always going to be true. She tires easily these days, and the shakes in her left hand will never go away."

"Any idea what she's going to do now?"

"I think she's going to try and continue working in veterinary medicine, but maybe as a vet tech instead of an actual vet. I don't know what her options are, and she's still looking into it."

"You guys ready to go?" Chloe bounced over to them, but the spring in her step was muted compared to the way she'd been before she'd been beaten.

"You want Frank's Diner?"

"Let me think. The best burgers in Halle, or anyplace else?" Chloe walked over to the door and threw it open. "What are you two baiting for?"

Glory laughed and grabbed her jacket. "I think someone is hungry."

"No, really?" Ryan stepped out the door before either of the women, taking deep breaths. It took Glory a moment to realize that Ryan was scenting the air for the Wolf who'd attacked them. "Coast is clear."

"Bye, Cyn. See you tomorrow, Heather."

Both women waved good-bye and continued cleaning their own stations. Glory could hear them discussing Chloe's new tattoo as the door shut behind her.

"Chloe?"

Ryan stiffened next to her, but it was Chloe's gasp that had her stepping between the Fox and whoever had spoken her name.

Chloe immediately moved past Glory, a hesitant smile on her face. "Jim."

Oh. So this was Dr. Jim Woods, the veterinarian Chloe had fallen in love with. He was pretty damn good looking, with his wavy blond hair and bright hazel eyes, broad shoulders and broader grin. He looked genuinely pleased to see Chloe…

…until he saw the way she was clutching Ryan's arm. Then his expression closed off, became cold. "It's good to see you're up and moving around."

Chloe whimpered. "It's good to pee you too."

Jim frowned. "Pee?"

Even in the dim light of the street lamp Glory could see the way Chloe's cheeks went bright red. "I mean tee."

"Chloe?" Jim took a step toward her, but stopped when Ryan growled. "Wait. I know you." The cold expression changed, warmed. "You're Ryan Williams, right?"

"Yup."

Oh shit. Glory knew that tone of voice. Ryan was pissed about something. She needed to head this off at the pass or the good doctor might find himself in chunky pieces. "Hi. I'm Glory Walsh, Ryan's girlfriend."

She blinked as Ryan's arm snaked around her waist. "Yup. Mine."

"Uh. Good for you?" Jim Woods winked at her, earning a small growl from Ryan. Jim checked his watch and grimaced. "Well. I need to get going. I'm meeting someone for dinner."

Jim either didn't see the way Chloe's face fell, or he chose to ignore it. "Oh." A weak smile crossed her lips. "May I gum visit the hospital and tree the animals?"

Jim eyed her for a moment, and Glory found herself holding her breath. She wanted him to say yes in the worst way. The hope in Chloe was almost tangible.

Slowly, he nodded. "I think it will be all right."

Chloe grinned. "Tanks."

Again, Jim seemed startled. Didn't he know about Chloe's affliction? Hadn't anyone filled the vet in on the extent of her injuries? "You're welcome." He looked past them and tsk'd. "But I really have to get going now. Be careful on the way home, okay?" And with a cheery wave he strode past them, calling out a woman's name as he went.

Chloe let off a strange half yip, half bark before covering her mouth with her bad hand. "Sorry."

"I swear I'm going to bite that fucker. Maybe if he feels the mating urge he'll finally get off his ass and come claim you." Ryan grimaced. "And I really don't want to think of my baby sister getting claimed, but I'm tired of seeing you miserable."

"It's my salt." Chloe looked ready to cry. "I didn't realize cow my relationship with Gabe hooked until it was already too rate."

From what Glory had seen in that brief second before Jim's expression had closed off, Jim had been jealous as hell at the sight of Chloe leaning on another man. "Maybe you should explain it to him?"

"I lied once, but he didn't want to ear it." Chloe began walking, her pace slow. She took a deep breath, obviously trying to get her emotions back under control. When she spoke again, she chose to do so slowly, sounding out each word. "He honestly thought Gabe and I were baiting, and then Gabe got together with Sarah and I was attacked while Jim was out of town."

"He didn't come back, not even once, to check on her."

She could hear the anger in Ryan's voice. "Maybe he couldn't." Glory shrugged when the siblings both looked at her. "If it was work related, he might not have been able to get away."

"Hmph." Ryan was less than impressed.

"I understand, mostly. He doesn't feel the mating wool the way I do."

"Which is why I want to bite his ass." Ryan held up his hands in a pleading gesture. "Just one little bite? I promise to only maul him slightly."

Chloe laughed. "No."

"But—"

"No, Ryan. Let me figure out a way to get out of my own mess."

"I agree." Glory patted Ryan's arm, hoping to soothe her savage beast. "Remember how you felt when that Wolf bit me?"

Ryan snarled, then huffed out a defeated breath. "Fine. Okay. I get it. I won't bite his ass." He shot his sister a look that Glory was glad the Fox couldn't see. She was willing to bet her favorite piercing needle that Dr. Jim Woods was going to meet an angry Bear in the very near future. She was sure of it when he muttered under his breath, "Yet."

CHAPTER TWELVE

It had been three days since the attacks on Ryan and Glory. Three days during which they'd heard nothing, not even from Barney. Ryan was slowly going out of his mind even as he quietly moved Glory into his apartment. Thank fuck Bunny understood, because his cousin had been instrumental in getting Glory's things packed and over to Ryan's.

Tabby still hadn't noticed that her old apartment key was missing. Once she did, she'd spill the beans to Glory and there'd be hell to pay.

But for now, Ryan was simply enjoying the fact that within the next week or two his mate would be a permanent part of his home, whether she knew it or not. Now all he had to do was find her father, find her stalker, make sure her brother and sister were on the up-and-up and get his ass trained as a Hunter before he did something irrevocably stupid, like get himself or his mate dead.

Too bad the man who'd come all the way to Halle to do just that had fucking disappeared on him. Not even Gabe could find the other Hunter, and Sarah, the Pride Omega, seemed blind to his presence.

So it was with some surprise that Ryan woke to the sound of voices in his living room. One held the sweet tones of his mate, making him smile as he stretched.

It didn't take him long to figure out who the other voice belonged to.

"Shit." Ryan rolled onto his back and dragged his hand over his face. "Why does he come over here so god damn early?" He rolled out of bed to his feet, ready to confront the man who kept barging into his home.

"Hey, Ryan." Barney poked his head into Ryan and Glory's bedroom and waved. "Your mate's making me breakfast."

Ryan snarled.

Barney merely grinned. "She's cute, like a Polly Pocket. I'm thinking of tucking her in my jacket and carrying her home."

"Shouldn't you be saying that about your own mate?"

"Pfft. I put her in my pocket and she'll bite my balls off." Barney winked. "But *your* mate is making me bacon. Can I keep her?"

Ryan slammed the bathroom door shut, ignoring Barney's bark of laughter. Glory hadn't made *him* breakfast yet. She usually made him pick up breakfast sandwiches from Frank's. So why was she making it for the pain in the ass Hunter?

When he was finally dressed and ready to face Barney he headed into his tiny kitchen, stopping short at the sight of Barney and Glory chatting and laughing together with ease. "So you're okay with it?"

Glory grinned and handed Barney a plate of bacon and eggs. "Sounds good to me."

"Excellent." Barney moaned happily as he bit into the bacon. "This is good. Marry me?"

Glory blushed and turned back to the stove.

She *blushed*.

Ryan wondered if his mate would like a new bearskin rug.

"Good morning, Ryan."

It mollified him a little when his mate walked over and kissed him on the chin. "Good morning, sweetheart." Ignoring the asshole sitting at his dinette set eating his food, Ryan claimed Glory's lips in a kiss that heated his blood and hardened his cock. He wanted to take her back to the bedroom and mark her again, prove to the world that this incredible woman was his.

"Knock it off, I'm trying to eat over here."

Ryan snarled. "What the fuck do you want, Barney?"

"To train you." Barney waggled his brows as he stuffed his face with some toast. "It's time."

"Don't talk with your mouth full." Glory, the dazed expression she'd had just a second before fading away, went back into the kitchen. "How do you want your eggs, Ryan?"

"Over easy?"

"Got it." She broke four eggs into the pan and began making his breakfast.

"What does the training entail?" Ryan settled at the dinette table and tried not to watch the way Glory danced around the kitchen. It was hard to keep his attention away from his beautiful mate.

He needed to look into buying a house in Halle. He could afford it. Hell, maybe Glory had something in mind. They could even pick something between where Tabby and Bunny had moved to and where Julian and Cyn lived if it made her feel more comfortable. He wanted his family close by, but her connection to Cyn was so close she'd probably be more comfortable living near the Kodiak.

Anything his mate wanted was fine by him. He would find a way to make it happen, even if he had to borrow money from his parents to get it done.

Glory could use some happy in her life, and Ryan was just the Bear to deliver it.

"Normally, I'd be taking you to different terrains, teaching you how to track and capture, or kill, each type of shifter." Barney's voice drifted over Ryan, but he barely paid attention. He was too busy watching his mate's ass as she bent over to pull the butter and bread from the fridge. "But since you refuse to leave Halle, and the Senate has declared these to be special circumstances—"

"What?" Ryan whipped around to stare at Barney in shock, his mate's backside forgotten. "What kind of special circumstances? Is this because I won't leave my mate?"

"It has nothing to do with you, Ryan, and everything to do with Julian and your sister." Barney grinned. "Did you think we didn't know about Chloe?"

Shit. He needed to head the man off. "Leave my sister alone."

Barney calmly ate another bite of toast.

"Barney." If he had to, there'd be one less Hunter in the world. Chloe was never going to be hurt again, not if Ryan had any say in it. His sister had been through enough.

"Look. I'm not the one who calls the shots." Barney shot Glory a glance. "If I had my way, your ass would be in Montana right now, and unmated, for the next six months." He shrugged, ignoring the spoon Glory dropped on the floor. "But it's not. I'm here to train you, yes, but I'm also here to observe Julian and Chloe." Barney smiled, and for the first time Ryan understood the man really was a Hunter. The look was grim, vicious, and Ryan almost shivered at the menace in it. "And I'm not happy that you tried to hide the fact that your sister is a white Fox from me."

"What would you do if it was your sister, Barney? Hmm? She nearly *died*." Ryan still had nightmares about the time when none of them thought she'd wake up. "She's linked to Julian because he had to do something to wake her up, something on so deep a level they're telepathically bonded now. She has trouble speaking and her hands don't work right, and she's had to give up every single damn dream she's ever had. What would you do if it was your sister?"

Barney's expression turned grim. "Tell."

Ryan rolled his eyes in disgust. "Sure you would. Cold-ass bastard."

"No. Worried bastard. There has to be a reason this happened, and I'm here to find out why." Barney held up his hand when Ryan began to protest. "She's the first white Fox *ever*. The Leo is...fascinated by the thought of her. He's the only white Lion in the world. It *has* to mean something."

"She has a mate." One she hadn't claimed yet, but still. No smarmy lion king was getting his hands on Ryan Williams' baby sister. He'd gnaw the fucker's mane off first.

Barney's brows rose. "Of course she does."

"You hurt Chloe and you won't live to regret it."

Ryan, startled, stared at his mate. She was growling, the spoon held out in front of her like a weapon. Tiny claws were beginning to break through her nail beds, and her baby blue eyes were dotted with brown.

His mate, his beautiful Glory, was changing, all to protect Ryan's sister. If he hadn't loved her before, he would have fallen for her now. Family meant everything to Ryan, and Glory was proving herself willing to defend it.

Barney held up his hands, but from the look on his face he didn't honestly see Glory as a threat. "Yes, ma'am."

"I mean it." She snarled, and tiny fangs peeked out from behind her upper lip.

"I get that." Barney downed his orange juice in one long gulp, then held out his cup. "More?"

Glory opened the fridge door and yanked out the juice. "Do it yourself." She put the carton on the table with such force orange juice fountained out of the top and all over Barney. "*Bon appétit*." She stormed off, every inch the outraged Bear.

Beautiful.

Barney, juice dripping from his face, his shirt, even his pants, licked his lips. "Never mind, Ryan. You can keep her."

Ryan smiled. "I plan on it."

***

Glory was fuming. It was bad enough Barney had said that he wanted to take Ryan away, but when the man got pissed at Rye for protecting Chloe? Glory saw red.

Barney should feel lucky that the worst thing Glory did was juice him.

"Sweetheart?" Glory snarled at Ryan, who threw his hands up in the air with a laugh. "Down, tiger."

Glory rolled her eyes. "I swear, Ryan. Barney needs to stay away from me." She was pacing, clenching her hands and ready to gut herself a Hunter.

"Hey." Ryan's arms went around her. "Calm down, SG. Your Bear is taking over."

She closed her eyes and took a deep breath, blowing it out in a raspberry.

Ryan laughed. "You have to keep your aggression under control. Brown bears are among the most combative bears in the wild, and we're no different."

"That's why Alex does yoga?"

Ryan snuggled her close, and the most amazing scent drifted over her. "Yup, and why Cyn does those deep breathing exercises you keep laughing at. We'll have to figure out ways to help you keep your temper under control."

Glory got up on her tiptoes, turning in Ryan's embrace to bury her nose against his throat. "Mm-hm."

Ryan tilted his head back. "If you d-don't, you could change in front of humans."

Glory licked Ryan's neck. Something about that scent, right there, had her wanting to...

"Fuck, Glory."

Yes. Exactly. She needed. Glory licked the side of his neck, her anger at Barney all but forgotten in the wash of desire that swept over her. She tugged on his shirt, needing to feel his skin under her palms, to stroke and tease until neither of them could stand it any longer.

But the very last thing she wanted to do was move away from the scent of Ryan, the taste of him drugging her as she continued to lick the side of his neck.

"Bite me, Glory. Please."

The sound of her mate begging for her was too much to bear. Glory bit, startled for a split second at the taste of blood filling her mouth.

"Shit." Ryan lifted her against him, holding her ass so that his cock and her pussy were lined up perfectly. "That's it, sweetheart. Claim me. Mark me as yours."

Hers.

Ryan Williams was *hers*, and she had every intention of making sure there was no mistaking it. The man was taken.

Glory bit down harder, unable to resist the urge to leave a permanent mark on his skin. She could feel something exiting through her teeth, but she couldn't think about that. Not when Ryan carried her over to the wall and pushed her up against it, grabbing hold of her thighs and forcing her to wrap her legs around his waist. He ripped a hole in her panties, the pain of the fabric digging into her skin a distant second to the feel of his finger sliding into her.

"Got to have you." Ryan was gasping, fucking her with his finger, his big thumb rubbing against her clit. "Jesus, how deeply did you bite me?"

"Ugh." Glory's head slammed against the wall as the quick and dirty orgasm raged through her. When the shudders had loosened their grip on her she found herself flat on her back, her skirt pulled off and her shirt pushed up to her chin. "Ryan."

He shuddered, ripping at the zipper of his jeans. He was going to give himself one hell of an injury if he wasn't careful. Glory bit back a snicker. *I'd love to see Julian heal cock zipper road rash.*

"Ryan, slow down. I might need that later." He paused when she cupped him through his jeans, moaning. His blue eyes became dark, his Bear staring at her with a hungry gaze.

There was a time when Glory would have been freaked the hell out. Now, she understood a little how he felt. Something inside her, foreign yet not, sat up and stretched toward their mate, eager for his touch.

Glory blinked.

Their?

Before she could ask Ryan if she really was changing, his hands were on her breasts and she just didn't care anymore. Let her turn fuzzy, let a strange Bear move into her head and rearrange the furniture. Just as long as Ryan kept plucking her nipples just like that?

She was one happy furry.

Her hands shaking, Glory reached for the tab of Ryan's zipper and pulled it down, careful not to damage anything she needed on the way. His cock was throbbing behind his briefs, hot and hard. The scent of his arousal actually made her giddy.

Licking her lips, Glory sat up and got on her hands and knees. "I need to taste."

"Oh shit." Ryan clawed at his jeans, wincing in pain as the material tore, but didn't come off. "You know, that works a hell of a lot better in the movies."

She laughed as he rubbed his abused hip. "Poor baby. Want Mama to kiss it all better?"

"Um, could we not talk about my mother in bed?"

"Ryan."

"Sorry."

"Do you want a blowjob or not?"

"Does a bear—"

She held up her hand, trying desperately not to laugh. "I will seriously end you."

He pouted and pointed to his cock. "The condemned have a last request."

Well. Nothing sexier than a woman on your bed, giggling so hard she cried, right?

At least, Ryan seemed to think so, because he finished taking off his clothes (the normal way, thank God) and crawled into bed with her. He then proceeded to ignore her laughter, gently removing her shirt and lace bra, tossing them on the floor next to his destroyed jeans and his T-shirt.

By the time he was done, the giggles were under control. She wiped the tears from her eyes and sniffled. "Oh God, I needed that laugh."

The warmth of his hands was seeping under her skin, but his smile was warmer than anything. "You're so beautiful."

"Even with my runny nose and red eyes?" She struck a pose, which was a lot more difficult than it seemed when you were lying on your side. "Oh yeah. You know you want me."

"Hmm." He kissed her, runny nose and all, soft and sweet and filled with something that absolutely terrified her. Something she recognized from the way Julian stared at Cyn, and how Bunny couldn't keep his hands off Tabby. "Yeah, I do."

"Ryan?" It was too soon, wasn't it? Love wasn't possible yet. They hadn't known each other long enough for real love, the kind that lasted forever.

Ryan smiled as if he knew exactly what was going through her mind.

No way.

Ryan, that sweet smile still on his face, nodded.

He loved her?

When the fuck did *that* happen?

"Shh." He took her lips again, the quiet peace of the previous kiss slowly replaced by heat and need. "Let me in."

She knew he meant more than her body, and while part of her spread its heart's legs wide, the other was still clenching her heart's knees together.

And man, I need more caffeine if I'm thinking… Oh. Oh.

While she'd been thinking, Ryan had spread her real knees and decided on an early lunch. She smacked him on the hip to get his attention. After all, she'd offered, hadn't she? "Me too."

His muffled groan sent vibrations through all her sensitive places. "Yes, please."

They rearranged themselves so she could taste Ryan to her heart's content. She took him in her mouth just as he began to lap once more at her pussy, driving her insane.

God, his scent. It was so strong here, so fierce. She licked the head of his cock like a lollipop, teasing him with what was coming.

But she couldn't tease for long. She wanted this just as badly as Ryan did. His cock slid between her lips, stretching them. It didn't take long to find a rhythm that pleased them both, and soon he was throbbing against her lips.

He was close, and she wasn't sure she wanted him to come in her mouth. She wanted him to—

She pulled away from his cock and screamed as Ryan's teeth pierced her inner thigh, the pleasure so intense she thought she might pass out.

Shuddering, vision dim, she barely felt as he rearranged her and slid inside her still-quivering body. "Mine."

She whimpered. He wanted speech?

"*Mine.*"

"Ugh." Her head was against the mattress, her ass in the air. The thickness of him stretched her almost to the point of pain in this position, but somehow the pleasure/pain of the bite he'd given her was intensified. His thigh kept striking the mark over and over, like stroking her clit but better, somehow. Like hitting her g-spot, but on the outside of her body. Glory could barely grunt and groan as Ryan took her, her hands scrabbling to grab hold of the mattress, the sheets, anything that would stop her from going headfirst into the headboard.

And he wasn't holding her down. His hands kept stroking her back over and over, tangling in her hair, cupping her ass. She could sit up at any time.

She just didn't want to. It was too fucking good to mess with.

"Say it, Glory."

Ugh. There he went with that whole speaking thing again. Apparently he didn't understand the meaning of "fucking her brains out", despite the fact he was doing an admirable job of it.

"I will bite you again." His voice was husky, the tone seductive rather than demanding.

She stared at him over her shoulder, unable to believe he'd said that. "This is a deterrent why?"

His grin was savage as he bent over her, completely blanketing her. His skin, his hair, his scent, all of it filled her even more than his cock did.

I'm doomed. She'd fallen, and she no longer cared.

"Say it." He licked the side of her neck.

"Pfft." She tilted her head. "Do your wor— Oh, right there."

The son of a bitch swiveled his hips again, and damn if Glory didn't want to sing hallelujah. His breath blew against the place on her neck he'd bitten before, the sensation teasing her with an orgasm that would make all the others look like a peck on the cheek. "Say it, SG."

She reached behind her, swatting at him, landing maybe one blow in three. "I swear to God, Ryan, if you don't bite me I will kill you."

He laughed. "That's my girl."

But damn if he didn't listen to her, because those big Bear fangs slid beneath her skin and Glory's body became one huge mass of bliss. She didn't even have the breath to scream as Ryan marked her once again.

And when it was over, and she could breathe, and think about the possibility of one day getting her sight back, Ryan curled up around her and rumbled happily, "Mine."

CHAPTER THIRTEEN

Ryan followed the scent of the Wolf right to Glory's old apartment. It was strongest here, now that he knew what he was looking for, covering the area right across the street from her bedroom window in a funk that left Ryan furious.

In order for this much scent to have covered the area the man had to have been here for quite some time, a month at least. How come Ryan hadn't noticed this before? He'd been haunting the area around his mate's home for a lot longer than that. He should have noticed someone else acting all stalkerish, but he hadn't seen, or sensed, a thing.

Some proto-Hunter I've turned out to be.

Barney's belief that they might be dealing with a rogue Hunter filled his head. He couldn't get it out of his mind. The thought that Barney might be right scared the shit out of him. If it was an ex-Hunter, the man would know exactly how to evade not only Ryan's clumsy attempts to find him, but Barney's and Gabe's as well. There was a possibility he could elude capture for months, maybe even get his claws on Glory once more.

Ryan would give all he was to keep that from happening. He needed to start training with Barney before that happened. Maybe he would have some tips on the best ways to keep Glory safe.

"Ryan, right?"

Ryan schooled his features into a blank mask. Why was he not surprised to find Glory's long-lost brother here? There was just something about the guy that made Ryan's hackles rise. "Temp."

"How's Glory?"

Ryan would have bought Temp's concern if he hadn't seen the strange flicker in the man's gaze. Temp was up to something, and Ryan was going to find out what. "She's good."

Temp studied him for a moment before he crossed his arms over his chest. Ryan's brows rose in surprise as Temp scowled at him. "Tell me about yourself."

"Excuse me?"

"I wasn't here to protect her before. I need to know what kind of man you are, and from what I've seen you aren't good enough for Glory."

"How so?" This Ryan had to hear.

"I remember what my father was like with my mother. I know the signs of someone who's overly possessive, and you're triggering every single one of them."

Ryan wanted to laugh. That's what that strange look had been about? The man was trying to protect his sister? "Glory's got a fucking stalker, but it sure as hell isn't me."

"How do I know you're not the one who's been doing all these things to terrorize her?" Temp took a step toward Ryan, ignoring the fact that Ryan was bigger than he was. Ryan hated to admit it, but he was impressed. Only Bunny really got in Ryan's face, and Bunny had a reputation that was far scarier than any Hunter's. Bunny had maimed the men who had terrorized Heather. Among the Bear community, his cousin was a legend. "You could be trying to drive her toward you. Without her family, you and Cyn are the only ones she trusts."

"And the fact that Cyn trusts me is irrelevant."

"I don't know Cynthia Reyes well enough to decide if she's a good influence on my sister or not. My dad hated her, so I'm inclined to give her the benefit of the doubt." Temp smirked. "You, not so much."

Ryan gave him the same look back. "I hate to tell you this, but I've already been in your sister's pants." He enjoyed the way Temp's face turned grim. "And I'm still looking for the man who sent her a dead rose."

"Dead rose." Temp froze before swearing under his breath.

"What?"

The man had the gall to start walking away from Ryan. "I have to speak to Glory."

"Tell me." Like Ryan was going to allow this guy anywhere near his mate without Ryan present. Until he was certain that Temp and Faith were no threat, he wasn't going to allow them any more contact than he had to. He followed after Temp, determined to find out what the man knew.

Temp turned on him again, his expression fierce. "I don't trust you."

"Good. I don't trust you, either, so we're even."

Standoff. The two men glared at each other, neither backing down one little bit.

Fuck. The human was stubborn. Ryan was becoming more and more impressed with the asshole. "I need to know to protect your sister."

Temp snorted. "Fine. Just before she disappeared, Hope told me someone left her a dead rose and a note that said '*Whore*'."

"Are you sure?" At Temp's nod it was Ryan's turn to swear. Glory was attacked right after getting the same message. "Was Hope getting gifts from a secret admirer?"

Temp seemed startled. "Yeah. Again, I didn't know about them until after Hope disappeared and Dad spoke to the cops. You're saying Glory is getting the same presents?"

"Champagne, roses, notes…"

"Fuck a duck." Temp took off again, heading for the apartment building's parking lot. "The gifts Hope got were more geared toward a teen, but the same thing happened."

"Any idea why she would have gotten the *whore* note? Glory got hers after our first real date."

"You *just* started dating?"

"We've known each other for a year, but your sister has…issues."

Temp turned on him again. Damn, the man had a temper, and apparently no problems aiming it at someone bigger than him. "What do you mean my sister has issues?"

Ryan just stared at him. Was he serious?

Temp rolled his eyes. "Fine. We all have our own tickets to board the crazy train. Where does Glory's train arrive at?"

Cute. The guy was growing on him. Ryan would say like a fungus, but that stuff in his crockpot had begun haunting his nighmares. He was pretty sure he'd heard it whimpering *help me* when he poured the bottle of bleach on it. "Abandonment Station, platform C. Your sister gets panic attacks whenever something serious changes around her. She has ever since your father beat her to a bloody pulp and left her alone, homeless and penniless."

Temp winced.

"They went away for a while, but they came back when all this shit started going down." Ryan wasn't about to tell the human about the attack on the girls that really started it. If Temp and Faith turned out to be everything Glory thought they were, Ryan would talk to the family about bringing them in.

If not?

For Glory's sake, he hoped both of them were exactly what they said. "Glory needs constants in her life, someone to lean on when everything else around her is spiraling out of control." He leaned in close, tempted to let

Temp see his fangs. "In case you missed it that would be me."

"If I find out you've hurt Glory…"

The threat remained unsaid, but Ryan decided to finish it. "You won't need to hunt me down, because if I hurt her, I've done worse to myself." Ryan sighed. "Whether you believe me or not, your sister means everything to me, and I'll protect her from anything."

"Including you?"

"Including you." And he stalked past Glory's brother, ignoring the way the man sputtered behind him. The scent of Glory's stalker was richest right around her bedroom window, and Ryan wanted to snarl and rip and tear.

"Fuck you, Williams."

"Not on your best night, Walsh." He batted his lashes at Temp. "Your hair just isn't blue enough."

***

"Ryan."

He froze, shoes in hand. "Hey, sweetheart."

She tapped her toe, her arms across her chest. She'd been terrified when she woke up alone, and only calling Julian had calmed her. "Where were you?"

He put his shoes down on the carpet by the door. "I was checking out your old apartment."

"*Old* apartment, huh?" She shook her head. She'd deal with that later. Fucker thought she didn't notice that he was sneaking her stuff over? Hmph. "And what did you find at my *old* apartment."

"Wolf signs and your brother."

"Temp was there?" Glory flicked the light on, enjoying the way Ryan flinched. That's what he got for not telling her he was leaving. "What was he doing there?"

"You know, I forgot to ask him."

"Uh-huh." She glared at him as he began stalking toward her, that *I want a taste of Glory* look on his face. "Don't even think you're getting out of this."

He whined, his shoulders slumping. "But Mo-om."

She bit her lip to keep from smiling. "Tell me when you're going out, okay?"

He flopped onto the sofa with a weary groan. "Your brother is a prick."

She choked on a laugh. "He's overprotective, like someone else I know."

Ryan grunted. "He knows more than he's telling me."

She settled on the sofa next to him, wrapping her long, silky nightgown around her legs. His apartment was always cold for some reason. "Ryan."

"I'm sorry." He cuddled her close, and she tried to ignore how safe she suddenly felt. Waking up alone had sucked monkey balls. "But there's something about him I just don't trust."

She stiffened. "Your Hunter instincts?"

"No." His expression was uncomfortable. "I don't even know if I have Hunter instincts yet."

"You do." It was one of the things she and Barney had discussed when he'd arrived on Ryan's doorstep so early in the morning. "But he also said you'd *know* if something was setting them off."

"So maybe I just dislike your brother?"

She bopped him on the shoulder. "You know, he didn't leave me behind voluntarily."

"Bullshit."

"Rye, Temp is only two years older than me." She stared at her mate, willing him to understand. "He was eighteen when my father kicked me out. He could have left Faith and come with me, yeah, but instead—"

"Instead he sacrificed himself to protect Faith." His arms tightened around her. "Except Faith said she has scars."

"I have scars too, Ryan." Her father was careful not to make them too deep, but yeah, they were there. She patted his chest when he grumbled. "But Temp managed to keep him from hurting us too badly. You have no idea how many times he stepped between my father and I, trying to save me. He's got more scars than I do. He's even gotten his jaw broken taking a blow for me."

Ryan relaxed beneath her petting. "He sets my teeth on edge."

She laughed. "Because you don't like another male, even a brother, horning in on your territory."

"Maybe?" He shrugged. "Until I know for certain he's not somehow involved in everything, I'm reserving judgment."

"I trust him, Rye."

He leaned his chin on top of her head. "I know, and I'm praying you're right and I'm wrong."

They sat like that for a while, simply enjoying each other's company. Glory was almost asleep when Ryan spoke again. "Your sister got presents."

Suddenly wide awake, she pushed away from his chest to stare at him. Or at least she tried to. Damn stupidly strong Bear. "What?"

"Temp says Hope got gifts just like the ones you've been getting, just geared toward a teen."

She snuggled closer to him since he wasn't letting her go. And, damn it, he did make her feel safer than anything else ever had. "We guessed the guy doing this was probably the one who had my sister."

Ryan tugged the braid she slept in at night. "I won't let him get you."

"You keep saying that, but you can't really promise it."

"I can."

The thought that Ryan could get hurt protecting her from a psycho filled her. "If anything happens to you, I'm going to be pissed." Damn it, her voice was shaking.

He hugged her tight. "Yes, SG."

"I mean it, Rye. If you die, I'll kill you."

"Yes, SG." He stroked her back, soothing her, but she could hear he was amused.

She blew out a breath and decided to rip off the bandage. "Tell me about the Wolf scent."

His embrace tightened almost to the point of pain. "It was strongest under your bedroom window. It was like he marked his territory."

"The dog pissed under my window?"

"Yeah."

She shuddered. "That's *so* gross."

"And one of the reasons you're moving in with me."

"I want a house." She hadn't meant to blurt that out, but it was true. It was something permanent, something neither of them could walk away from.

His grip eased. "Near Bunny and Tabby?"

Oh, God. He was going for it. "I was thinking between them and Cyn and Julian. I'd really like that." Glory couldn't hide the yearning she felt for a real home.

She could feel his smile as he pressed his face to her hair. "Me too, SG. Me too."

CHAPTER FOURTEEN

"Wakey wakey, little Bear."

Ryan was gonna kill him a Bear. "Fuck, Barney."

"No thanks, you're not my type. Not enough jiggle in your wiggle."

Ryan groaned and rolled over, glaring blearily at the clock. "What fucking time is it?"

"Five a.m." The shadowy figure of the Hunter crouched down beside Ryan. "I think I found Hope."

Ryan pushed up. He'd gotten maybe three hours of sleep, so his brain wasn't quite working yet. Otherwise he might have been more surprised that Barney had possibly found Glory's sister so quickly. "Where?"

"She's in a little rundown hotel outside town." Barney sighed roughly and stood up, backing away from the bed. "She looks like she's been through hell."

"If we're right, she has." Ryan stood, not really caring that he was naked. He made sure Glory's ass was covered, though.

"Get dressed and let's go." Barney leaned up against the wall. "We don't have much time before she runs again."

"What makes you think that?" Bleary eyed, Ryan pulled some clothes out of his dresser.

"She's got her bags packed. I think she's going to run sooner rather than later, especially if she thinks the guy who took her is here."

"Then I'm going too."

Ryan turned back to the bed to find Glory sitting up, holding the sheet to her naked breasts. He could barely see her blue eyes in the mostly dark room, but the determination rolling off his mate was loud and clear.

"No."

For once, Ryan was in total agreement with Barney. "He's right. It's safer if you stay here."

She just stared at them for a moment, and Ryan felt his heart sink. "Okay."

"Shit." Barney pushed away from the wall. "You're going to follow us."

"Nope." She curled up against Ryan's headboard, the sheet clutched tightly against her chest. The puppy eyes she gave them were almost as good as Tabby's. "I'm gonna stay right here, *all alone*, where a stalker could get to me at any time." She sighed deeply. "Too bad I haven't changed yet. Then I might stand a chance of defending myself against a shifter if I was attacked." Big eyes blinked up at them. "Not that the stalker will know you left me all alone or anything."

Ryan was already tossing a pair of his mate's jeans and one of her gauzy tops onto the bed. "Hurry up, sweetheart."

"Are you sure? I wouldn't want to be in the way." Her tone was sugary sweet.

"This is why Hunters shouldn't mate." Barney stormed out of the bedroom. "You have five seconds."

As soon as he was out the door Glory was scrambling into her clothes. "Thanks."

"You stay near either me or Barney. We could be leading the Wolf right to your sister, you realize that?"

She made a rude noise. "And you know I'm right. He's after me, and if you leave me alone he'll get me." Her voice was muffled as she pulled her top over her head. "By the time you call the clan and get me a babysitter Hope could be gone."

"If a fight breaks out—"

"I'm not stupid, Rye. If a fight breaks out, I run. I'll grab Hope and get my ass out of there, I swear it." She pulled her braid out from under the top and buttoned her jeans. After slipping her feet into a pair of ballet flats, she grabbed hold of his arm. "Ready."

"We could drop you off with Bunny and Tabby." Ryan trusted his cousin before all others to keep Glory safe. Bunny would kill anyone who threatened their women.

"Nope." She tugged him into the living room and snagged her purse, ignoring Barney's snort of disgust. "You don't have time. Besides, I'll know if it really is Hope you've found." She tapped her forehead. "My twin senses will tingle."

"Uh, I think I can figure that out on my own, Super Grover." Barney titled his hat down over his eyes. "I've been doing this for a while now, ya know."

"And you're not Hope's twin, so shove it up your trunk, Snuffleupagus."

Ryan allowed his mate to drag him out of the apartment. "Snuffleupagus?"

"He appears and disappears when you least expect it, but at least everyone knows he exists now."

"Okay." He wasn't going to question it.

He.

Wasn't.

There were just some places in his mate's mind Ryan did not want to go, and this was one of them. "Get in the car, SG, and let's go see if this really is your sister Snuffy found for us."

She got quickly into the back seat of the car, yawning and curling up against the door when he shut it. Her eyes were drifting shut as he slid into the passenger seat. "Wake me when we get there."

"Sure thing, sweetheart."

Barney slid behind the wheel. "Are you sure about this, Ryan? She could be a liability."

Barney's hat flew off his head as Glory's hand whipped out and smacked him one.

"All right then." Barney picked up his hat, placed it back on his head and began driving. "Here's how this is going to work. Glory will stay in the car while Ryan and I verify that Hope is still in her hotel room. Ryan, you'll scout around and make sure we don't have the Wolf sniffing around either the hotel or the car. Once we're sure we're clear, we'll have Glory knock on Hope's door. That will either prove it really is Hope or not. Once we verify whether or not it is Hope, we get her out of there and someplace safe."

"Should we call in Gabe?" The other Hunter would come in handy.

"He's already on the scene, watching the hotel."

Ryan blinked. "Oh."

Barney chuckled. "Don't feel hurt, cub. Gabe is fully trained, and you're not. You've got a ways to go before I pull you fully into a hunt."

"Thanks." Ryan's gaze was drawn to the rearview mirror. Glory was asleep, her blue curls framing her face, her braid hanging over one shoulder. She looked like a powder-blue Rapunzel, and he'd get smacked faster than Barney had if he dared say it out loud.

"You love her, don't you?"

He turned back around and faced the road. "Yeah."

Barney drove out of town, his expression solemn. "Then the sooner you get trained the better." He grimaced. "You might want to invest in getting her some hand-to-hand training as well."

"Why?"

"Because the mate of a Hunter is his or her weakest point. Attack the mate, take out the Hunter." Barney turned down a quiet, tree-lined street, not a single lamppost in sight. "It's happened before, and it's one of the reasons Hunters shouldn't mate, at least until they're trained."

"Too late. We've marked each other." And Ryan, training or no, wouldn't give that up.

"I'm aware of that. I just…" Barney frowned. "I don't want to lose another Hunter."

"Another one?"

"When I first found Gabe, we'd lost one of our Hunters in this area. One I'd trained." Barney shook his head. "It's always difficult when one of us gets taken down, but Daniel was a friend. He'd been a Hunter for five years before a rogue took him out."

"I'm sorry to hear that."

"He'd been hunting a serial killer." Barney pulled up outside a dilapidated roadside motel. "The guy got to him first, and used his mate against him. Neither one survived."

"I get that, I really do." Ryan blew out a breath. "And I'll make sure all the girls at Cynful take some self-defense classes."

"It may not be enough. It took three of us to take the killer down. The Atlantic City Hunter had been a good friend of Daniel's and his mate's, and insisted on helping." Barney seemed haunted by the memory of the Hunter he'd lost. "Look. I'm not telling you this to be a Debbie Downer. You need to know the life you've been born into. It's going to be rough, and if you're not careful your mate could become a liability."

"You're wrong." The soft voice of his mate filled the car. "Ryan's the reason I would keep fighting."

Ryan nodded. "You're not mated yet, so you don't understand." He almost felt sorry for Barney. He had no idea what he was trying to deny himself, and Ryan hoped like hell that he'd find out one day soon just what that wonderful something was. "Glory is my strength, not my weakness."

"If you say so. Your cousin…" Barney grimaced, his expression clear as he glanced in the rearview mirror. "She's small, Ryan, and so god damn young. Until I know she can protect herself I won't mate her."

"You keep telling yourself that." Ryan could already tell Barney was going to have a hard time with that. Every time he said Heather's name he got this wistful expression before he covered it up with banter or determination. "The pull is going to be too strong to resist. You'll claim her because you won't have any other choice."

The stubborn set of Barney's jaw said otherwise. "I'm doing what's right for her."

"I'd ask Heather what she thinks is the right thing to do. You might be surprised at what she has to say." Glory sat up and put her hand on Barney's shoulder. "Now, go get my sister."

Ryan nodded. "I'll be right back."

"Ryan, damn it."

But he ignored the Hunter and got out of the car, taking a deep whiff. If Gabe was in the area, odds were good it was safe enough.

And he was proven right when Gabe strolled out of the woods. It was strange to see the sheriff in casual clothes, the dark jeans and jacket causing him to blend into the night. Even his face had patches of darkness on them, and Ryan realized he'd put on camouflage. "All clear, Ryan. Let's go get Hope."

With one last glance at the car, Ryan followed Gabe to the motel, and Glory's past.

***

Glory waited as long as she could, which was about two seconds longer than she'd thought she'd be able to.

Ryan and Gabe were standing in front of a motel door, quietly talking, neither one making a move toward knocking on said door.

"Glory, I know what you're thinking, but you need to stay put until they call for you."

She glared at Barney, who'd wound up staying behind by default. "Yeah, let's keep the liability in the car."

His jaw tightened. "I'm not going to apologize. If it saves Ryan's life, then I'll call you whatever the hell I want, whether you like it or not."

As much as she wanted to argue with him, he was right, damn it. "Fine. But you're not invited to the family barbecue."

"Story of my life, and one I can live with." Barney climbed out of the car and took up a sentry-like pose outside. He leaned against the driver's side door, his gaze glued to Ryan and Gabe, but Glory was willing to bet his attention was focused more on the surrounding woods. It was there the Wolf who'd been stalking her and her sister would be waiting for them, if he was even in the area.

At a gesture from Gabe, Glory got out of the car. She was shaking like a leaf. The knowledge that she might finally have found her twin rushed through her like a tsunami.

Hope was here. Glory was certain of it. That twin sense that told her that Hope was alive was tingling now, driving her toward Ryan and the door that separated her from her long-lost sister.

Ryan took a couple of steps forward and took her hand. "You ready for this?"

She nodded, barely able to speak. "She's here."

Ryan smiled. "Good. Then we'll have her home with us, safe and sound."

"We'll put her in a safe place, guarded by Pumas. We won't let anyone lay a hand on her, I swear." Gabe gave her a brief hug. "Knock on the door, Glory."

She took a deep breath and squared her shoulders. Butterflies danced the jitterbug through her veins. "Here goes."

The sound of her knuckles rapping on the metal-clad door was loud in the quiet, but Glory could still hear the sound of someone breathing behind it. Her senses had sharpened considerably since Ryan marked her.

Going with her gut instinct, Glory called out to her sister. "Hope? It's me." The door remained shut, but Glory could no longer hear breathing. "It's safe, Hope, I swear. Open the door, please?"

The door remained stubbornly shut.

"Temp and Faith are back. They've been looking for us." She shared a glance with Ryan, who shrugged. "The man who took you? I've got friends here. Strong ones. We're going to stop him."

The door flew open, and Glory found herself staring into a face she'd never thought to truly see again. For all they were identical, there had always been minute differences between them. Glory was a quarter inch shorter than her twin, and Hope's blue eyes had been a touch darker than Glory's baby blue. It had somehow made Hope's disappearance even harder on her.

Cyn thought it was the reason Glory dyed her hair wild colors and pierced her skin. So she wouldn't see that not-quite-right face in the mirror every day. But Glory knew better. It was about being Glory, not Hope. She wanted people to see *her*, not her missing twin, and it had worked.

But the differences between the Hope of her childhood and the worn, battle-scarred woman before her were night and day. Hope's blonde hair was chopped off, cut so short it was almost a buzz cut. Even Chloe had more hair than Hope did. A vicious scar ran down one cheek, a cheek so thin Glory immediately had the urge to buy a couple of pizzas to fatten her up with.

Worst of all was the sheer terror Glory saw as her twin took in Ryan and Gabe.

Glory held out her hand, taking hold of Ryan. "This is my fiancé, Ryan, and Gabe is a police officer. They're both friends of mine, and they're here to help you." Better than saying they were both Hunters.

"Hi, Hope." Ryan held out his hand to her twin, trying to appear non-threatening.

Hope didn't take his hand. "I…Hello."

Ryan lowered his hand. He didn't seem at all phased by the fact that Hope had essentially refused to touch him. "The local Wolf Pack will want to meet you."

Hope sucked in a breath. "What are you?"

"Bear."

A big hand reached over Glory's head and pushed open the door. "Hi. My name's Barney." Barney very gently pushed past Glory and into Hope's hotel room. "I'm here to help you too."

Hope's eyes grew wide with fear before her expression turned bitter. "No one can help me."

"I can." Barney crouched down, putting his head below Hope's. Glory knew a submissive gesture when she saw one, and Barney was going all kinds of shades of gray on her shaking sister. It was a shock to see the strong, in-your-face Hunter be so gentle with Hope. "I'm what's called a Hunter. I'm a cop for the shifter world, and I'm here to take in the man who abducted and changed you against your will. He did, right? Change you against your will?"

Hope nodded.

"If you come with me, I can protect you from him, even introduce you to a Wolf Pack that will welcome you with open arms and protect you." He held up his hand, patiently waiting for Hope to place hers in it.

"I know what a Hunter is." Hope took a step back. "*He* told me all about them."

Barney nodded. "He was one."

"Was?"

Glory closed her eyes as Hope confirmed all their worst fears. No wonder they'd never found her.

Barney didn't move a muscle. His expression remained serene, calm in the face of Hope's overwhelming fear. His hand was still held out for Hope to take, or not. "Yes. Was. A Hunter who turns bad is just another rogue."

"Just like a human cop who goes bad is just another criminal." Gabe held up his badge. "He *will* be brought to justice. I swear it."

Barney smiled so sweetly Glory was shocked. She'd never seen such a soft expressionon the Hunter's face before. "Come with us, Hope. See your family. There are three Hunters here just to protect you, and the Senate knows who you are. All you need to do is tell me the man's name."

She barely heard Gabe's indrawn breath. "Of course. If we know his name, we know everything about him."

Barney never stopped looking away from Hope. "Yup."

Glory wanted to drag her sister out of this depressing room and into Ryan's car. "Please, Hope. I missed you so much."

"I missed you, too." Hope eyed her warily. "What are you?"

Glory didn't pretend to misunderstand. "Grizzly. Ryan is my mate, and we just claimed one another, so I haven't even gone through my first change yet."

"Whoa." For the first time Glory saw some of the girl she'd known in the suspicious woman before her. Hope's eyes lit up, a small smile creasing the scar on her cheek. "Your ass will finally be bigger than mine."

Glory laughed, aware she was close to tears. "Bitch, you always had a fat ass."

She grunted as Hope dove into her arms. "I really did missed you. It's why I came back. I wanted to see you, just once, before I ran again."

"Missed you too. So much." She held tight, terrified Hope would disappear like she had all those years ago. "I'm glad we found you before you left."

"He'll come back." Hope was shaking so hard Glory was afraid she'd rattle to pieces. "He always finds me."

"Then we'll be here to stop him." Glory said the one thing she could, closing her eyes at the irony of it. "You're not alone anymore."

Hope sobbed.

Glory wasn't that far behind her. She couldn't seem to stop the tears that came. She finally had her twin in her arms, and she had no intention of losing her again. "Let's get you home, okay?"

Hope sniffled. "Okay."

"Can you tell me his name?"

"His name." Hope turned toward them, tears running down her cheeks. "Tito Salazar."

Barney quivered, but that was the only sign he gave that he might recognize the name. "Good. Thank you, Hope." Still using the unusually gentle tone and touch, he guided Hope and Glory toward Ryan's car, careful not to touch Hope. "I'm a Bear as well, a Grizzly, and Gabe is a Puma. The local Pride has taken your sister and her friends in, made them Pride."

"I'm authorized to inform you that Max and Emma, our Alpha and Curana, are willing to extend the same protections to you that your sister enjoys." Gabe held open the backseat door for Hope. "We want you to have as many options as possible."

"I just never want to see Tito again. I barely got away from him. If he finds me again…" Hope bit her lip, and even in the early morning darkness Glory could see how she shook. "You don't know what that son of a bitch did to me."

"We'll stop him." Barney gestured for Glory to climb into the car next to her sister. "Is there anything in the motel room you can't live without?"

Hope shot a despondent glance toward her temporary home. "I've learned there's very little I can't live without."

Glory couldn't stand it anymore. She took hold of Hope's hand. "Let's see if we can change that, hmm?"

When Hope leaned her head against Glory's shoulder, it took everything in her not to break down and weep like a child.

CHAPTER FIFTEEN

Hope had been through a rougher hell than any of them had dealt with before. Barney had done his best to seem as unthreatening as possible, and all of them were treating her like a china doll that could break at any moment. Hope was impossibly traumatized, and might never fully recover from her ordeal.

He very much doubted Hope had slept with her abductor willingly.

Gabe sighed. "I've got more bad news."

"What now?" Crap, could this night get any worse?

Gabe shot him a worried glance that had Ryan's claws extending, ready to protect and defend. "I'm not just smelling the rogue Wolf around here."

"Fuck." Ryan took a deep breath, sneezing as the strong odor of dust, mold and a very familiar, very frightening Puma filled his nostrils. "Is that...?"

Gabe nodded.

"What the fuck is *he* doing around here?" Last Ryan had heard the good doctor was secluded with his family, refusing to speak to anyone.

"I have no idea, but I'm worried."

"You think he's gone crazy on us?" It was possible. Ryan didn't know of anyone who survived the traumatic loss of a mate the way Jamie Howard had. If Julian hadn't saved him, there would have been a double funeral in Halle.

Marie Howard had been the daughter of the previous Alpha, and much loved in the community. Her death had hit the Pumas of Halle hard, none more so than her mate.

He was just glad that Jamie was the only one who seemed to place his mate's death at the feet of the Cynful girls. Even if it wasn't fair, he could almost understand why. It was Tabby's ex-Alpha who had taken his mate from him, and Julian who had saved Jamie's life, leaving him forever denied his mate.

"It's possible. Hope has victim written all over her. And Ryan…" Gabe shot him an unreadable glance, "…Jamie used to take care of…*certain things* for the Alpha that were better left to the Hunters."

"Shit." The easygoing, affable man Ryan remembered wouldn't hurt a fly, but if what Gabe was saying was true, it could spell big trouble for the Walsh family. "Tell me."

"Only because you're a Hunter, Ryan."

He got that, he really did, but this secretive stuff was going to get old fast. This might be Puma business, but right now it was Ryan's business as well. "Whatever helps you sleep at night." He made an impatient gesture. "Spill, damn it."

Gabe almost chuckled at that, but his expression remained grim. "When Emma Carter first mated Max, there was some opposition to her becoming our Curana, specifically from a woman named Livia Patterson. She'd been Max's girlfriend in high school and always assumed she'd become his mate and co-ruler of the Pride. She lorded it over anyone and everyone, even the people who called her friend."

"But then Max met Emma?"

Gabe shrugged. "They all went to the same high school, but Emma was younger. I think the mating instinct didn't kick in until he met the adult Emma. Anyway, he met up again with Emma, he marked her, and declared her his Curana instead of Livia. Livia was furious, and in a fit of rage attacked Becky Holt at the annual masquerade ball."

"Which is when Becky got those scars." The Beta mate had deep, savage-looking scars on her shoulder, ones she hid in the long, curly fall of her hair, but Ryan had seen them.

Gabe nodded as he led the way out of the motel room. "Yup. She bit her, but didn't try and change her. She just wanted to prove that Emma's weakness for her friend would be her downfall, but she wasn't aware that Becky was Simon Holt's mate." The glass artist and Beta of the Puma Pride was an easygoing man much in the same mold as Bunny. Ryan was willing to bet he had the same protective instincts Bunny had too. "Emma forced Livia to submit to her, cementing her place as Curana, and she and Max Outcast Livia."

"Let me guess. Livia couldn't let it go?"

"Of course not. Bitch always thought she was owed more than she was worth. She came back and went after Emma and Becky a second time, poisoning Becky and threatening her with a gun. Simon wound up killing Livia when she attacked Becky, and Jamie made the body…disappear. And it wasn't the first time he'd done something like that for the Pride."

"And you know that because you're a Hunter?"

Gabe stared at him. "Because I'm Marshal's Second. This wasn't something that could be hidden from Adrian and me, not when we're part of the ruling hierarchy. Max had to tell us, but the rest of the Pride has no idea that Livia is dead."

Ryan would never understand the whole Pack/Pride thing. They took their whole "ruling hierarchy" thing far too seriously. In his family, they all would have known what happened and done their best to make sure no one ever found the body. It was what family did for each other. "No one questioned it?"

"Nope. Everyone assumed Livia was gone, that she took her Outcast ass and just disappeared. There wasn't any need to tell anyone what really happened. I think the only people outside the Pride who know are Rick and Belle Lowell, and that's only because Livia was Belle's best friend before she went after Emma."

"So why is Jamie Howard hanging around here?" Ryan sniffed the air, recognizing the lingering traces of Dr. Howard now that he was looking for them. "He's not here now."

"I have no idea. Maybe he decided to go after Glory's attacker?"

"That doesn't make sense. He still blames Cyn and Julian for losing Marie. The last person he'd help would be Glory."

"Then he's here for Hope." Gabe shrugged. "If he's been watching her, I have to wonder how he'll react when he realizes she's gone."

"He's not a rogue yet." Ryan knew it the way he knew his mate's scent, or that little gasp she gave just before she came.

"No, but he's come close. Too close. And now this, watching a woman who was on the run from an abuser?" Gabe sighed roughly. Jamie's actions were wearing the Second down. Everyone had loved Jamie Howard, but now several Pumas feared him. "I don't know what to think."

"Are we certain he's watching Hope? He could be here for some other reason." Ryan stared out into the darkness, trying to see if he could find the hidden Puma.

"I don't know for sure." Gabe sighed. "But for some reason I don't think he's out here hunting bunny rabbits."

"That Spidey sense of yours is tingling?"

"More like fizzing." Gabe shook his head. "I have no idea what's up with him, but we need to figure out what the hell is going on."

"We'll watch for him, then." Ryan clapped Gabe on the shoulder, hoping to offer some reassurance. If one of his relatives went bug-shit insane, he'd be weary too. "His scent wasn't anywhere near Glory's apartment."

"So maybe he's not interested in Hope at all. Maybe it's something else he's come out here for." Gabe put the shopping bags in the trunk. "Here's hoping he's just out here taking his aggression out on poor, defenseless Thumpers and Bambis."

Ryan nodded. The last thing they needed was Doctor Demento going after Glory's sister. Hope had been through enough. She didn't need to add a brand-spanking new stalker to her list of woes. "How do we deal with Hope? She's been changed against her will. She may not want to be around other shifters." A lone Wolf, one who wasn't rogue, wasn't unheard of. It was rare, but it did happen. Packs and Prides would view such a Wolf warily, but the shifters who formed family groups would be more open to them.

"We let her decide." Gabe shut the trunk. "If she chooses to stay in Halle, we talk to Max and Emma about bringing her into the Pride. If she needs other Wolves around her, we send her to Rick and Belle."

Ryan didn't know Hope well enough to guess what she might choose, but he did know her sister. "Glory won't be happy if Hope decides to go to the Poconos rather than stay here."

"It's not about Glory. It's about Hope, and what she needs in order to heal." Gabe stared at the two women in the back seat of Ryan's car. "If the closeness and security of a Pack are what she needs, that's what she gets."

"And Glory will be torn between following her twin and staying in Halle with Cyn and Tabby."

"Maybe Temp and Faith will go with Hope. Rick Lowell isn't nearly as backward as his grandfather was. He's accepted humans into his Pack. Hell, his Omega just mated one. He'll be fine with it."

"And if Faith becomes a Wolf as well, she'll be better able to protect herself from her father if the good Reverend ever comes back for her." He couldn't see a man like Temperance Walsh bowing down to any Wolf, even Rick Lowell. They'd have to figure out something else to do with the man.

Gabe nodded. "In the meantime, let's get the girls back to Halle." He glared around at the darkness. "Something doesn't feel quite right."

"Do we need to check it out?" The Wolf who'd hunted his mate could be in the woods, watching them, but Ryan didn't scent anything.

"No, it's not that. I think we're being watched, though."

"I think you're right." Barney sauntered over to them, keeping the women in his sight at all times. "But whatever it is doesn't feel hostile."

"I'm not an Omega. I couldn't tell you whether or not it's safe." Gabe blew out a breath. "I'm going to follow you back, get Hope settled with Max and Emma. I called on the way over here, and they told me that if Hope really was here they'd take her in, no questions asked."

"Will she be all right with them?" Ryan's mate was talking quietly to her sister, her voice a barely audible buzz against his senses, but her tone was easy to distinguish. She was keeping her twin calm, Hope leaning against Glory as if weary beyond endurance.

"Max is *pissed* that this shit keeps happening in his town, and Emma has declared she'll neuter anyone who goes after Hope. So yeah, I think they'll be safe." Emma Cannon was one hell of a scary woman, almost as frightening as the Poconos Pack Luna, Belle. "Besides, Adrian and I have some enforcers watching the Alpha's house. They'll keep watch for this asshole."

"Good." Ryan headed for the passenger seat, yawning his head off. "Let's go home."

***

"C'mon in, we've been expecting you."

The quiet sympathy on the face of the Puma Curana nearly had Glory in tears once more. "Thanks."

"Sheri is here. We were hoping, with what she's been through, she might be a little bit of help." Sheri Giordano was the mate of the Puma Marshal. She'd also been kidnapped, but Max Cannon had saved her life. He'd turned her into a Puma, and when she'd come back to Halle years later and met her mate, Adrian, he'd given her a new home. She was now a happy, important member of the Halle Puma Pride. If anyone could understand what Hope had gone through, it would be Sheri.

Max Cannon, Emma's mate, stood behind his spouse. The man was almost inhumanly beautiful, with golden-blond hair that brushed his shoulders and stunning blue eyes that crinkled at the corners when he laughed. He had a small scar at the side of his nose, the only mark that marred the perfection of his face.

If Thor and Black Widow had a baby, and that baby had a baby with Brad Pitt, he *might* turn out half as handsome as Dr. Max Cannon.

"We called in Sarah too." Emma yawned, her mobile mouth going wide. She was still in a pair of pink Hello Kitty sleep pants and a white tank top, a pair of fuzzy, bubblegum-pink slippers on her feet. She was much shorter than her tall mate, with deep brown hair in a sloppy bun and big brown eyes that watched the world around her with quiet intensity. She was like a chubby little bunny in a lion's den, ready to be eaten—

"Jesus fuck, I need coffee."

—until she opened her mouth. Glory chuckled, by now used to Emma Cannon's unusual personality.

"Who's that?" Hope's eyes were so wide in her face Glory was afraid they'd roll out of her head and go click-clack down the wooden floors like a pair of dice.

"The Curana."

"The who?" But Hope followed her into Max and Emma's Craftsman-style home without a protest. Glory pretended not to notice how badly her sister startled at every little sound, how she shook like a leaf or shied away from Barney as the man followed them in.

"The Curana." She helped her sister into the great room. The sage-green walls, cherry floors and white trim helped create a homey look in the Cannons' home. A vaulted ceiling with skylights gave the room the feeling of being huge, while a large, reddish-brown leather sofa invited you to sink into it. It rested on a bold area rug done in a geometric pattern of reds, blacks and greens and faced a set of built-in cherry cabinets along one wall that doubled as the entertainment center. The fireplace, on the opposite wall, was decorated with the same fieldstone that was on the outside the house.

Glory loved this place every time she came to visit. She soaked it in, dreaming of the day she'd own her home and the little changes she'd make to give it her personal stamp. The place wore its age well, and Max and Emma clearly loved it almost as much as they loved each other.

"That's better." Emma sank into one of the leather armchairs, a mug cradled in her hands.

"That had better be decaf." Max stared at his mate, one brow cocked, his arms crossed over his chest.

"Sure it is." Emma blinked innocently and took a sip. "Mmm. Coooffeeee."

Max shook his head. "I'm throwing the coffeemaker out."

Emma merely smiled, the expression secretive and terrifying. "You're cute."

Max smiled back, but his was predatory. It was obvious who had his undivided attention. "Keep that up and I might just ask you to prom."

Emma snorted out a laugh.

"Um. Excuse me." Hope was staring at them like they were crazy. "Why am I here?"

That quickly, Glory was brought back to her sister and Hope's predicament. "The Puma Alpha and Curana are taking you in while the Hunters search for your kidnapper."

"Oh." Hope collapsed onto the leather sofa. She took a deep, shuddering breath. "You meant it."

"Meant what?" Glory took the seat next to her twin and brushed that brutally short hair back. It felt like peach fuzz in spots, the locks uneven. It was like Hope had taken a lawn mower to her head and missed a few spots.

"You're really going to help me."

Glory wanted to scream. "Of course I am."

Hope curled up around her stomach. "No one looked for me."

"He lied to you."

Glory kept her gaze on her twin, but out of the corner of her eye she saw Ryan kneel before Hope.

He placed a hand on Hope's knee, ignoring the way she flinched. "Whatever he told you about your sisters and brother, the fucker lied to you. Glory never stopped looking for you."

"The others?"

Hope wouldn't look at them, trembling slightly under Ryan's hand as Glory wrapped her arm around her sister. "Temp stayed with Dad to protect Faith."

One sharp nod was all that said Hope even heard. "He…did things to me." Hope stared past her toward someone else, and some of the trembling eased. "Tito. He raped me."

Glory turned to see what, or rather who, Hope was giving such rapt attention to. It was Sarah Anderson, the Omega of the Halle Pride. Glory didn't know what the Omega was doing, but it flowed over her like gentle sunshine on her soul. "We know. We're going to find him and Gabe is going to kill him for you."

"That's right." Gabe spoke softly from behind Glory and Hope. "We'll get him."

"If I don't find him first." Ryan darted a glance at Glory, and she noticed his eyes were completely brown. "I'll kill him for you. I swear it on my bond with your twin."

From Barney's gasp, that was no small vow. "Or me. We're going to get him, I swear it." He glanced at Gabe. "I know Tito. I know how he thinks, what to look for. He fell off the grid when…" His gaze cut to Hope. "Yeah. I also know he wasn't ever a member of Tabby's old Pack, so the rogue Alpha had nothing to do with this."

"That's something, at least." Tabby's mind would be eased. Her possible connection to the Wolf that had been hounding them didn't exist.

Hope shuddered, her eyes closing tight before she opened them again. This time, she looked, actually *looked* at Ryan. "Thank you."

Ryan smiled, a bit of fang showing, turning it feral.

"When he comes for me, you have to let him…" Hope was shaking again, her gaze turning once more toward Sarah. "He says I'm his mate, that he'll kill anyone who tries to take me away from him."

"Bullshit."

The abrupt curse came from Emma, whose power briefly rolled through the room like a fog, blanketing them all. Glory instinctively ducked her head, bowing before the force of the tiny brunette who now stood scowling at Hope. "He comes after you, and we'll eat his balls with a side of garlic mashed potatoes, that's what we'll do."

Every man in the room choked, Gabe even going so far as to cover himself with his hands. "Emma!"

Max laughed. "That's usually my line."

"Hmph." Emma plopped down next to Hope. "Is anyone hungry? I'm hungry." The men shivered as she yawned again. "Hey, Lion-O. We still have the number for that all-night pizza place?"

Max rolled his eyes. "Yes, dear."

"Extra mushrooms."

"Yes, dear." Max was already on his way to the kitchen.

"God, I love watching that man, coming or going." Emma quivered, her expression wicked before she turned her attention back to Hope. "So. We have a turd that needs to be covered in kitty litter. Any idea where we can find him?"

This was directed at Gabe, who shrugged. "We've found his scent around Hope's hotel room and Glory's apartment."

Hope whimpered.

"We also scented Jamie Howard."

Emma flinched at Gabe's soft warning. "Shit. Max?"

"I heard." He held up his finger as he placed an order for enough pizza to feed several Bears, a pregnant Puma and a traumatized, half-starved Wolf.

Emma grumbled something under her breath. "Gabe. What's *he* doing there?"

"We have no idea." Ryan answered Emma and ran a hand through his hair. "His brother Gray seemed to think he was staying holed up in his parents' home."

"He hasn't been to the mansion since Marie passed." Emma sighed. "Sarah?"

Sarah shook her head. "He's still cold, but…" She continued to stare at Hope. "Something is different. He's angry and…scared?"

"Who is Jamie Howard?" Hope relaxed in Glory's arms, her gaze still locked on the Omega. Whatever Sarah was doing, it was helping, because Hope's trembling lessened. "Is he like Salazar?"

"No. I don't think he's a threat to you—" Sarah nodded, confirming Glory's guess, "—but he *is* dangerous. He survived losing his mate."

Hope stared around at them, obviously lost. "What does that mean?"

"It means you're not Salazar's mate." Barney's tone was still strangely soft. "You would know if you were, and the thought of losing him would be unbearable for you."

"When a mate dies, especially as suddenly as Marie did, the mate almost always follows." Emma smiled softly over at Max, who blew her a kiss. "I wouldn't want to go on without Max."

"So was Marie really his mate?"

When everyone turned to Hope, shocked, Glory tightened her grip. "It's a valid question."

"Yes, Marie was Jamie's mate. Julian saved his life, but in losing Marie, something inside Jamie broke. He's closed himself off, turned cold." Gabe took hold of his mate's hand. "Sarah says, and I agree, that he's not at the point of going rogue, but he's come close to it."

Hope nodded. "Then keep him away from me. I've had enough of crazy shifters to last me a lifetime."

"He's not crazy. He's hurting, desperately missing something he'll likely never have again. He's a junkie whose fix is permanently out of his reach, and the pain can be unbelievable." Sarah snuggled closer to Gabe, who put his arm around her tightly. Sarah didn't seem to mind. "I wish there was something I could do for him, but he's doing everything he can to shut me out. I can't help someone who doesn't want it."

"I know what it's like to lose everything that matters." Hope's expression was somber. "You say he's dangerous, but in the next breath you say he's in mourning."

"He's both. We don't know how he'll react at any given time." Max picked Emma up, over her protests, and settled back down on the sofa with his mate firmly ensconced in his lap. "He's not the man who danced at my wedding."

"But he's no monster, either."

It sounded like a familiar argument between the Omega and her Alpha, one that had probably been going on ever since Jamie woke from his coma a changed man. Glory hadn't known Jamie and Marie Howard all that well, but Ryan had, and he'd liked them both.

"Can I ask you something?" Gabe kept his tone easy. "How did you manage to get away from Salazar?"

Hope shrugged, but she didn't fool Glory. Her twin's face had gone so pale Glory was surprised she hadn't passed out. "He didn't latch the shackle the right way."

"Shackle?" Glory looked down to where Hope pulled up her pant leg and cursed. There was a huge mark on her ankle, the skin rough and red and bruised.

"Yeah. When he finally fell asleep, I got up, stole the car keys and ran for it. I ditched the car somewhere in Louisiana and began going cross-country in my Wolf form. He almost caught me a couple of times, but I'd learned some things after being with him for so long. It took me a couple of months to make my way here, but I'm pretty sure he isn't far behind."

"He's not. We're pretty sure he bit me outside the tattoo parlor I own with Cyn and our friend Tabby." Hope swayed in her arms. "We'll keep you safe. You aren't alone anymore. You found me, okay?"

For the first time that night Hope smiled. "I knew where you were."

"And I knew you were still alive." Glory hugged Hope, trying to convey how much she'd wished to see her sister again. "I never stopped believing you'd come home, I swear."

Hope sniffled. "Thanks."

The knock on the door startled them all. Gabe and Barney made their way to the front door, both wary, while Ryan placed himself between the door and everyone else.

But Sarah smiled. "Ease up, guys. It's Julian."

"You called him?" At Sarah's nod, Gabe grinned. "Smart girl."

"Your girl."

Gabe winked at his mate as Barney opened the front door. "Hey, look. Snow White and his dwarf are here."

Cyn pushed past Barney with a snarl, cursing him out roundly in Spanish.

Barney's eyebrows disappeared under his hat, clearly understanding whatever it was Cyn had said to him. "And my little dog too?"

Julian laughed as he sailed into the room behind his mate. "Hello, Hope."

Hope stared up at Julian with fear. "How do you know who I am?"

Cyn snorted. "You think Glory could find her twin and Super Bear *wouldn't* find out about it?"

Julian just gave them that mysterious smile that drove Cyn insane. "Let's take a look at you, sweetie." He ignored Hope's quiet protest and knelt at her feet. The silver streak that indicated the Kermode was using his powers slid down his hair, marking him as a Spirit Bear. His dark eyes glittered with silver specks as they focused on Hope. "Hmm. You've been sick? We need to get some nutrients in you." He shuddered hard, gasping as his hair suddenly blazed snowy white. His eyes turned completely silver. "One becomes three."

"What?" Glory stared at Julian, who'd slumped over Hope's lap. "What does that mean?"

"The prophecy, the one Bear delivered to Julian." Ryan's tone was filled with wonder.

"The same one Fox gave Chloe." Gabe and Sarah exchanged a quick glance.

"What the fuck is going on?" Hope shoved Julian off of her. "What…prophecy?" She laughed, the sound bitter, unnerving. "Oh, God. I've gone from one crazy shifter to a fucking town full of them."

"Sorry about that." Emma held out her mug, looking apologetic. "Um. Coffee?"

Glory didn't blame Hope one bit for the hysterical crying fit that followed.

CHAPTER SIXTEEN

It had taken the rest of the night, but they managed to get Hope settled down in Max and Emma's spare bedroom. They'd all been exhausted, especially Julian, who said he'd gotten an "unexpected call" while healing Hope. When Julian and Cyn left, Julian's hair had still been mostly white.

Cyn had to drive Julian home. He was shaking too badly to operate a can opener, let alone a car. And none of them, not even Julian, knew how Hope was part of the prophecy, or why Julian had such a strong reaction to her.

So when Ryan pulled up in front of his apartment, he wasn't surprised to find his father, his mother and his sister all waiting for him in the parking lot. They were shivering in the dawn light, holding take-out coffee cups from Ryan's favorite place, and chatting quietly with each other.

Ryan got out of the car and approached his family, aware Glory was following closely behind him. "Hi, Mom, Dad." He hugged them both, then tugged on his sister's hair, laughing when she batted at his hand. "What are you doing here?"

Ryan's mom shrugged. "Chloe said you needed us."

Chloe blushed and hugged Glory tightly. "I don't know why, but I just knew you were going to want the whole family around you."

Glory yawned. "Oh. That's nice." His mate was exhausted, and Ryan wanted nothing more than to—

"Wait. Did you say the *whole* family?"

Glory didn't sound quite so sleepy anymore. Ryan bit back the urge to laugh. The panic in her tone was endearing. It wasn't like his parents were *that* scary, after all. And having the entire Bunsun-Williams clan ready to protect her sister would ease both their minds.

"Yup. Alex and Eric will be here shortly. Uncle Ray and Aunt Stacey are watching over the girls at the shop. Tabby and Heather are there today."

"And Uncle Will and Aunt Barb?" Ryan let his family into his apartment, taking their coats and draping them over the back of the sofa.

"You have a closet," Glory muttered, picking them right back up and hanging them behind a door Ryan barely ever bothered to open.

"So I do." Ryan hung his own jacket, ignoring Glory's sniff of approval. "Why don't you go get some rest? I'll deal with my family."

She shot him an evil look that was totally ruined by baby-blue curls and red-rimmed eyes. "I can handle it."

"You can barely lift the bags under your eyes." He brushed those curls away from her face. "Go to bed, love. I'll be here when you wake up."

Her brows rose. "Love, huh?"

He smiled, noting she hadn't kneed him in the groin. Things were looking up. "Yup." He kissed the tip of her nose, thrilled when she didn't pull away. "Deal with it."

"Pfft." But her cheeks were flushed, her lips turned up with pleasure. He could sense her heart pounding, but smelled no hint of fear, and the zing of arousal nearly knocked him to his knees. "You're going to have to work harder than that to get me to say it back."

He threw his head back and laughed. *Mine.* And nothing would ever keep them apart. "That's my girl."

"Fuck you, Rye. Like I'm going to bare my soul in front of your parents." She wrinkled her nose. "That's just…ew."

He hugged his mate, ignoring the avid way his family was watching them. "You willing to bare anything else after they leave?"

She made a rude noise and shoved at his shoulders, squealing when, instead of letting her go, he picked her up. "Ryan."

"Oh, scary."

She snarled, a fang peeping over her lip. "I'll show you scary, asshole. Put me down or I'll let Tabby make your breakfast."

Ryan flinched and dropped his mate. "You're evil."

"I may be evil, but I can operate the coffee machine." His mate's usual swagger was gone, her steps barely a stumble as she moved away from him toward the kitchen. She was far more tired than she was willing to admit. "Go sit with your family. I've got this."

And she didn't want to acknowledge she loved him? She showed it, with everything she did. Ryan could wait for the words.

The feeling was there, apparent to any who looked at her, at them.

"Ryan." Chloe was clutching his arm, demanding his attention. She'd always been that way, touchy-feely, before the attack. It was nice to see his baby sister returning to herself. "The family wants to help with Glory's sister."

He turned his attention back to Chloe and away from his exhausted mate. "How did you know we'd found her?"

"Fox told me."

Fox. The elusive spirit that ruled over all Foxes, never seen except by those who had a connection to the spirit world. Of those, Ryan had thought he only knew one: Julian DuCharme.

Now, apparently, his sister was also connected to the spirit world. What else could she do that other shifters couldn't? *Gods and spirits, please don't let this be harmful.* The thought that something could get in his sister's head, pull her into a world he barely understood, freaked him the hell out.

How could he protect her from spirits?

"Don't be afraid. One becomes three. Things are happening that are supposed to, and some wrongs are going to be righted. Balance *will* be restored."

"What wrongs?" Glory's voice floated out of the kitchen.

"Fox didn't say, and I was too terrified to ask." Chloe shivered. "It's weird. Fox visits me, tells me something, and I just nod and pray I don't get eaten."

"He's that scary?" Ryan had heard both Cyn and Julian describe Bear. The spirit was large, and calm, but not frightening at all once you got to know him.

"No. That *strong.* He—" Chloe tilted her head toward the front door, and Ryan heard what she did. "Bunny and Eric are here."

The brothers were arguing in fierce whispers. No humans would hear them, but the shifters in Ryan's apartment could. Ryan opened the front door and waved to his cousins to come inside. "C'mon in." He smirked at Bunny. "Glory's making coffee."

Bunny moaned. "Oh, sweet Glory. I brought chocolate donuts in tribute to Your Coffeeness."

Glory's laugh was evil. "Get your buns in here, Bunny-boy."

Eric chuckled as Bunny sprinted for Ryan's kitchen. "He sorely misses his caffeine fix. I don't think he realized how much of it he drank until Tabby couldn't stand the smell."

"The things we do for our mates."

Eric grunted. "Speaking of which…" He tugged Ryan toward the bedroom, waving at Ryan's parents and sister before shutting the door between them. "I did some research on one James Woods, doctor of veterinary medicine."

"And?" Ryan wasn't above using his cousin's overprotective streak to keep Chloe safe.

"He's smart, he's making a good living, and he used to date the Curana."

"I knew all that, and I'm pretty sure Chloe did too." He'd thought Eric would dig up more than that. The Bear had quietly scared off more than one suitor for their female cousins with his blackmail, educating them on the error of trying to get into the girls' pants. When that didn't work, his size and muscles had made more than one man turn tail and run.

Lighter skinned than his brother, with short-cropped hair and thick eyebrows, he was considered by a lot of the women Ryan knew to be handsome. He wore a business suit and black-rimmed glasses with the same ease that he sported cargo shorts and a tank top. Eric Bunsun looked at home no matter what he wore, and rarely failed to impress when he wanted to.

And when he wanted to impress upon someone the need to leave, he wasn't above showing what he could do with those large, accountant's hands. Eric had never been quite as rough and tumble as Bunny, but only because the man was more subtle. If Eric decided Dr. Jim Woods wasn't good enough for Chloe, the poor guy wouldn't stand a chance of getting close to her. Almost as large as Bunny, Eric could be downright frightening when he chose to be. His dark eyes would go ice cold, and the thick muscles that corded his neck would flex. He went from smiling money man to menacing hit man with a simple look.

But Eric didn't comprehend the siren song of a mate, how hard Chloe would fight to stay by Jim's side. Chloe would take Jim and run if she thought for even a second that Eric was a threat to him. It's what Ryan would have done if Eric had taken a dislike to Glory and tried to drive a wedge between them. Luckily, Eric didn't seem to mind his mate nearly as much as Julian's. "He's Chloe's."

Eric scowled. "He's not."

Ryan chuckled. "Marked or not, trust me. He's Chloe's." He patted his cousin on the shoulder when the man grunted unhappily. "Look. Did you find anything really bad in his background? Anything that would raise a red flag for Mom and Dad?"

Eric fidgeted with his glasses before shrugging. "Not yet."

"Then trust in the mate bond. Chloe knows what she's doing." At Eric's disbelieving look, Ryan opened the bedroom door. "A mate can't be denied, no matter how much you might want to. The dreams alone would eventually drive you insane."

Eric followed him into the living room, muttering under his breath. But Ryan heard what his cousin said. "Then I hope I never meet mine."

Oh, but Ryan did. And he prayed that, whoever it turned out to be, they got a look at the *real* Eric Bunsun, the one who thought his family hung the moon and the stars. Whoever it was would become Eric's sun, bringing sunshine to his cousin's life. Eric needed someone to protect, to turn all that need onto. As annoying as he could be, Eric had a big heart, even bigger than Bunny's. If—no, when—he found his mate, she'd be utterly adored.

"So." Ryan pulled his attention away from Eric and back toward *his* mate. Glory was holding out a mug of coffee, yawning so wide he thought her lips might split. She'd managed to clip her waist-length curls into a high ponytail, with two thick curls coming from her temples to brush against her breasts. The hairstyle made her look even more like one of Bunny's manga characters, and Ryan loved it. "What did Eric the Awful want?"

Behind her, Bunny laughed as Eric rolled his eyes. "I'm not *that* bad."

"You called Cyn a freak because you didn't want her around Heather, remember?" Glory shot Eric her best glare. "As far as I'm concerned, you're lucky I don't call you Eric the Ball-less."

"Eric!" Stacy Williams smacked her nephew upside the head.

"Ow!" He rubbed the spot his aunt had hit, staring at her with an outraged expression.

"Wait, wait." Bunny held up his hands, ever the peacemaker. "Mom and Dad already laid into him for it."

"Oh." Ryan's mom settled back down. "In that case, what can we do for you, dear?" Stacey turned all her considerable charm on Glory, who blinked in shock. "Your sister will need family around."

"Family that can protect her from a shifter." Raymond Williams put his arm around his mate, his Bear peeking out and dotting his green eyes with spots of brown.

Before Glory could respond Ryan pulled her close, careful of both their coffee mugs. "The asshole changed her. She's Wolf."

"Then we protect her from the rogue Wolf and introduce her to the local Pack." Stacey sipped her take-out coffee serenely. "I'm sure Belle Lowell would love to meet her."

Glory went stiff. "I've met Belle Lowell. She's overwhelming on her best days. Maybe we should let her get used to Tabby and being around non-psychotic Wolves, before we introduce her to the Queen of Scream."

The Queen of... Ryan started to laugh. Where did she come up with this stuff?

Bunny shook his head sadly. "You *really* think the Curana hasn't already called her?"

"Bunny's right." Ryan held tight when Glory made a move to get away from him. "From what I've seen, Emma and Belle are tight. She'd want Belle to know what's going on, and to hell with what Barney wants."

Bunny nodded. "Besides, Belle and Rick will do their best to protect Hope, just like they do Tabby."

"And so will we." Chloe looked determined, and there was a strangely familiar silver glint in her eye. "Hope won't live in darkness anymore."

Well. That wasn't freaky as fuck. "Chloe?"

She tilted her head, the silver gone, just his little sister looking at him like she usually did. Like she totally knew something he didn't. "Yeah?"

"Nothing." Julian was keeping a close eye on her. The Kermode would tell him if Chloe was in danger. And if he didn't, out of some half-assed sense of privacy or to protect Ryan, Cyn would tell Glory.

"We're moving up the plans to take Bunsun Exteriors to the East Coast." Ray and Stacey exchanged a quick glance. "Tiffany and Keith will be coming here as soon as they wrap up some jobs they've been working on. Once they do that, corporate moves to Halle."

Ryan wasn't surprised that Heather's brother and sister would be moving closer to the rest of the family. Keith was far more laid back than even Bunny, and would follow the family flow without a quibble. Keith and Bunny even had the same love of manga and anime, and would watch *Ranma* and *Sailor Moon* for hours together, cackling like hyenas.

Tiffany, on the other hand, was hell in heels, and would eviscerate anyone who bothered her baby sister. He bit his lip to stop a laugh as he pictured introducing his hell-raiser cousin to Barney. The Hunter wouldn't know what hit him until he was plucking a four-inch spike out of his balls.

Tiff would just bitch about blood on her Pradas.

"I've already agreed to go back to Oregon in Ryan's place and wrap up some final business." Eric poured himself some coffee. "Thanks, man." Ryan relaxed. Now that he knew for certain he wasn't going to leave Halle any time soon, he could take the same step Bunny had. "I should look for a house."

Glory froze.

"What a good idea." Stacey wrapped an arm around Glory's shoulder. Ryan knew from experience how amazingly strong her grip was. She'd used it more than once to discipline him and his cousins. "What kind of house do you like, dear?"

Ray chuckled. "I think we can handle the landscaping, so don't worry about that."

His mate's eyes glazed over. "Uh…"

"She wants to be between Tabby and Cyn, and she loves the look of Max and Emma's house, so maybe a Craftsman style?"

Deer, meet headlights. Glory looked ready to pass out, and not from exhaustion.

"Not as easy to find here as it is out west." Eric grinned. "You have enough money. Buy a plot of land and put up your own."

He nodded, thinking Eric might have the right idea. That way, they could build something that would suit both their tastes. Maybe he could find something that faced the forest just outside the city limits. "I could do that."

The strangled noise his mate made was going to make it all worthwhile.

"But I don't have a lot of money." Glory looked panicked. "Ryan, I can't afford a house that size. It will be years, if ever, before Cynful makes that kind of cash."

"You're mated to a Bunsun-Williams." Eric sounded frustrated with Glory's lack of understanding, but a single glance at his expression revealed nothing. "Despite what Bunny says, our company takes care of us."

Ray and Stacey nodded, but it was Ray who spoke. "We're not stinking rich or anything, but we do well enough."

"Ryan can afford a home for you, don't worry about that."

Oh, there was that strangled noise again.

"Sweetheart?" Glory turned to him with a panicked expression. Ryan needed to get that look off her face, so he suggested the one thing he figured would ease her mind. "We should make sure there's a room for Hope."

Her panic was suddenly mixed in with something else, something he couldn't quite put a name to. Gratitude, maybe? "That…sounds *so* good."

"Glory." Her tone, and her expression, both were off. She'd been hit with far too much tonight. Ryan extended his senses and felt his mate's pulse racing. Her heart was beating far too fast as her adrenaline levels rose. Her pupils were dilating as the panic set in. He strode to her side and pulled her tight against him, using his healing gifts to calm her. "I'm here, sweetheart."

For just a second he thought she'd fight him, but in the end she leaned against him, hard. He took her weight, loving the fact that she felt secure enough with him to give him this gift. "I'm okay." She squinted up at him. "You're using your power on me, aren't you?"

He shrugged. What was he going to do, lie to his mate? "You were starting to panic." In fact, he was monitoring her closely, keeping her body from its fight-or-flight response. Her adrenaline was still a little high, so he adjusted it slightly.

She blew out a breath and snuggled close, burying her face against his chest. "It's just so much all at once."

"I know." Ryan rubbed his hand up and down her back, hoping to soothe her. When she leaned into the touch and practically purred, he smiled. "But we'll get through it, I swear."

Everyone was silent as he got his mate's panic attack under control. Finally, she relaxed in his embrace, her arms tight around his middle. "A house, huh?"

He nodded, pressing his chin against the top of her head so she'd feel it.

"Hmph." She was quiet for a moment. "I want all the trim-work and details you'd see in a really old house, but with all the modern amenities."

"We could talk to a realtor, find something—"

Her fingers were on his lips, shushing him. "I want to make something that belongs just to us."

That was what he wanted too. "With a lot of stone on the front."

He felt her smile. "And a wood-burning fireplace."

"More than one."

"And one of those big, wrap-around porches that can sit, like, twenty people." She grinned up at him. "If I'm gonna spend your money, I'm gonna spend it *all*."

"Uh-huh." Sure she was. And, hell, if she really did, it was their forever home, so he was okay with that.

"You think Hope will want to live with us?"

He sighed. "I don't know, but we'll make sure she knows she's welcome. It will give her options. Just being safe, being able to make her own decisions will be huge for her."

"I can't even imagine…" Glory's shoulders sagged. "I don't know what to do for her."

"We'll figure it out." He kissed the top of her head. "I promise."

When she rested against him again, he took it for the gift it was.

CHAPTER SEVENTEEN

God, she was exhausted. Ryan's family left soon after breakfast, and Glory had gotten maybe four hours of sleep before she had to join Tabby and Heather at Cynful. There was a time when that would have been plenty for her, but it had been a couple of years since she partied till dawn.

I'm getting too old for this shit.

She huffed out a laugh and drained her soda can dry. No coffee meant sleepy Glory, but she didn't dare make a pot. Tabby's sensitive nose would sniff it out, and then Glory would have Technicolor yawn to clean up.

She scratched absently at her arms, the itch that had been building all morning becoming unbearable. Her vision kept blurring in and out as her muscles jumped and quivered.

She needed sleep, badly.

Glory scratched grumpily at the top of her head, hoping to ease the itch at least a little. Ugh. The itchiness was driving her crazy. She'd already snapped twice at Heather and once at Tabby, who'd actually growled at her in that big, bad Wolf voice of hers. The only bright spot of her day so far was Ryan, and Ryan's family.

Ryan's family was beyond awesome. They'd all agreed to table the house discussion—and hadn't *that* thrown her for a loop—until after Glory's first change, when she and Ryan would begin hunting for land. The fact that Ryan had paid enough attention to notice how much she loved Max and Emma's home hadn't been lost on her. The man knew her better than anyone. Not even Cyn and

Tabby were aware of her desire to have a large family home.

Hell, that wasn't all of it, either. Glory wanted to have a large family, period. It was a dream she'd never dared voice, especially after being abandoned by her parents and siblings. The thought of a little Ryan running around their home, driving them both insane with his smirk and his big blue eyes?

She banged her head against the counter. She did not need another too-cute Williams boy wrapping her around his finger.

But it would happen. She knew it would. The sun would rise in the east, the coffee maker would remain distressingly empty, and Ryan Williams's children would drive her insane.

She couldn't wait.

The Bunsun-Williams clan seemed determined to fulfill her desire for a huge family, and Glory was just selfish enough to grab hold with greedy hands and never let go. She thought she'd cried herself out holding Hope, but Ray and Stacey had made her feel so welcome that she'd been unable to stop herself from sobbing on her new mother-in-law's shoulder.

She hoped Ryan didn't find out about that. He'd fallen asleep on his sofa, utterly exhausted, and Glory had lost it in front of her new family.

"Glory?"

"Hmm?"

Heather, who'd snuck up behind her, poked her arm. "You're fuzzy."

Glory grimaced, but refused to lift her head off the counter. It was cool against her forehead, keeping the threat of what promised to be a doozy of a headache at bay. "Thank you so much for pointing out my hairy embarrassment. I know I haven't shaved my arms in a while—"

"No, silly. I mean you're *fuzzy*. I think you're changing."

Glory blinked blearily down at her arm, amazed to see the rich brown fur sprouting in patchy spots. She laughed, aware how hysterical it sounded. "Fuzzy Wuzzy *was* a bear."

"Fuzzy Wuzzy has some hair." Heather grabbed hold of her, ignoring Glory's tired giggle. "Ryan!"

The sound of him running thundered through her head, louder than anything she'd ever heard before. "Wha—oh shit." He grabbed hold of her arm and tugged her into the back room. "I need you to concentrate."

"On what?" Holy shit. She was changing? Now? Fuck a duck.

"Glory!"

"What?" Why did he have to be so *loud*?

"Do not let your Bear out. Now isn't the time."

"Really? You think so?" She stumbled as Ryan whirled her around, closing the curtains into the back room so that no one could see in.

"Listen to me." He cupped her face in both hands. The feel of his skin on hers was intoxicating, his scent enveloping her in a cocoon of calm. "Breathe deeply. In." She took a deep breath. "Out." She let it out slowly. "Again."

She repeated the exercise until Ryan seemed satisfied. "What now?" The itch was slowly becoming a burn, and something inside her, something large, was waking up.

"Damn it. It's too late." Ryan grimaced. Whatever he saw in her face had him pulling back. He tugged his T-shirt over his head. "You're going to change here, whether we like it or not."

"Oh." Glory licked her lips as smooth, golden skin was bared for her gaze. *Yum.*

"Get naked."

"Whu?" Glory dragged her eyes from his abs. "I'm sorry, what?"

His smug grin was strained. "Get. Naked."

"Is this really the time?" She was all for a little back-room loving, but—

"Glory." He growled out her name, and she shivered. "I want you bare."

She laughed. "Don't you mean bear?"

Ryan undid his jeans, pushing them down his legs. "Yeah. I need you Bear naked." He rolled his eyes at her. "Now, sweetheart. You do not want to try and shift while wearing clothes."

"What's the worst that could happen?" But she tugged off her skirt, trusting her mate's judgment.

"You'll hurt yourself when your clothing rips away. It's not like the movies, you know." Ryan kicked off his jeans and underwear, leaving him completely naked. "Most clothing is pretty sturdy. You tug on it, and it doesn't rip right away."

"It constricts." It made sense. She'd had a boyfriend once who thought it would be cool to rip off her panties.

That had been one hell of a super-wedgie.

"At best, you'll try and claw it off. You'll have to sit back here, with no clothes, while I run home and get you some."

"Or I could work in your T-shirt and boxers."

His eyes went wide and deep brown. Someone liked that, a lot.

"You like the thought of me in your clothes?" She reached out to brush a hand down his chest, startled to realize that she had five-inch claws. The little ones she'd been sporting since he'd bitten her had finally grown. "Whoa."

"Get the rest of it off." He tugged on her shirt, pulling it over her head.

Glory managed to take her own underwear off, though the claws made undoing the bra a pain in the ass. Ryan didn't help, laughing his butt off when she began twirling in place, trying to get the hooks undone with nails in serious need of a trim.

"Ass. Hole." She glared at him, her shoulders feeling strangely humped, her voice far lower and more gravelly than it had ever been before.

Ryan stopped laughing. "All right. Deep breaths."

She drew in a quick breath and blew it out with a snarl.

"Okay then." Ryan chuckled. "Down, SG. No eating the tasty mate."

She couldn't help it. Her lips curled, mostly in a smile.

"Now, let your Bear out. She wants to come out. Close your eyes and scent…" He looked around. "Well, scent the shop. We'll head into the woods later, let your Bear *really* out."

Glory closed her eyes and sniffed.

The chemical scents of the inks and antiseptic, the metallic ting of needles and the dust and cardboard—it was overwhelming. "We have a mouse."

He nodded. "I can set out a trap if you want."

She shook her head, entranced by all the new scents filling her nose. Her mouth began to water. "I smell Kung Pao chicken too."

"Bears are omnivores, so what tastes good in human form will usually taste good in Bear. We're taught that a Bear's sense of smell is much stronger than that of a bloodhound. We can track prey over miles, and our mates even further than that."

She opened her eyes. "Sight?"

"Our night vision is better in Bear form, and we aren't color blind the way most other shifters are. We have the full human spectrum."

"That's cool." Her voice was almost gone, lost in a deep bass rumble, totally inhuman.

"It's okay, sweetheart." His voice had gone gravelly as well. Ryan was changing with her. "Let go. Follow the spiral path you sense before you. Your Bear will guide the way."

She could feel it more than see it, the spiral path Ryan was talking about. It swirled inside her, strange yet familiar at the same time, leading her to the presence that had woken inside her. The creature stirred, stretched, filling her thoughts with its own.

Her Bear was curious, proud, and filled with need for their mate.

Glory's skin rippled, flowed over muscle and bone that was suddenly way too big for her frame. Everything tingled, as if her limbs had gone to sleep and were just now waking up, but the pain she expected didn't come. Instead, it was seamless, a flow of water over rocks rather than grating of bone over tissue.

It felt…good. Different, but good, and she understood now why Tabby needed to run in her fur. Glory wanted out, wanted to roam the forest, finding new scents. She wanted to go exploring in her new badass furry skin, and woe to anyone who wanted to stop her.

She looked up from her hands to find herself nose to nose with another Grizzly. Ryan had changed as well, following his own path to release his Bear.

Glory made a chuffing noise, running her nose along his chin, his neck, taking in his scent until she was satisfied she could find him no matter where he went.

Ryan did the same, sniffing around her, rubbing against her until she couldn't tell her scent from his any longer. The scents mingled, melded together, marking them both as taken.

Ryan's massive Grizzly head whipped around, a low snarl startling her. He positioned himself in front of her, his shoulders bunching as he went to two feet in an aggressive stance that shocked her.

Ryan was protecting her, but she had no idea what from.

After a minute, he settled back down with a chirring noise, a remarkably satisfied sound that had her rumbling what should have been a laugh.

She watched as Ryan slowly shifted back to human. It was like watching water flow through him, moving him and bending him, blending man and animal together until one was gone and only the other remained. She wished she'd been able to watch him shift into his Bear, to see the strength in him made flesh, but all that naked skin was worth missing out on the transformation.

"Change back, Glory." Ryan began picking up his clothes, laughing when she whined. "Tonight, I promise. We'll strip down to our skin and just enjoy each other. But until I can get you into the woods and show you what being a Bear is really all about, you need to go back to work."

She could call out sick. Hell, she owned the damn place, along with Cyn. Tabby would—

"No." Ryan was laughing, but his eyes were still dotted with brown. His Bear was all for her idea of ditching work, but the man ruled. "Shift back, sweetheart."

She did as he asked, settling into her human skin with a pout. "You are no fun."

He leaned his forehead against hers. "Tell me that again when you're writhing in my lap, screaming my name."

Glory gulped. "Okay."

For some reason, it took her just as long to get dressed as it did to get naked. It might have had something to do with the way her hands shook, but she refused to give Ryan the satisfaction of knowing how badly he'd affected her.

From the grin on his face, he already knew.

***

Well. This was going to get awkward.

Temp had seen them change.

Ryan didn't know how to tell Glory that her brother, whom she trusted, had caught how they shifted in Cynful's back room. Chasing after the man when he ran wasn't an option. A Grizzly—or a naked accountant, for that matter—chasing a man down Main Street Halle wasn't a sight the locals were ready for.

Glory had needed him, needed his strength, his ability to guide her through her shift and back again. And leaving her alone, when she'd been attacked in broad daylight, wasn't an option. He'd do something about Temp later, maybe after he spoke with Bunny and Julian. The Spirit Bear would know what to do. In the meantime, he'd enjoy the fact that his mate had finally changed.

My God, she'd been a gorgeous Bear.

Ryan pulled his mate into his apartment after her shift was done at Cynful, desperate to feel her skin to skin. Seeing her change, watching the flow of her animal over her, had made him realize that Glory really *was* his. She would forever be his mate, his woman, his to love, to fuck, to have children with.

"Rye? What's going oh… *Oh.*"

He'd dropped to his knees as soon as the door shut behind them, lifted up her skirt, and kissed her covered pussy.

"I'm going to go with…you're horny."

The laughter in her voice would disappear soon enough. Ryan had every intention of feasting on his mate.

His.

God, he still couldn't get over it.

"Bed?" Glory's voice was breathless and filled with desire.

Nah. He'd never make it. "Sofa."

She whimpered. "You're going to kill me."

He smiled and picked her up. "Consider me baby bear."

She quirked her eyebrow at him. "Just right, huh?"

He loved the fact that she got him, even when they were both exhausted. "Yup."

She laughed when he dropped her on the sofa, careful not to hurt her. The only pain she'd feel tonight was sexual. He had every intention of draping her over the arm of the sofa, of pounding into her until they were both screaming.

But first, he had a mate to taste.

A bunch of filmy fabric hit him in the face. Apparently Glory was way ahead of him. While he'd been daydreaming about what he wanted to do to her sprawled, naked body, she'd gotten her clothes off. He tossed the clothes aside, moaning at the sight of her splayed legs.

"Ryan?"

"Yeah?" Whoa. His voice hadn't cracked like that since he was a teenager.

"You might want to check and see if I'm too hot or too cold."

The blush on her cheeks was in direct contrast to her bold words. "I'll have to eat a lot to make sure." He knelt at her feet, ready to worship her. "You know, blow on it if it gets too hot, warm it up if it gets too cool." He stroked a finger down her stomach until it rested just above her clit. "Until it's just right."

She shivered, her hips thrusting toward his hand. Her expression was filled with desire as she buried her hand in his hair. Instead of the pressure he expected, the demand, her caress was soft, pleading. "Yes, Rye."

He took his first taste of the night, ready to set aside their game. The need to make her come was overwhelming, almost as intense as when she claimed him. So instead of gentle touches, he took her into his mouth and suckled her, enjoying her startled, pleasure-filled cries.

The hand that had been softly stroking his hair clenched, holding him in place while she thrust her hips against his face. Ryan did his best to follow, but a sharp tug told him to stay still.

Glory was beautiful, wild, her curls spread out beneath her. Her pink nipples stood, ripe and ready for Ryan's mouth. He wanted to taste her there, too, to suck and bite and scratch the flawless skin with his beard, just to watch her quiver. He'd mark her with his beard, his teeth, his come until they were both a pile of satisfied goo on the floor.

But first, he had to make his mate come.

She was muttering, tugging at him with impatient hands, demanding that he do *something*, anything, but Ryan refused to give up his prize. He growled, loving her choked cry as the vibrations of his growl rocketed through her, triggering an orgasm.

Well, now. Wasn't that interesting?

Ryan continued to lap at his mate, soothing her, building her back up as the shivers began to turn once more into moans. But this time he growled for her, kept the sound going, giving her his own version of a hummer, Bear style.

Glory went wild beneath his mouth. The grip in his hair became painful, but he couldn't care less. His mate was taking from him, accepting the pleasure he gave her, and nothing could drag him away.

This time, when she came, her eyes scrunched shut and her whole body shook. Her breath came in panting gasps, her skin flushed, and Ryan nearly came in his jeans at the sight.

Ryan waited for the spasms to pass, for her eyes to open and focus on him. The precious, rare smile, the one she only gave to him, crossed her face. "Mmm."

She stretched, thrusting her breasts up, tempting him. "Just right?"

She nodded and moaned softly again, a happy, sated sound.

"My turn, then." And he wouldn't last long, not at all. Just watching her had him throbbing, aching. He needed to bury himself inside her again, both fang and cock.

Glory stood, almost toppling over. He righted her, laughing when she made a face. "What?"

"Mm. Nothing." No way was he going to say he was proud that he'd made her knees weak. If he did, she might show him how *not* weak they were. Once he was certain she could stand on her own, he moved the end table out of the way and gestured toward the sofa. "Over the arm, sweetheart."

Maybe she was just as eager for this as he was, because she did what he asked without arguing. Or maybe she was finally done with arguing.

"Are we fucking, or are you going to frame it?"

Ryan laughed as he realized he'd been staring absently at her naked ass. "I'm thinking."

She reached behind her and cupped his erection. "Think harder."

Hissing, he pulled down his zipper, pulling his cock out for her to stroke. "Fuck. Touch me, please."

Glory turned, kneeling for him, sucking him into the hot, wet cavern of her mouth. He closed his eyes, trying desperately not to come as she languidly stroked her tongue up and down his length.

As much as he loved the feel of her lips wrapped around his cock, he was going to have to put an end to it soon. Just as he thought to move away, Glory swooped down, taking almost his whole length into her mouth.

"Shit." Ryan backed up, his cock sliding out of her mouth with a pop. He gripped the base and prayed like he'd never prayed before. He had to make her come at least one more time, and he intended to do it by marking her again. "Over the sofa."

With lazy grace she draped herself over the arm of his sofa. "Too hard?"

He snorted. He hadn't forgotten their game. "Better than too soft."

She giggled, spreading her legs farther apart when he gently nudged at her feet. "Will it be too big?"

He smacked her ass cheek, making sure not to hurt her. He knew his strength, how to temper it, and wouldn't intentionally hurt her for the world.

Still, the sound was loud, startling, and she went up on her toes. Wide-eyed, she glared at him over her shoulder. "Fuck you."

"Okay." And before she could move away Ryan slid inside her until his thighs touched hers.

She was laughing, her shoulders shaking. "You suck."

"Yup, I do." He started moving, the urgency not as intense, the need tempered by affection for his quirky mate.

"You'll suck again?"

He leaned over, bracing himself on the arm of the sofa, hands on either side of her head. He licked the mating mark, groaning as she clenched around him. "Again." He nipped the mark, letting her feel his teeth. "And again." He dragged his fangs over it, smiling when she bucked under him.

"Rye."

Her voice was breathless, her body trembling. She needed as much as he did, so Ryan began to truly move, keeping his thrusts deep and long. He wanted to feel all of her, the slide and drag of skin on skin, the feel of her beneath his teeth drugging his senses. Her scent flooded him, mingled with their desire until he felt drunk.

She was so much smaller than he was, so much stronger than anyone gave her credit for. But Ryan understood, and gave her what she needed. For all that her tiny frame was under his, held down by him, she was in charge.

"Harder, damn it."

Ryan began moving with such force the couch began to slide across the carpet.

"Yesss." She hissed, her head thrown back, her curls sliding around, tempting to him grab hold. Her nails bit into his sofa, morphing to claws, ripping the leather in her passion. "More. Fuck, more, Rye."

So he gave her more, setting a bruising pace that would leave them both sore at the end.

"Oh, fuck. Fuck me, Rye." She was moaning, taking what he gave her, lost in the pleasure of their coupling. He doubted she even realized when her head tilted, giving him access to her vulnerable neck.

Shuddering, Ryan took the invitation, sucking on her mating mark with all the hunger he'd felt when feasting on her.

Glory collapsed, crying out, so close even he could feel it. "Bite me!"

Ryan obeyed, sinking his fangs into his mate, marking her again.

Her whole body froze, her muscles locking around him in a vise grip that was so fucking tight, so good, Ryan followed her over the edge. The orgasm ripped through him, blinded him as he poured himself gladly into his mate.

"Shit."

Glory's gasped curse had him laughing weakly. "Tuckered you out, did I?"

She pushed a curl out of her face with a trembling hand. "The bed would be just right."

Staggering, holding each other up, Ryan led his mate to the only place he really wanted to be.

CHAPTER EIGHTEEN

"It's simple. You're going to try and find me, and I'm going to do my best not to be found."

Glory shook her head. Barney sounded so sure of himself. The man had no idea how tenacious Ryan could be. He'd be found. She had no doubt of that. He couldn't hide from someone like Ryan Williams, not for long.

"I'll stay here and keep Glory safe." Gabe, who'd come to Cynful with Barney, settled on the gray chaise. He pulled out a tablet PC, but instead of the video game she expected, he opened an e-book. "I swear I won't go anywhere until you get back. Between Alex and me, Glory will be safe as a baby Grizzly in her den."

"Thanks, man." Ryan smiled, obviously relieved.

Glory should be used to Barney showing up in Ryan's apartment unannounced, but today he'd startled them with the news that Ryan's training would begin today. Nothing, not the threat to Glory or Ryan, Hope's reappearance, or Ryan's need to keep Glory in sight at all times, could persuade him that they needed to wait. As far as Barney was concerned, Ryan was already on a hunt, and that meant he needed training, badly. Glory had agreed, making it two against one. She wanted Ryan safe, and Barney could help him.

So despite Ryan's reservations, Ryan and Barney would be leaving her alone for the day, relying on Gabe to make sure that the rogue Wolf did not get a hold of Glory.

"We've got it covered. Get on out of here, guys." Bunny shooed both Barney and Ryan toward the door. "Go teach Ryan how not to get dead."

"Ha. Ha. Very funny." Ryan kissed the tip of Glory's nose. "Do not leave the shop under any circumstances without Gabe or Bunny, you hear me?"

"Loud and clear." Even with her new Bear abilities Glory didn't feel safe. She was still more Goldilocks than anything else, and the thought of trying to face down the rogue Wolf made her want to hide under something, preferably Ryan. Tito Salazar would get what was coming to him, but not by Glory's hand. Glory just hoped Salazar didn't hurt anyone else before he was caught.

"Are you sure it's safe for me to be here?"

Glory waved good-bye to Ryan before turning her attention to her twin. It had taken some persuasion, but Hope had agreed to come to Cynful with them that day. Glory had been ready to have Ryan just pick her up and put her in the car, but Gabe had stepped in and convinced Hope that it would be easier for him to keep track of the girls if they stayed together. Because the Hunter made Hope feel safe, she'd agreed. In fact, instead of staying with Max and Emma like they'd originally planned, Sarah had insisted that Hope stay with her and Gabe. The Omega wanted to be close to help Hope with the trauma she'd suffered, and Gabe had assigned sentries to keep watch over her and his house when he wasn't there. While Glory couldn't say Hope was thriving, she was at least beginning to put on some much-needed weight.

Hope had refused to leave the Anderson house for any reason, and Glory couldn't blame her. But she wanted to spend a little time with her sister in an environment where they'd be fairly safe, and Hope had finally caved.

Hope had not agreed to let Faith and Temp know they had found her. Like Ryan, she wasn't certain she trusted them anymore.

Her twin was still very skittish. Glory just hoped that, between Julian and Sarah, they'd be able to help her.

Glory finished buzzing down Hope's hair, evening it out until it was a pink fuzz on top of her head. She wondered if she could convince her twin to dye it. A pretty sapphire blue would look stunning on her. "If Salazar shows up here he's in for a surprise." Glory hitched a thumb toward Alex. "He may look like a big old teddy bear, but he'll rip the arms off of anyone who touches you."

Hope didn't look convinced, and Glory couldn't blame her. Alex was busy chasing Tabby around the glass and wood counter, making kissy faces at his mate. He looked about as threatening as his nickname.

"Why does his cousin call him Bunny?"

"I can answer that." Alex finally managed to catch Tabby and planted a wet kiss on her neck. "My cousins gave me that nickname because I hate fighting. After a while, they started calling me Bunny, and it stuck."

"That's not the whole story." Tabby leaned back against Alex, who easily took her weight. "Alex has a cousin named Heather. She's a Fox, and she works here now. When she was young, about twelve years old—"

"Ten. She was ten." Alex looked extremely uncomfortable. The big Bear didn't like being reminded of why he chose not to fight.

"She was a baby." Tabby scowled, pissed on Heather's behalf. "Anyway, about seven guys ganged up on her and tried to get her to change."

"Shifters don't change until puberty." Gabe snarled, his book forgotten. He'd heard the story secondhand, and taken a liking to Heather when he finally met her. Even Sarah was careful around the shy little Fox, helping her come out of her shell.

"They were trying to force her into puberty." And as someone who had almost been raped, Tabby was particularly upset on Heather's behalf. "So Alex taught them the error of their ways."

"I hurt them, maimed one of them permanently. I forced them to their knees and made them apologize." Alex grimaced. "But instead of making Heather feel safer, she became afraid of me. She wouldn't look at me, come near me or speak to me. She was terrified every time I was in the same room with her. I decided then and there that I didn't want any of my family to be afraid of me ever again. I started to learn anger management techniques like yoga and meditation, and refused to fight at all unless it was absolutely necessary."

"But that doesn't mean that he can't fight." Tabby patted Hope's hand. "If Salazar comes in here looking for you, he's gonna face an overprotective Grizzly chock-full of pent-up aggression."

"Can you take on a Hunter?" Hope still didn't seem convinced that she was safe here, and Glory wasn't sure how to go about doing that.

Alex nodded slowly, reluctantly. "I've never lost a fight, and I don't plan on starting now."

All of them turned as the bell over the door jangled, startling them. In sauntered the last person Glory expected to see, his hat pulled low over his eyes. "What the hell are you doing here?"

Barney winked at her and quietly made his way to the back room.

Glory blinked. *What the…?*

She followed Barney into the back room, leaving Tabby to finish dusting the hair off of Hope. What the hell was the Hunter was up to? Wasn't he supposed to be showing Ryan what to do? Shouldn't he be out there, with Ryan, keeping her mate safe? How was Ryan supposed to learn what he needed to do if Barney was back here, stealing her cherry cola? "What do you think you're doing?"

Barney opened her soda and chugged half of it before answering. "Didn't you know? I'm a fugitive on the run. So where is the last place he would look for me?"

"Back at the beginning?" Glory smirked. "You really think this is gonna work?"

"Of course it will. It always works. Baby Hunters always think they know more than I do." Barney leaned back against the mini fridge, practically sitting on it. "Gabe was one of the few who knew what I did. The bad guy almost always goes back to where he feels safe. He'll run to his mama or his girlfriend and beg them to take him in, or give him money. The successful ones are the ones that cut off all ties with their past, creating new identities in different cities."

"Like Salazar."

Barney's upper lip lifted in a silent snarl. "Salazar is an ex-Hunter. He knows better than anyone what to do and how to hide." Barney huffed, the sound remarkably Bearish. "I should know. I didn't want to tell your sister, but I trained the fucker."

That explained why Barney was taking this so seriously. "Do you think he's taken people other than Hope?" Just the thought of it sent shivers down her spine.

"No. I think he was obsessed with your sister. He had the one he wanted, but when Hope got away, he focused on her identical twin. I think if he was going to go after a type instead of a specific person he would've tried to snag someone closer to home." Barney shook his head. "No, it's definitely your sister that he wants, and he'll use whatever means necessary to get her back, including you." Barney grimaced. "I think he knew your likes and dislikes from Hope. He probably talked to her about you, or got her talking about you. Maybe at one time he thought to have you both. I'm not sure, but I'm inclined to think he was hoping taking you would make Hope come back to him."

"That makes me feel so much better." Glory rubbed her hands up and down her arms. "Do you think—"

"Gotcha."

Barney's eyes went wide as he was yanked off of the mini fridge and thrown to the ground. His arms were pulled up behind his back as Ryan straddled him with a saucy grin.

"You're under arrest. You have the right to remain stupid. Anything you say can and will be used to mercilessly taunt you. Do you understand your idiocy as I have described it to you?"

"Get off me, asshole."

Ryan laughed and helped Barney to his feet.

"How did you find me so fast?" Barney wiggled his shoulders. He didn't sound nearly as cocky as Ryan dusted him off.

Ryan shrugged. "I used to play hide and seek with my cousins. Some of us took the game pretty seriously." He pounded Barney on the shoulder, ignoring the other man's pained wince. "Besides, it wasn't like you tried all that hard to hide."

Barney mumbled something under his breath and finished the rest of the cherry cola. "The next test will be harder."

"I'm sure it will be."

Barney shot Ryan an evil look. Glory had the feeling that Ryan's smugness had just earned him a test that was ten times harder than it was originally going to be.

Glory heard the muted sound of the bell out front. She didn't think anything of it until Alex started growling. Dashing through the curtains, she was surprised to find Jim Woods standing there, staring at Alex with a frightened expression. "Look, I just want to talk to your cousin."

"Don't you think you've hurt her enough?"

Jim ignored Alex's growl, returning Alex's scowl with one of his own. "You don't know everything that happened, and you have no idea what I've been through."

"What *you've* been through? What about what my sister has been through?" Ryan stomped over to Alex and stood next to his cousin, shoulder to shoulder. "Where were you when she was in the hospital, crying for you?"

Jim sighed wearily, and ran his hand through his hair. He really did look tired, bags under his eyes and his shoulders slumped. "My mother is —"

"Shit." Barney raced past and out the front door. "Ryan, Gabe, get your asses in gear. I smell Salazar."

The two men quickly followed Barney out the door, their expressions grim.

"Go."

Alex snarled, indecision on his face.

"Sugar." Tabby cupped her mate's face between her hands. "Go keep your cousin safe."

"No." But Alex was clearly torn, the need to protect Ryan almost as strong as his desire to keep Tabby safe.

"Trust me. I can take on one Wolf." Tabby turned her mate toward the door. "Go on, now."

"Tabby…"

"Alex." They stared at one another, a titanic showdown that Alex lost the moment Tabby lifted one dark brow at him. "Trust me, sugar. Glory's changed now, and Hope and I are both Wolves. If this guy comes after us, he's supper."

Alex's shoulders sagged for just a moment before he pulled his mate into a quick, hard kiss. "Stay put, baby."

Tabby nodded, her expression fierce, and Alex raced out the door after the Hunters. Barney and Ryan wouldn't be thrilled that the Grizzly had followed them, but if it came down to a fight Alex would be one hell of an asset.

Jim Woods looked totally confused. They'd completely forgotten he was there in the chaos caused by Salazar's scent. "What the hell is going on?"

"Um." The girls exchanged a quick, uneasy glance. They'd have to educate the man on shifters, thanks to Tabby's little scene with Alex. "You see—"

Glory was shoved violently to the side as someone raced past her from the break room. A dark-haired man Glory had never seen before snarled, reaching for Hope as Hope screamed in terror.

Jim put himself between Salazar and Hope, holding his arms out and crouching for all the world like he'd fight the Wolf if Salazar took one more step. "Who the fuck are you?"

Salazar grinned, his mouth full of his sharp Wolf teeth. "You're about to find out, human."

Tito Salazar grabbed hold of Dr. Jim Woods so quickly none of them could stop him, and bit him right through his shirt.

***

Ryan raced after Barney, Salazar's scent barely detectable on the afternoon breeze. The guy had some balls coming so close to the shop during the day. The lure of Hope must have been too strong for the rogue Hunter to resist.

Barney silently pointed, and Gabe broke off, heading down an alley between the Chinese restaurant and the small curio shop Glory loved to splurge in. Ryan stayed close to Barney, aware the other Hunter wouldn't allow him out of his sight. Until he was fully trained and Barney gave his stamp of approval, Ryan would not be allowed to hunt on his own.

Something was off. Wrong. Ryan sniffed, growling when he realized what was bugging him.

Salazar's scent seemed to be fading rather than increasing, and Ryan cursed under his breath. Unless Gabe had the scent, they were going to lose the son of a bitch.

Barney stopped, panting and cursing under his breath. He punched the brick wall of the storefront he was standing next to. "It's a red herring. Gotta be." Barney sniffed the wall, making a disgusted face as he pulled back. "He fooled me."

"What you mean?"

"The son of a bitch scent marked the walls."

Ryan froze.

Shit. He knew about scent marking. Wolves weren't the only animals who felt the need to mark their territory. Brown Bears would rub their backs up and down trees, marking their territory and warning away other Bears. Ryan, Alex and several of his other relatives had done the same when they changed shape, marking the woods they shared with the Pumas, who thankfully found the whole thing amusing.

If the Bunsun-Williams clan hadn't been accepted by the Puma Alpha, it might have been a different story. Pumas were just as territorial as brown Bears, and the shifters had the advantage of working in a group, unlike their wild counterparts.

For Salazar's scent to start off so strong and then slowly fade away, he had to have been marking things for a day or two, only marking the final spot just before Barney scented him. He also had to have been heading *toward* the shop, not away. "He's going after the girls."

Ryan didn't wait for Barney's response. He took off back toward Cynful at a dead run, praying he wouldn't be too late. Rounding the corner he caught sight of Alex sniffing the wall and snarling.

Terror filled him, the metallic taste of adrenaline jolting him. "Who's watching the girls?"

"Tabby. She insisted I come after you, that they were all safe." Bunny's voices barely human, his Bear close to the surface.

Nothing more need be said. Both of them started racing back toward the shop, well aware the pregnant Wolf would be no match for a Hunter, even an ex one. And while Glory had gone through her change, she wasn't a fighter on her best day. He didn't call Glory Super Grover for nothing. As for Hope, Ryan prayed Hope would run rather than be captured again. It would destroy Glory if anything more happened to her sister.

With a bit of luck, Ryan, Bunny and Barney would arrive in time to stop Salazar before he hurt anyone.

Ryan didn't want to think about the worst they might find. When this was over, he was going to have a little chat with Bunny. His cousin should have stayed behind despite Tabby's orders and protected their mates, not chased after Ryan. This wasn't the first time Bunny had been worried about family, though. It was the memory of what had happened to Heather that had sent Bunny after Ryan. Bunny should know better. Ryan was more than capable of taking care of himself. But there was no way the girls plus one unaware human were going to hold off Salazar.

They slammed through the door of Cynful together, snarling and claws unleashed. What he saw made him want to howl like a Wolf.

Tabby lay on her side unconscious, her arms curled protectively across her middle. Jim Woods was right next to her, bleeding from a gaping wound in his neck.

Glory and Hope were missing.

The bell jingled and Ryan turned with a snarl, claws and fangs extended.

"His scent... Shit." Gabe held up his hands. "Tell me he didn't take the girls."

Bunny was kneeling at Tabby's side, running his hand through her hair over and over and cursing himself.

Ryan could sense his cousin calling on his healing powers, and knew Tabby would be all right.

He wasn't so certain about Jim. The man was bleeding profusely, and his skin had taken on a grayish pallor. Without Julian, Ryan wasn't certain they could save the vet, but he had to try.

"We need to see if we can heal him enough to wake him up. We need to know if he saw anything that can help us track the girls." Barney knelt by Jim and took a deep breath. "C'mon, Ryan. Show me what you've got."

Ryan put his hand near the wound and closed his eyes. He wasn't as good at healing as Julian, or even Bunny, but he'd do what he could to save his sister's mate.

Ryan followed the spiral of the healing path, dancing down into Jim's body, marking the worst of the damage. He began the slow process of knitting together flesh and blood vessels, muscle and bone. The bite had gone far enough, deep enough, to break the man's clavicle.

"Oh shit."

Ryan saw it just as Barney cursed. "Son of a bitch." It looked like Dr. Jim was going to learn about shifters a lot sooner than they'd anticipated, and in a way Ryan wouldn't have wished on anyone. The bite the Wolf had given him was a changing bite, the same kind he'd given Glory and Hope. Because it wasn't linked to a mating bite, it would have been horribly painful and traumatic for the veterinarian.

Worse, because Chloe wasn't here to bite him quickly a second time and claim him, there was no way to stop the process. If any of the Bears bit him, nothing would happen. He'd wind up with two bite marks, but the Wolf would be predominant because it came first.

"Why? It doesn't make sense to change him." Barney continued healing the vicious wound, but the puzzled anger in his voice echoed what was going through Ryan's mind.

Ryan suddenly sensed the presence of his cousin on the healing path. Tabby must be awake, or Bunny would never have left her side. His tone was weary as he asked, "You think Salazar had anything to do with the attack on Chloe?"

"Anything is possible, but somehow I doubt it." Barney's tone was absent as they continued to close the vicious wound.

"Ugh." Tabby's moan nearly distracted him from the blood vessel he was attempting to patch. "Oh no!"

"What?" Alex was already pulling away from Jim, his attention caught by the distress in his mate's voice.

"He got between us, tried to protect us from Salazar."

"Shit. That's why he got bit." Barney took over from Alex, fixing the last of the damage to Jim's clavicle.

"But why make it a changing bite?" He finished closing the blood vessel and began working on the damaged skin.

"Because he's a sick motherfucker and probably thought it would be funny?" Barney sat back with a sigh, most of the healing done. "Shit. We really need to contact Rick Lowell, let him know there are two new Wolves in town who are going to need a hell of a lot of therapy."

Ryan swayed, exhausted, as he too finished his healing. Jim would have a horrible scar, but he would live. "Bunny. Sit. Stay. Good Bear."

Bunny nodded as he crooned to his mate.

Good. That took care of Tabby and Jim. The way he was acting, Alex was probably never going to leave his mate's side again.

Ryan got to his feet, staggering as a wave of exhaustion rolled over him. If the rogue hurt one powder-blue curl on his mate's head, Ryan would rip him limb from limb. He scowled at Barney and Gabe, the Grizzly rage that rode all of his kind barely held in check. "Now. Let's go get my mate back."

CHAPTER NINETEEN

Glory was freaking the fuck out. She'd come to, ready to fight the man who'd hurt Jim and Tabby, only to find herself stuffed behind the driver's seat with her arms bound behind her back. She thought of changing, shifting into her Bear, but her Bear whined at the thought. With her arms bound, she couldn't shift without dislocating or breaking both her shoulders, which would render her useless in a fight. Just because she was a shifter that didn't mean she could automatically heal anything just by changing into her Bear.

Fuck. A. Duck. Ryan could have filled her in on that little tidbit. Stupid werewolf romances. Why'd they have to get it wrong? The hero or heroine *always* healed by shifting, didn't they?

But no. Glory wasn't that lucky, and now she was in a car with the psycho of the month, heading toward Hell and unable to do anything about it.

A small moan had her looking sharply to her right. Hope lay next to her, right behind the passenger seat, equally turkey-tied and still unconscious from the blows Salazar had landed. Hope's cheek was swollen, her eye bruised, and blood trickled from her lip.

They'd fought. God knew, they'd fought fucking hard, Tabby in mid-shift when the first blow took her out. Hope had been terrified, huddled in a corner away from her tormentor when Glory placed herself between Salazar and her twin. But Salazar had easily taken Glory down, landing two solid blows that dropped her to her knees before he'd knocked her out. Whatever happened to Hope had been done after Glory lost consciousness, but, from the looks of her twin, Salazar had beaten her down as well.

Maybe Ryan was right. Super Grover really *did* suit her. She'd been about as useful as limp spaghetti when it came time to protect her family.

Ryan.

God, why hadn't she told him she loved him? She was such an ass. She'd die here, at the hands of Salazar, and Ryan would never have heard the words she should have told him long ago. If she lived through this, the first thing she was going to do was finally say it. Her mate deserved the words, deserved to see her as naked and bare as he'd laid himself out for her. He was so much braver than she was.

He deserved a mate who'd fight for him just as hard as he fought for her, and Glory was finally going to be that mate.

The scent of Hope's blood filled her senses. Without thought Glory reached for her Bear, wanting to heal her twin before the psycho driving the car to fuck knew where realized Glory was awake. Her Bear answered, its anger over her twin's state and her own injuries nearly causing Glory to shift in response. She didn't have the control the others had, not even Cyn, who'd only been a Kodiak a few short months.

Hell, if Cyn had been there, Salazar would be scattered into tiny little pieces while Cyn bitched about getting gore in her curtains.

Her Bear liked that thought. It was odd, gentling the creature that lived within her. She assured her Bear that they'd get their revenge on Salazar, but first they had to take care of Hope. Their twin was far more important than the asshole who was going to die no matter what he tried to do to prevent it. There'd be no shifter jail for his ass, no Bubba Bear using him as their personal bitch.

Nope. Rye was going to shred him into itty-bitty pieces when he found them.

If he found them.

"Stop it."

Glory jumped, startled, at the deep tone of Salazar's voice. She scowled at the back of his head, wishing she had the nerve to rabbit kick him until his eyes bugged out. But she could feel how fast the car was going and was terrified she'd take all of them out if Salazar lost control of the vehicle and crashed. "Fuck. You."

"Sweetheart, I plan on it."

Glory gagged.

"Shut it. You're just leverage to get the other Hunters off my ass." She caught a glimpse of Salazar's dark eyes in the rearview mirror before he turned his attention back to the road. "Trust me, you're not nearly as good as your sister."

Glory froze. He couldn't mean…?

Her Bear snarled. If Salazar had touched her…had done things to her while she was unconscious, Glory was going to go all SG on his ass. And she didn't mean Super Grover. A Grizzly versus a lone Wolf, no matter how powerful the Wolf, would always win.

Always.

And somehow, she doubted the rogue had a Pack to call on for assistance.

Within seconds, her Bear settled down, and the knowledge that she remained untouched filled her. Her Bear could sense no tearing, no invasion of her person, easing one worry. Salazar was just fucking with her, messing with her head, possibly in an attempt to keep her off balance. If she was too busy being angry, she wouldn't be able to heal her twin.

Glory tuned him out, ignoring the sound of his voice and the vile things he was spewing as she focused on Hope. She reached out with her foot, barely touching

Hope, but it was enough for her Bear to fully assess Hope's injuries. Thank God the damage to Hope was minimal. The unconsciousness was because of a blow to the head, and the concussion was the only thing that worried her. Glory healed the damage carefully, aware she wasn't sure what she was doing but unwilling to wait for Ryan, or even Julian.

And she knew, without a shadow of a doubt, that Ryan would come for her. The man had bared his soul for her, stripped himself naked until she saw him inside and out. The thought that he would abandon her to her fate almost made her laugh out loud.

Oh, he would come. It was the only thing that staved off the panic attack she could feel nibbling at the edges of her mind. Ryan *would* come.

And Salazar would die.

Glory finished healing her twin, concerned when Hope remained unconscious. After Ryan showed up and kicked Salazar's ass, she'd have to make sure Julian got a look at her. The fact that she wasn't waking up scared the piss out of Glory.

"I knew she would run to you." Glory brought her attention back to Salazar. "The twin who stayed behind. She'd speak of you, of how she wished you were the one I'd taken."

Glory doubted that. For all that Hope had been unwilling to trust them at first, she'd never once mentioned blaming Glory for what had happened to her. But Glory answered anyway, hoping the fucker would actually start to monologue. If he was distracted enough, maybe he wouldn't notice that she was trying to work her hands free. "So you're telling me she wished I was the one getting raped by a skeezeweasel?"

He growled, low and feral. "She's my mate."

"She's no more your mate than Tom Cruise is." She wrinkled her nose. "God, please tell me he's not a shifter."

"Who?"

"Tom Cruise." She called forth her claws, all five inches of them. Curling her fingers, she began picking at the rope around her wrists, praying the Wolf wouldn't hear the *skritch-skritch* sound over the road and his own voice.

He shrugged. The feel of the car going up scared the shit out of her. Were they getting on the highway? If he hit I-76, they could be heading toward Ohio. She began picking at the rope a little bit faster. If she could just get her hands free, she'd be able to take Salazar down and get Hope out of here. "He's not, as far as I know."

"So you're saying he could be." *Keep the pyscho distracted, Glory. Don't let him hear you breaking free.*

"Don't you want to know where I'm taking you?"

"Not particularly. You're not going to survive long enough to arrive." Glory continued to saw at her bindings. "Ryan is coming for me."

He laughed. "Your mate is probably healing his sister's mate as we speak." He grinned, looking oddly handsome despite the fact he was nuttier than a squirrel in a vat of peanut butter. "I kind of did them a solid."

"Excuse me?" Poor Jim. He'd tried to put himself between Salazar and Tabby and gotten his ass mauled. If he lived, Glory was so sending him a fruit basket.

"Oh, don't worry. He'll survive what I did to him."

Shit. "You changed him."

"Yup."

Damn. That had to have hurt. He must have done it after he knocked out Glory and Hope. She remembered the pain of Salazar's bite, the way Ryan's had hurt right before the pleasure kicked in. For Jim there would have been no pleasure, only pain and blood and fear. "Tabby?"

"The pregnant Wolf?" He rolled his eyes. "She'll live, despite what the Se…" He sighed. "You know what? Never mind. You'll learn soon enough."

"About what?"

Salazar ignored her, gazing in the rearview mirror and cursing up a storm. "Who the fuck is that?"

Glory dug her claws into the leather seat to drag herself upright and peered out the rear window. Behind them, a motorcycle weaved in and out of traffic, and for a moment her heart skipped a beat as relief washed through her.

Ryan.

But, no. The lean body wasn't her mate, the black helmet with the mirrored visor obscuring the features of the man chasing them down. Ryan was bulkier than the sleek individual who raced down the highway, drawing alongside of them. The mirrored helmet turned to the car, and Glory shivered.

There was a menace she had never sensed before, not even from Salazar. Salazar was crazy, but he didn't seem it, not at a glance, anyway.

Something about the man in the faceless helmet scared the ever-loving shit out of her. Glory moved, hiding the sight of her twin from the man on the motorcycle.

The rider gunned the cycle, swerving in front of their car. Salazar swerved, an instinctual response as he tried to avoid a collision.

"Fucking Hunters. They aren't going to catch me." He glanced toward the passenger seat and smiled. "I'll deal with him."

Salazar took the first exit he came to, one that lead to a sleepy little town with plenty of farmland and few inhabitants that Glory recognized as being about twenty miles eastbound outside Halle.

The rider reversed on the shoulder, doing a high-speed turn that had Glory gasping in disbelief. Either the rider really didn't give a damn if he lived or died, or he was channeling the spirit of Ghost Rider, complete with flame-covered head. Dirt and small stones flew in an arc as he twisted the back wheel before gunning it down the ramp, catching up to them easily. He followed Salazar through the town, staying on the rogue's ass until the Wolf was growling and snarling in frustration. Glory sawed faster at the ropes, feeling them loosen a bit just as Salazar pulled over near a thickly wooded area. She was almost free.

She was shocked when the man pulled a gun and pointed it right at her head. "Get out."

"What?"

"Get the fuck out of the car." He glanced over her shoulder and winced. "He wants you, he can have you. But I'm leaving with Hope."

"No."

The sound of the gunshot was loud, the burning fire in her shoulder shocking her. Glory screamed. Shit. She *hated* getting shot.

"Get out of my car."

Glory whimpered, but refused to move. She couldn't abandon her twin. "No."

Before Salazar could pull the trigger a second time, the driver's side door was wrenched open. A pair of black-gloved hands reached in and grabbed hold of Salazar's hand, driving the gun up. It went off, leaving a smoking hole in the car's roof.

Salazar struggled with the stranger over the gun, kicking the rider in the thigh. The pained grunt was the only sound the rider made.

It was freaky as hell.

Glory worked harder to get her hands free. She needed to get Hope and get out of the car before the two men turned on her. She had no idea who the stranger was, but a familiar scent was beginning to override the scent of leather and gunpowder and Wolf.

The rider was...a Puma?

Maybe?

Hell, she'd been a shifter for so short a time she was lucky she knew what Bears smelled like, but the man currently struggling with her captor had a distinctly feline scent to him that she recognized in Gabe, Max and Emma. The smelled like they belonged together.

They smelled like family.

Even so, the strange sense of menace rolling off the rider had her double-timing her work on the rope. She was rewarded when it finally gave way, freeing her hands to grab hold of Hope's shoulders and shake her twin. "Wake up!"

Nothing. Hope's head lolled on her shoulders, rolling with Glory's movements.

"Shit." She grabbed hold of Hope under her armpits, ignoring the screaming, red-hot agony in her shoulder, and dragged her twin to the car door. "We're getting out of here, I promise."

"No." Salazar finally managed to get the rider off of him, pointing the gun once more at Glory's head. "You're not going anywhere."

Then his eyes went wide as the rider drove his fingers into the side of his head, claws first. Glory could hear the bone snap as Salazar screamed.

A Puma's claws weren't nearly as long as a Bear's, so Salazar wasn't killed instantly. He was wounded now, a bleeding Wolf who thought he was defending his mate. So he did what any wounded shifter would do.

He shifted, desperately trying to wriggle free of his clothing. Because he shifted into an animal that was smaller than his human form, he didn't risk hurting himself by trying to burst through his clothing.

Must be nice. It would have been a hell of a lot easier to fight Salazar back in the shop if she could have changed. Glory redoubled her attempts to cut through the ropes binding her wrists, grunting in satisfaction when she felt them begin to give way.

The familiar-smelling Puma didn't change. He backed up, making come-hither gestures with his hands, shooting the Wolf the finger when Salazar crouched down in the driver's seat.

As soon as the fucker was out, Glory would be in. He'd left the keys in the ignition. Glory had no trouble stealing the psycho's wheels and making her getaway, whether Hope regained consciousness or not. She had to get Hope to Julian, had to—

"Mother pus bucket!" Glory swore, using Cyn's favorite curse, her vision blurring as she twisted wrong. It pulled at the wound in her shoulder, and pretty stars danced around her head, nearly sending her tumbling into unconsciousness along with her sister.

She had to be more careful, or she and Hope were going to be in bigger trouble than they were now. She healed a little of the damage the bullet had caused, closing the bleeding blood vessels and torn flesh, the moves instinctual. Her Bear guided her, showed her what to do and how to maximize what little energy she had left. And she had precious little. Healing Hope had taken most of it. By the time she was done taking care of her shoulder she was panting, gasping, her vision blurred at the edges. And not all of it was from pain and exhaustion. Her Bear was showing her how to stave off the panic attack that threatened to stop her breath.

The Puma whistled, that sound one used to call a dog to heel, and Glory would have laughed if she wasn't terrified of the pain. This whole thing was so surreal.

From Salazar's answering growl, the Wolf was less than amused. He stayed hunkered in the driver's seat, glaring and baring his teeth at the Puma who was trying to taunt him out of the car. From the way he positioned himself, Glory would swear he was trying to keep Hope safe. He kept his eye on the Puma, his back to Hope, but every now and then he'd snarl at Glory. If Glory didn't know better, she'd swear he was acting exactly as Ryan had when he'd been protecting her.

But Salazar was *not* Hope's mate, no matter what his delusions told him. There was no mingling of their scents, no permanent mark on her body. Cyn smelled of Julian; Tabby, of Alex. Glory was aware how her own scent had mingled with Ryan's.

Hope smelled like Hope, and nothing else. Ditto with Tito Salazar.

But that didn't stop the psycho wolf from *acting* like a mated shifter. He was keeping the Puma from getting too close to Hope while remaining close enough to keep her safe.

The Puma shrugged, reached in his jacket, and pulled out something Glory could barely see. He sauntered back to the car, his stride certain, the object half hidden in the palm of his hand.

Salazar tensed, ready to spring at the Puma who dared come close to them once more. The man in the leather was going to get savaged unless he changed, and Glory wasn't certain how much more she'd be able to heal. The exhaustion that rode a Bear who'd used his or her powers, the price they had to pay for their gift from the spirits that had made them, was riding her hard.

But if the Puma got hurt trying to save them, Glory would try and heal him. It was the least she could do.

The rider reached the driver's side of the car.

Salazar pounced, snarling and snapping like the rabid Wolf he was. Glory tensed, certain the Puma was about to get his throat ripped out, high-necked leather jacket or no. Salazar was just that fast.

But the Puma was faster, his hand whipping out and jabbing the object he held into Salazar's side.

Salazar cried out, a canine yip of pain, his momentum shattered as the Puma used it to pound him into the ground. She saw his thumb press down, and realized he was injecting the Wolf with something.

Salazar began to thrash almost immediately, his body contorting as whatever the Puma had given him killed him so quickly it was over before it really began.

Fuck. A. Duck. No fucking way.

But it had to be. There was no one else she could think of, no one else who would have fucking poison and an injector on him. And they'd scented him at Hope's run-down motel, but none of them had known why.

"Jamie?"

The helmet swiveled in her direction as the Puma lifted his finger to his helmet in a shushing motion. He turned his attention once more to Salazar and nodded.

Salazar wasn't breathing. He'd shifted back, a naked human with half-closed eyes and grayish skin.

He was dead.

Jamie—if it *was* Jamie—backed away from Salazar and the car. He didn't do anything more. He simply stared into the back seat, at Hope, for a long moment before walking over to his motorcycle.

Glory shivered. If the insane doctor had fixated on Hope, they were in more trouble than anything Salazar had been capable of giving them.

But Jamie's shoulders weren't nearly so tense, the sense of menace dulled to a quiet river rather than a raging storm. He was still dangerous, still unstable, but whatever had driven him after Glory and Hope seemed satisfied now.

Glory leapt out of the car, ignoring the body of the man who now lay where the Wolf had been. Salazar deserved to be found naked and dead of whatever Jamie had done to him.

Hope yelled from the backseat, staring at the man in the helmet. "Wait!"

Jamie paused, shuddering violently at the sound of Hope's voice, but didn't turn around.

Her sister took a deep, shuddering breath. "Thank you. For saving us."

For a second, Glory didn't think he'd respond, but then the helmet briefly dipped before Dr. Jamie Howard got on his cycle and roared out of her life once more.

Hope kept her gaze on him until he disappeared from sight, before collapsing again in the back seat. "Who was that?"

"I'm not sure, but I think it was Dr. Jamie Howard."

"The one who lost his mate?" Hope's tone was full of…something. Fear, maybe? Longing?

Glory couldn't tell. She was too busy trying to get her breathing back under control. "Yeah." Glory sat in the driver's seat, her hands shaking as the panic she'd barely allowed herself to feel began to kick in. Her vision was going white around the edges, her breath coming in panting gasps.

She had to get herself under control, or she'd wind up killing both herself and Hope.

Glory reached for her Bear and prayed that what little she knew would be enough to keep her from losing herself in the fear.

CHAPTER TWENTY

Ryan followed the sweet scent of his mate, his head
hanging out the window like a dog's. "There. Down the
ramp."

He tried not to panic as the scent of Jamie Howard
mingled with that of Hope, Glory and Salazar. If Jamie did
anything to hurt his mate, there'd be war in Halle,
Pennsylvania. Jamie wouldn't live to see the dawn.

"Julian says Jim is awake." Gabe hung up his phone,
but his eyes were still Puma gold. The sheriff was *pissed*
that Salazar had tricked them, had hurt people under
Gabe's protection. Ryan wasn't certain which of them
wanted Salazar's blood more. "He's confused, and asking
a lot of questions."

"Julian called Chloe?"

Gabe nodded as Barney followed the scent of Jamie,
Glory and Hope through a small town. Gabe had his badge
ready in case the local police decided to pull them over.
Technically, he should have called the kidnapping in to
state police, but time was of the essence and they didn't
want a crazy shifter set on a bunch of humans. The bite
Jim had gotten proved the rogue Wolf couldn't be trusted
not to try to harm or change them, thus endangering them
all. Even if Ryan didn't get to him, Tito Salazar was a
marked man. "Chloe's making her way to the shop as we
speak. She'll try and help Julian explain everything to
Jim."

God, what Jim was about to go through. No one
should have their choices taken away like that. But it was
too late to do anything now. If Chloe had been there, she

could have bitten her mate, given him the mark and changed him into a Fox.

But Chloe hadn't been, and now Jim would become a Wolf against his will. Chloe had to be heartbroken.

It was just one more reason to rip Salazar apart. No one made Ryan Williams's baby sister cry.

"Julian used their freaky mind-link to call her to him. She's on her way." Gabe was leaning forward, his gaze glued to something outside the front window. "Wait a minute. You see that?"

Barney, driving the car, was also leaning over the steering wheel. "Yup. Looks like they've stopped."

Ryan leaned farther out the window, trying to see what they saw.

A dark car, front and back driver's side doors open. A body on the blacktop, naked and grotesquely distorted.

A fall of powder-blue hair spilling out of the driver's seat.

Glory.

Ryan was out of the car before it came to a full stop, running toward his mate, terrified as the scent of blood, *her* blood, filled him. "Glory!"

Her head snapped up. Her pale blue eyes were glazed, her clothing dripping with her blood. There was a gaping hole in the shoulder of her filmy top.

Fuck. She'd been shot again. His Grizzly roared, wanting to rend, to tear at the son of a bitch who'd harmed his mate.

"Ryan?"

He was growling, his eyes changing to his Bear's brown, his claws extended in anticipation of ripping through flesh.

But his mate needed him. She was wounded, hurting, terrified and on the verge of one hell of a panic attack. Ryan soothed his Bear, reminded him the body had to be that of Salazar, but his Bear wasn't ready to listen yet. It wanted revenge for his mate's suffering, and wouldn't calm until it knew Glory was safe and whole. "I'm here, sweetheart." He pulled her the car, cradling her close as she collapsed against him. "I'm here."

God, he'd almost lost her. The smell of gunpowder on her skin, her clothes, terrified him. Hell, he might have a panic attack right along with her.

She was trembling against him. "Ryan."

Ryan was still tired from healing Jim, but his mate needed, and he would provide. His Grizzly agreed, and together they danced down the healing spiral, checking her wound and repairing what little damage was left. She'd done very well for someone who hadn't been formally trained in her gift, leaving little sign of the damage the bullet must have made.

The panic was easier to soothe than he'd thought it would be. She'd begun to calm the moment he took her in his arms.

"I knew you'd come. I waited for you." The trembling increased as Glory clung to him so tightly he was surprised he could still breathe.

"Good." He sighed as she snuggled up against him. "Good." He eased her racing heart, damped down the surge of adrenaline. She relaxed, already easier in his embrace.

"Jamie was here."

"I know. I smelled him."

She pressed her face harder against his chest. Out of the corner of his eye, he saw Barney checking on Hope while Gabe studied Salazar. "He saved us."

"How?" Ryan refused to let his mate go, even when Gabe gestured for him to come and check on the dead body. And it was obvious that Salazar was dead. The gray color of his skin alone would have marked him. The knowledge that his mate was safe, healed, and the offender was beyond his reach finally eased the Bear's rage and the man's fears. Ryan relaxed, closed his eyes and buried his face in his mate's curls.

"He followed us, injected Salazar with something when the Wolf shifted and attacked him."

Shit. "Did he hurt you?" Jamie might have been a friend once, but Ryan had no trouble hurting the Puma if he'd laid one claw on Glory. His mate had been hurt enough to last a lifetime.

"No. He didn't speak to us, didn't do anything. Just…assassinated Salazar and left."

Ryan took a deep breath and let it out as relief flooded through him. "Thank fuck." He was dizzy from relief, ready to lie down on the blacktop and just hold his mate until the shakes passed.

"He kept staring at Hope. I think she's the reason he saved us."

"And then he left you both here alone." Ryan wasn't certain what to make of that. If, as he suspected, Hope was Jamie's second mate, why had the man left them here alone? Ryan would never have been able to walk away from his wounded mate, and it was obvious from Hope's unconscious state that's exactly what Jamie had done. He could sense Barney attempting to heal her, felt the touch of his mate on her twin's wounds. Hope's condition was worse than Glory's had been, but it looked like Glory had done everything she could for her sister. Hope was speaking quietly to Barney, possibly telling him everything Glory had just told Ryan.

"He scared the hell out of me at first, but when Salazar was dead, he seemed…calmer, somehow. If that makes any sense whatsoever." Glory shivered. "I think he's still cold, still grieving Marie, but maybe he's finally starting to snap out of it."

Either that, or the fact that someone had taken his mate from him again had broken him out of his grief-fueled rage. Ryan wouldn't be sure until he saw the two of them together, but how would he go about bringing Hope, scared of her own shadow, to the psychotic doctor who'd sworn to kill Julian if he ever saw him again? Was Jamie finally starting to heal, or was something more sinister going on?

Ryan sighed. At least their life was never boring.

"Rye?"

"Hmm?"

"I have one more thing to tell you. Something I promised myself I would if I lived long enough."

"What's that?" God, she killed him. Just the thought of never seeing her again...

He could understand now why Jamie had broken. If he lived through losing Glory, he'd be a basket case too.

"Love you."

He stilled, frozen as her muffled words filled him, quieted the fear that had driven him ever since he found she'd been taken from him. Her reluctant, aggravated tone amused the hell out of him. "I love you too, SG."

She snorted against his shirt, but for once she didn't argue with him about the nickname. "Good. Now take me home."

He chuckled as he looked down at his mate. She was smiling up at him, a trembling one, sure, but that cocky, confident grin was peeking out of the fear, dazzling him. "Yes, dear."

She shook her finger up at him, nearly poking his nose. "Remember those words, Rye. You'll be saying them a lot."

"Yes, dear."

She laughed, and the sun came out from behind the clouds once more.

***

They were back in Halle, seated on Max and Emma Cannon's comfy leather sofa, and clutching each other while Ryan, Barney and Gabe filled the Alpha pair in on what had happened. "I want to call Temp and Faith, let them know you're safe."

Hope whimpered. "I'm not sure…"

"Dad isn't in their lives anymore." At least she hoped so. If that proved to be wrong, if Temp and Faith had fooled her…

No. No, she knew Temp. Her brother would never betray them that way. He'd tried to intervene, to accept the beatings for her. He wouldn't turn on her, she was sure of it.

Hope took a deep breath. "We have to tell them about us."

Glory nodded. Ryan had already told her he'd sensed Temp was present when she changed for the first time. Telling Temp about her shifter status, and what it meant for both her and Hope, was the next step. Odds were good the local shifters would insist on changing Temp and Faith as well, for security reasons. She didn't envy them that. "I know."

"I want you there when I tell them what happened to me." Hope took a deep breath. "They really looked for me?"

"Yeah. We really did."

Hope nodded, her expression turning incredibly fierce. "Then they deserve to know."

The determination in her twin's tone was almost scary. "You're going to be fine. Ryan and I, we're going to build a house and we want you to live with us."

"No." Hope winced. "I can't. I don't want to be around—"

"Shifters?" Glory could understand that, even if it hurt.

"Men." Hope's tone was so soft, Glory could barely hear her. "I don't want to be around men."

"That could be...problematic." Max Cannon smiled softly at Hope. "Since the Poconos Pack Alpha is male, and so am I." He took her hand, ignoring when Hope visibly tried to remove it. "But I give you my word, you'll be safe here. You're ours now."

Hope sucked in a breath and shivered hard, but Glory understood what Max was saying. "He means you're Pride now."

Max nodded, grimacing. "Sorry. I should have worded that better."

"Yes, you should have, Lion-O." Emma settled on the sofa next to Hope with a soft sigh. "But I get it."

"It's okay. I feel like..." Hope's eyes were wide, confused.

"Like you finally belong." Gabe placed his hand on Hope's head and ruffled her hair, ignoring the way she tried to get out from under his touch. "You're definitely ours now. I can feel you."

"And if things go well with Rick and Belle, you'll have dual status, becoming a member of both Pride and Pack." Emma grinned. "We'll share you like we do Tabby Garwood."

"It will mean you'll have a choice of living here, or in the Poconos with the Pack, and have the freedom to move between both." Max's smile was gentler than his mate's, but no less sincere. "Glory is already a part of the Pride, along with Tabby, Alex, Cyn and Julian."

Glory shivered as the Alpha reaffirmed her place in the Pride. The sensation of belonging somewhere, of being accepted flaws and all, filled her.

She had family again, family that accepted her just because she was Glory Walsh, not because she was Ryan's mate. And the feeling was heady.

"Oh." Hope relaxed, giving them a genuine smile for the first time since they'd found her. "I can feel that."

"I can feel you now, and…" Gabe stuttered to a halt. "What *is* that?"

"I don't know." Max stood, rubbing his chin as he stared down at Hope. "I've never felt anything quite like it before."

"It's like…sunshine?" Gabe shook his head. "We need Rick and Belle on this."

Emma appeared intrigued. "You think Hope is an Omega?" Emma looked intrigued.

"I don't think so. An Omega's powers only come into play when they meet *their* Alpha, and Max already has one." Gabe grimaced. "Maybe Adrian or Sarah can shed some light on this. There could be something I'm missing here."

"God, I hope so. This is confusing the hell out of me." Max plopped down into the overstuffed chair that had his scent all over it. She could tell it was his favorite. "When did Rick say he could come?"

"Belle is having some issues with her hip, and without Jamie…" Emma shrugged. "She's looking for another shifter doctor, so it could be a few days."

"What about that kid we sent up there, the one who loved coming into the shop?" Tim had seen Cyn partially change when Glory was shot, and had quickly figured out what was going on. To protect themselves and Tim, they'd given him the option of becoming a Bear, a Puma or a Wolf, depending on who he wanted biting him. Tim had chosen to go to the Wolves, and had left Halle about a month ago. The fact that he was pre-med had delighted the Wolves, who had to travel either to New York or Halle to see a doctor. They'd all agreed to allow Tim to continue attending college in Halle once his Wolf emerged, and he'd agreed to work at the Red Wolf Lodge once he earned his doctorate.

The last time she'd seen him he'd been happy as a pig in mud, and had hugged Tabby and called her "sister". Tabby had been thrilled to have a Pack member so close. As much as she loved the Pumas, having Pack in Halle made her feel even safer and settled in the town. Sometimes Glory felt it was one of the reasons Max and Emma had agreed so readily to having Tim stay in town.

"He's not a doctor yet, so Rick isn't allowing him to do much." Max smiled as Emma joined him on the overstuffed chair, settling on his lap like it was something they did every day. "They're talking to the Coyotes, making sure that traveling in and out of their territory for the next ten years until Tim graduates is all right with them."

"The pass-through treaty allows it, but they've only recently become friends with the Coyote Alpha, Nathan Consiglione. They don't want to stress that too far or too soon." Gabe took Emma's spot on the sofa with a weary sigh. "Sarah should be here shortly."

Hope stood up and walked toward the windows, staring out into the darkness with her arms wrapped around her stomach. Glory kept an eye on her, barely paying any attention to what the others were saying.

"Someone is out there." Barney, who'd barely spoken since they arrived, startled her.

Ryan's head swiveled toward the window. Toward Hope. "What do you mean?

Barney shrugged. "I mean, someone is out there. Watching us."

"Jamie?" Gabe stood, placing himself behind Hope.

Hope reached out and touched the glass. "Who is that?"

Glory tried to join her sister at the window, but found herself held back by Ryan. The man's eyes were speckled with brown. "Rye. I don't think he'll hurt me."

"I don't want to take that chance."

He was being unreasonable, but the slight tremble in his arms forced her to forgive him. He was still dealing with the scare of her kidnapping, just as she was. "It's okay, Ryan." She leaned against him, needing his nearness, his strength, just as badly as he seemed to need to give it to her. "Besides, if he was going to hurt me he would have done it after he killed Salazar."

"Why would Jamie be outside?" Max stood, headed toward the front door.

"I think he's Hope's mate." Glory kept her voice down, but Hope's indrawn breath indicated her sister heard her anyway. Damn it. She hadn't wanted to scare her sister, but the way Hope trembled in front of the window left her in no doubt her sister was terrified.

Max froze. "That's not possible."

"I think it is." Barney was also staring out the window, but his expression was bemused rather than concerned. "Wolves sometimes have more than one mate."

"Oh, shit." Emma paled. "You mean, Hope, Jamie and Marie would have been mates together?"

Barney nodded. "Odds are good, yeah."

Max closed his eyes and cursed viciously. "Does he know?"

"I think so. It makes sense. It could be why he's been sneaking away from his parents' house. He sensed Hope, her pain and her fear, and his Puma forced him to go to her."

"And it's doing the same thing now." Barney edged closer to Hope, keeping his motions slow, unthreatening. "He lost his first mate. His Puma won't allow him to lose his second."

Hope stroked the glass, her brow furrowed. "So he's hurting."

"Yes."

She nodded and took a step back, her expression tormented. "So am I. I don't think I'm ready for a mate."

She sounded terrified, but Glory remembered her soft tone when she'd spoken to Jamie. The need was there, but both Jamie and Hope had some healing to do before they'd be able to act on their instincts.

"We'll figure this out, Hope." Glory ached for her twin, for everything she'd been through.

Hope wrapped her arms around her waist protectively, her gaze drawn once more to the window, and the shadows beyond. "I sure as hell hope so, because he's hurting even more than I am."

"You can feel him?" Glory exchanged a look with Ryan.

Hope nodded. "Sarah's right. He's lost in his pain." She smiled wearily. "Just like me."

EPILOGUE

He hadn't been expecting a confrontation so soon, but there he was, waiting for Ryan and Glory on Ryan's front step.

"Want me to talk to him?" Glory was yawning, her body worn out from the kidnapping, the healing and Hope's revelations. The last thing she needed was to deal with her brother.

"No. I'll talk to him."

"Ryan. He's a good man."

He'd be the judge of that. "Go on up, sweetheart. Get some rest." He wouldn't take the man into his apartment until he was certain he was no threat to Glory.

They'd agreed, after much arguing, that Glory would officially move in with him. Hope would take Glory's old apartment, and each of the male members of his family had agreed to keep an eye on her while she healed. Hope had agreed to multiple sessions with both Sarah Anderson and Adrian Giordano, the Pride's Marshal. The Poconos Pack Omega and Marshal, Chela Mendoza and Ben Malone, had also agreed to counsel her. Hope would need all that help if she ever hoped to live a normal life again. Ryan was glad, both for her sake and Glory's, that she'd agreed to the counseling.

Glory's twin had a shit-ton of healing to do, and he wasn't certain how long it would take before she could get over the constant fear she lived in. She'd been scarred, inside and out, in ways that would take years to overcome if she even could. He hoped if she really was Jamie

Howard's mate that the man had some patience left, because he doubted she'd be ready to mate any time soon.

"You sure? I can talk to him." Glory was eyeing both her brother and Ryan with some misgiving.

"I swear, unless he threatens you, I won't eat him."

She wrinkled her nose. "I don't think either of you swing that way."

He stopped dead, staring at her. She'd borrowed some of Emma's clothes so that she wouldn't be wandering around drenched in her own blood. He was grateful to the Curana for that. It helped keep his Bear calm, taking away the scent of his mate's pain. "SG?"

"Hmm?" She swayed on her feet, blinking huge blue eyes up at him. She was so tired it wasn't even funny. She did not need to be dealing with her brother right now.

Ryan caressed her cheek, practically purring like a Puma when she leaned into his touch. "Go to bed."

She yawned so wide he thought her lips would split. "M'kay."

Ryan escorted her up the steps, holding up a finger when it looked like Temp would follow them in. "Wait here, Temp. I want to get your sister settled first."

Temp nodded, reluctance in every line of his body. The man shoved his hands in his pockets, staring at Glory with a wistful expression. "Yeah. Okay."

It didn't take long for Ryan to get Glory settled. She was asleep as soon as her head hit the pillow, her clothing barely off her body. He left her under the covers with a soft kiss.

Now, to deal with her brother.

Ryan made his way out the front door, snagging two beers on the way. If Glory was right, and her brother was no threat, then Ryan hoped to make this a peaceful little chat.

If Temp *was* a threat...

Well. Glory had lived this long without her brother, hadn't she?

"I know what I saw." Temp stared up at him, his expression defiant and fearful at the same time. "I'm not crazy."

Ryan blinked. He hadn't expected the man to go immediately on the attack. "What did you see?" He held out the beer can and waited.

Temp scowled, but took the offered drink. "My sister became…something else."

"She became a Grizzly Bear, yeah."

Temp popped the top and took a long swig.

"Tell me you're not driving." Fuck, if he had to he'd put the guy up on his couch. That would please his mate.

"I'm not driving." Temp sighed and settled on the step below Ryan. "What the hell is going on? Is that really my sister? Is this something that could hurt her?"

"Glory is a shifter now, and yes, it's really her. No, it won't hurt her. Nothing will ever hurt her again, not if I can help it." Ryan settled on the step above Temp and took his own sip of beer. "Glory is my mate."

Temp blinked. "Okay. Back up and start from the beginning. You're like, what, a werewolf?" Temp sounded calm, but his hand was shaking.

"No. I'm an accountant." When Temp blinked at him, confused, Ryan laughed. "I'm also a Bear. A Grizzly, in fact."

Temp's hand froze on the way to his mouth. "Aren't they the most aggressive species of bear?"

Ryan shrugged. "Kodiaks are worse."

Temp swigged more beer. "There are Kodiaks?"

It was almost cute, the way the man's voice squeaked. "Yup."

"Shit." Temp slumped, his hands between his knees, the almost empty can held loosely. "Are you sure this isn't going to hurt her?"

"It's not going to hurt her." Ryan smiled as Temp relaxed, at least marginally. The man really *had* been worried about his sister. "You're taking this pretty well."

Temp snorted. "I'm holding on for her sake. I'll freak out in private, where she can't see it."

"Good. She's been through enough."

Temp finished his beer and crumpled the can. "Tell me about bears, Ryan. I want to know what my sister is going to have to deal with."

Ryan nodded. "Bear, like all the other animal spirits, chose his people and offered them a gift."

"Wait. You mean there really *are* werewolves out there?"

"Yeah." This was the part Ryan dreaded. "Look, man. It turns out Hope was held by one."

"Was? You found her?" Temp's expression was so relieved Ryan began to believe Glory might be right about him. "How is she? Is she safe? Where is she?"

Ryan held up his hands. "The Wolf who took her is dead, she's alive, but she's…traumatized, deeply." Ryan grimaced. "He…did things to her. Turned her into one of us against her will. Temp, she's broken."

Temp sat, stunned for a moment before he closed his eyes with a pained expression. When he opened them, Ryan caught sight of tears. "Fuck."

"Yeah." Ryan ran his fingers through his hair.

"She's a Grizzly too?" Temp shuddered.

"No. She's a Wolf, like her captor was."

"Was?"

Temp had picked up on that quickly. "He managed to get his hands on both Glory and Hope. One of the Pumas chased them down and killed him before he could get too far with them."

"Good." Temp sounded fierce, as fierce as Ryan ever had. "I hope the fucker burns in Hell." Temp sighed and lifted his head. "She's going to need us to get through this."

"She is, yeah."

"So I'm really not crazy."

"Nope."

"Shit balls. You couldn't lie to me and tell me I'm stuck in some padded room having hallucinations, could you? You just had to tell me the truth."

Ryan chuckled. "Sorry, man. You're not crazy."

Temp blew out a breath. "Both my sisters are shifters?"

"Yup."

"And they're all right?"

"Glory is, yeah. Hope, not so much, but she will be."

Temp fiddled with his can nervously. "Are you going to change me too? Because I'd guess it's either that, or…" He drew his thumb across his throat.

Ryan smiled. Temp was turning out to be okay. The man was smart, he'd give him that. "That's up to you."

"What do you mean?"

"You know about us. Usually, humans who discover what we are do so because they're mated to one of us. It's how Glory wound up changing."

"And Hope?"

Ryan snarled. "The son of a bitch changed her against her will. He had some weird delusion that she was his mate, but she wasn't."

"Did he…?" Temp sighed. "I can't even say it."

Ryan patted Temp's knee. "Yeah, he raped her."

"God damn it." Temp wiped his eyes with the back of his hand, and Ryan pretended not to see the moisture still gathering there.

"We're going to do everything we can to make her feel safe and heal her wounds, inside and out. But you're going to have to help us."

"Damn straight I will." Temp slumped. "So. My choices are…?"

"Let me or one of my family change you, or choose one of the local species to do it." There was no way Temp wasn't going to wind up changed.

"So I'd be a Bear like you and Glory."

"Or a Fox, if one of my cousins changes you, yeah."

Temp blinked at that, but didn't say anything about Foxes and Bears. "You said each spirit gave each species gifts. What are they?"

"Bears have the ability to heal, but it drains our energy, makes us tired. Foxes can hide their scent, enabling them to hide from other shifters remarkably well, but when they *want* to be found it can be…difficult." They'd been lucky that Bunny had stumbled across Heather and her tormentors all those years ago.

Temp snorted. "Man, I need more beer."

"No." Temp looked startled at the fierceness of Ryan's reply. "You want to be sober when you make this decision. Whatever you decide will tie you to the shifter group you choose to belong to. If you pick a Wolf, you *will* need a Pack. Same if you pick a Puma. Bears and Foxes live in family groups, and because I'm mated to your sister you would belong to mine." Ryan leaned forward.

The wistful expression on Temp's face disappeared almost as quickly as it came. "I can't leave Faith behind."

Ryan had figured as much. "We can change her too, if you like." Pretty little Faith would make an excellent Fox. The ability to hide in plain sight would soothe her brother's need to protect her.

"That's up to her. I won't take her choices from her. It's bad enough Hope didn't get that choice. I won't do that to Faith."

"It won't be up to her if we tell her about all of this." He held up his hands when Temp rounded on him. "For the safety of your sisters, and all of the shifters in this town and beyond, you'll need to decide if Faith becomes one of us or not."

"Shit." Temp slumped again. "This is…"

"Crazy?"

Temp nodded. "This is a lot of information, Ryan." Temp blew out a breath. He glanced toward Ryan's apartment, his expression wistful. "Glory really is all right?"

Ryan nodded. "Exhausted, scared and ready to kill a man who's already dead, but yeah. She'll be fine."

They sat in silence, listening to the sounds of the night. "Ryan?"

"Hmm?"

"I can't let this happen again." His expression was tormented. "I failed them both." His gaze, when he turned it on Ryan, was determined. Ryan knew that look. He'd seen it with Bunny, and in his own mirror. Temp might not have a mate to protect, but his sisters really did mean the world to him. The last of his suspicions about Temperance Walsh fell away. "I need to be able to protect my family."

Ryan smiled. He'd thought Temp would pick this option. It seemed Glory's opinion of her brother was spot-on. "I know how you feel."

"Will it hurt?"

"The changing bite will, since you won't be getting marked by your mate. A mating bite feels…different." And that was all he was willing to say to his mate's big brother. There were just some things a man couldn't share with his mate's family.

Temp looked confused. "So it didn't hurt Glory when you changed her?"

Ryan's cheeks flushed. No fucking way he was telling her brother that it had been far from pain his mate had felt. "Nope."

"But Hope, she *was* hurt."

"Yeah. And not just by the bite."

"Fucker. I am so glad he's dead." Temp sighed. "Ryan?"

"Yeah?"

Temp took a deep, cleansing breath.

Ryan prepared himself for what he knew was coming. Glory, he felt, would approve.

"Bite me."

Ryan nodded, and silently gave his brother-in-law his wish.

***

Glory closed the curtain as her brother bit back a scream. Ryan would take care of Temp, just like he took care of her.

She smirked as she made her way to her bed. Their bed.

Okay, maybe not *quite* the way her mate took care of her. And when he crawled into bed with her half an hour later, Glory made sure she showed Ryan that she could take *very* good care of him.

Look for these titles by Dana Marie Bell

The Gray Court
Dare to Believe
Noble Blood
Artistic Vision
The Hob
Siren's Song
Never More

Halle Pumas
The Wallflower
Sweet Dreams
Cat of a Different Color
Steel Beauty
Only In My Dreams

Halle Shifters
Bear Necessities
Cynful
Bear Naked
Figure of Speech
Indirect Lines

Heart's Desire
Shadow of the Wolf
Hecate's Own
The Wizard King
Warlock Unbound

*Maggie's Grove
Blood of the Maple
Throne of Oak
Of Shadows and Ash
Song of Midnight Embers

The Nephilim
*All for You
*The Fire Within
Speak Thy Name

Poconos Pack
Finding Forgiveness
Mr. Red Riding Hoode
Sorry, Charlie

True Destiny
Very Much Alive
Eye of the Beholder
Howl for Me
Morgan's Fate
Not Broken

**Published by
Carina Press*

CPSIA information can be obtained
at www.ICGtesting.com
Printed in the USA
LVHW090050311218
602236LV00001B/86/P